I0663604

Glass Trilogy Book 1: Glass House

By Max Overton and Ariana Overton

Writers Exchange E-Publishing

http://www.writers-exchange.com

Glass Trilogy Book 1: Glass House
Copyright 2013, 2024 Max Overton and Ariana Overton
Writers Exchange E-Publishing
PO Box 372
ATHERTON QLD 4883

Published by Writers Exchange E-Publishing
http://www.writers-exchange.com

Cover art by Julie Napier
www.julienapier.com
From an original concept by Ariana Overton
Photographs by Julie Napier

Prologue

He raised his bloodied face from the fresh kill, the antelope forgotten as the voices filled his head. They called to him, a siren's song, stroking every cell and fibre of his brain. Picking up his spear, he rose onto his knees, listening. He anxiously fingered the black stone hanging around his neck, its angled facets catching the light in a rainbow of colours. Fear twitched thick, knotted muscles as he aimed his mind toward the message he knew he must listen to and obey. He could hear Umbra, his grown son, in the next valley, and the other men of his tribe. They all froze, joining their thoughts to his, listening to the distant message.

Garagh, my father, do you hear? The 'Others' call again, Umbra's thoughts connected with Garagh's mind, which now filled with images alien to memory.

Yes, I hear, my son. It is stronger this time. We must answer, as we have been taught to do. Call the men. We must go--now.

No resistance was possible, or offered, as he rose onto trembling, muscular legs. Slinging the kill around his thick neck, Garagh scanned the horizon for the other hunters of the tribe, his dark, penetrating eyes protected from the fierce sun by a thick brow. He could hear their thoughts and feel their reactions, and he knew they were aware of his inner workings as well.

Come, my brothers. We go to the cave. We must ready our people for the journey. It is time...at last.

Aiming his resolute face toward the south, he took his first step into a journey that would last 40,000 years and change the fate of humankind.

1

The tropical rainforest of Far North Queensland is lush and close, the tangle of thickets, vines and that particularly nasty prostrate palm, *Calamus*, with its rows of wicked barbs along its petioles, makes progress through parts of the forest difficult and sweaty.

Rick Jennings decided the easiest way to penetrate the jungle around Mount Thornton, north of the Daintree River, was along the streams. This fitted in with his plans anyway, as he was up there on a two week research trip looking at the endangered frog fauna of the area. He was a PhD student at James Cook University in Townsville, and this would be one of his last trips to Mount Thornton before he settled down to write his dissertation. The results in his files were depressing, showing a steady decline in numbers and health among the commoner species, and the possible local extinction of at least three of the rarer ones. The Sharp-snouted Day frog and the Armored Mist frog had been totally missing from his survey, but he still had hopes of finding the Northern Tinker frog.

There had been a severe lightning storm the previous night as he waded through the shallow streams armed with a torch looking for frogs. Curiously, there had been no accompanying noise of thunder, indicating the storm was further away than he supposed, so he was able to hear frog calls. One of the ones he thought he had heard had been the distinctive soft metallic tapping sound of *Taudactylus rheophilus*, the Northern Tinker or Tinkling frog. The calls had originated from a stretch of Bell's Creek on the flanks of Mount Thornton and he started to investigate until the lightning display above the treetops gave him pause. He could feel the electricity in the air, with the hairs on his forearms standing up in waves as the lights rolled above the canopy. Realising he was standing in water with possibly several million amps of current fifty metres above him, he decided it was prudent to withdraw.

Rick returned the next morning with his digital camera determined to search the stream for any signs of the elusive frog. His search was slow and methodical, probing into cracks between boulders, turning over stones but being careful not to create too much of a disturbance as he waded up the splashing torrent. So absorbed was he in his search that it was not until he felt the sun hot on his back that he realised he had left the forest cover. He stood and stared about him in growing disbelief at a circular scar in the landscape, the tiny torrent stream of Bell's Creek cutting across it like a silver ribbon.

The scar was a hundred metres across, an area totally devoid of plant growth. Rick looked closer, his forehead wrinkling in wonder at the total lack of anything organic on the soil surface. It was as if it had been wiped clean, leaving just soil and rock. Every vestige of plant life, even down to mosses and lichens, had vanished, along with leaf litter and every animal trace. Not a single footprint or stray leaf marred the pristine earth and nothing scuttled across its surface or flew through the vacant air above it.

Rick stepped out of the stream onto a flat rock, half wondering if it was safe. "What the hell has happened here?" he muttered. He rapidly thought of and as quickly dismissed a handful of possible explanations, ranging from a localised fire--*no ashes*--to logging--*they'd only take trees*--to a toxic spill--*there's nothing dead, it's just gone*--to...to...

He remembered the curiously silent electrical storm of the previous night, and his mind slipped unwillingly to stories he had heard of crop circles and UFOs. "Bloody nonsense, the lot of it," he growled, annoyed for even thinking it. "There's got to be a rational explanation." Remembering his digital camera, he switched it on, raised it...and jumped. There was a dark figure standing in the middle of the circle, looking at him.

Rick stifled a cry and lowered the camera, staring back and quickly saw it was not a figure--*why did I think it was?*--only a black post or a rock. He raised the camera again and took a picture before walking slowly across to the object. The closer he got, the more mystified he became. It was definitely a rock, or rather a shiny black mineral, so black it almost seemed to suck light out of the air. *No, that's wrong*, he thought. *It's shiny, so it reflects light--just not very well*. About a metre and a half in height and about half a metre across, it would have come up to Rick's chest if he had stood beside it. He stared at it in distaste, the thought of getting that close to it making him uncomfortable.

Something moved within the blackness and Rick stifled a scream, leaping back. Staring at it from several metres away, he decided it was only his imagination. He took another picture then moved closer again, edging forward. When the movement came again, he trembled but stayed where he was, examining the black obelisk intently. Rick laughed suddenly, feeling relief flood through him. The smooth surface of the stone was carved into forms, human and animal, in low relief. As he moved, the light reflected off the curves, slipping and sliding and giving the impression of movement. He squatted down and took a series of pictures, though the effect of black carvings on a black surface produced poor images. *Maybe I can clean them up a bit on my computer.*

Rick realised he had to tell someone and took out his cell-phone to call his supervisor, Ross Everington, at JCU. The phone just crackled and hissed, before suddenly winking off as if the battery was drained. He cursed, looked at his watch and cursed again. It had stopped too. Raising the digital camera to take some more photos, he found a blank screen. "Shit! I changed those batteries this morning," he shouted in frustration. He turned and stamped back across to the familiar territory of Bell's Creek and down the stream to his camp. Camera and cell-phone worked perfectly there and Rick called his supervisor while he waited for his pictures to download onto his laptop.

"Ross? Rick...yes, I'm fine...no, I had a bad storm last night but no rain...no, nothing much there...yes, I think I heard a Tinker last night...Mount Thornton...look, Ross, I found something...no, not a Tinker, a black rock...yes, a rock, an obelisk in a bare circle of...no...shit, you won't believe me until you see it...I'll send you an email. The pics are uploading now...okay...talk to you later...cheers."

Rick disconnected the camera from his computer and deleted the pictures on his memory card. Then he sent an email to his supervisor, attaching all his photos of the black rock, plus the location using a map reference. He sent the message, then carefully deleted all traces of the images, and emptied the trashcan before packing up his computer. An hour later he found himself sitting in front of his tent staring idly at the burbling stream. Several mosquito bites itched fiercely on his arms. He stared upstream, trying to think what it was he had meant to do that morning, but the thought eluded him. *Well, there's nothing here. I think I might pack up and try Mossman gorge before I head home.*

*   *   *

The torrent stream on the flanks of Mount Thornton rushed and tumbled past the little flat glade where Rick's tent had been pitched. As evening fell, a metallic 'tink-tink-tink' sound could be heard above the sound of the water, but the sound went uninvestigated. A little further north, a shiny black obelisk sat silently in a circle of lifeless earth, waiting. The call had gone out; the wait would not be long.

2

D r James Hay ran long artistic fingers through thinning brown hair and pushed his shoulders back, grimacing at the twinge that racked the muscles at the base of his neck. "I'm getting too bloody old for this," he muttered. "I ought to retire and leave it all to you youngsters."

"For a man of learning, you really do talk a lot of nonsense at times, uncle." The speaker, a tall powerfully built Torres Strait Islander woman, looked nothing like the man save in height, but the look she gave him was one of amused affection. "You know you'd fret if you stayed back at the university."

James grunted and got up from the moss-covered log and dusted the seat of his shorts off before picking up his wide Akubra hat and stepping to the edge of the clearing. Squinting in the bright sunshine after the dim filtered light of the forest, he stared across fifty metres of totally bare soil to a densely black obelisk outlined against the yellow-brown clay. Around it were three young people, two men and a woman, busily engaged in taking a variety of readings on various pieces of equipment. James watched them for a while before turning back to the forest and re-examining the edge of the clearing. The vegetation had been sliced through where it stood, cleanly and without ripping or shredding what was left. The wounds did not ooze sap or become discoloured from the action of the air, yet neither were they scarred from any continued plant growth. James shook his head wonderingly.

"The wounds look fresh, Ratana," he called to the Torres Strait Islander woman. "It's as if it happened an hour ago."

"A week last Thursday, I gather," she called back. "If Everington's student was telling the truth."

"Yes, it was good of Ross to let me know..."

Screeches from the treetops attracted James' attention and he turned toward the sound wondering if he would see a repeat of a performance he'd seen a dozen times since they'd arrived at the site the previous day. A flock of rainbow lorikeets, busy lapping nectar from a tall flowering Firewheel tree, took flight and speared through the air toward the bare circle. As they crossed the boundary from unbroken rainforest to naked soil, the flock broke up in a flurry of beating wings and raucous cries, racing back to the cover of the surrounding vegetation. At the same time, annoyed cries came from the trio around the obelisk and James knew all the instruments had stopped working again.

A dozen times in the last twenty-four hours, birds or animals had broken through into the circle and each time had run or flown rapidly back into cover. On five of those occasions, a pulse of energy had knocked out the instrumentation for about half an hour. It might have happened the other times too, but nobody had been working at the time. Even insects avoided the circle, though they did not seem to show signs of panic and did not trigger a surge in electromagnetic energy.

The three students left the obelisk with its ring of non-functioning instruments and trudged back to the welcome shade of the rain forest. "Hi, Dr Hay, the instruments have packed up again," called one, a young, rather attractive woman of Chinese extraction.

"Sure, Maggie," James answered. "Take a break. It'll probably be half an hour again."

"We thought we'd upload some data while we're waiting," added one of the men.

The surge seemed to originate from the obelisk but extended no further than the hundred metre diameter of the circle, which was one reason that James had decided to camp just inside the forest boundary. The other reason was an uncomfortable feeling of being watched when he was out in the open.

James walked back with the three young people to the makeshift camp. Ratana looked up from her laptop as the others arrived.

"Where's Nathan?" she asked.

"No idea," Maggie replied. "He was with Robbie earlier."

Robbie had plunked himself down by his tent and was rummaging in his backpack for a muesli bar. "I think he went back to the road."

"And you let him wander off alone?" Ratana asked.

Robbie shrugged. "How am I going to stop him? Nathan Wambiri has a mind of his own and nobody--I mean nobody--better get in his way."

"He said he was meeting some of his mates," chipped in the other young man, a sallow faced youth by the name of Ed Sanders.

James grimaced. "I really hope he's not going to bring them up here. I have a lot of sympathy for his militant Aboriginal friends, but sometimes I think they go looking for trouble."

"They only want what's theirs, uncle." Ratana smiled, robbing her words of their sting. "After all, this land is ours, or was before the white man came."

Ed groaned. "Don't let's start that again. It's not as if you do anything with the land you have. Now you want it all. What's next? Chuck us all into the sea or sink a spear into our ribs while we sleep? My uncle, Peter Howard, says..."

"I'd like to sink one into yours," Ratana muttered. Louder, she added, "We all know your uncle is the Head of Department, Ed, but it doesn't make your opinions any more valid. Especially when they come unchanged from him."

"Okay, guys, let's cool it," James said quietly. "We should all be able to work together professionally. Now, how about filling me in on what we've found?"

"But you know it all already," Ed objected.

"I know, but I'd still like to hear it again. Every new measurement adds something to the pool of our knowledge, and something meaningless when taken alone might reveal insights when added to what has been found out before. Maggie, why don't you start?"

"Sure, Dr Hay. The obelisk measures one metre fifty-seven centimetres in height, is half a metre in diameter and has an average circumference of a metre fifty-seven too. It's sunk into the earth by about twelve centimetres. I dug down to see," Maggie added. "It's made of quartz as far as I can determine without a full lab analysis. I was wondering about how I could take a sample but I found these buried in the soil about a metre out from the base. I think there's a whole ring of them." She took a smooth black object out of her pocket and handed it to James. "Looks like the same material, so I took one for analysis."

James nodded and turned the object over in his hands. It was a thin, flat oval of shiny hard crystal like the obelisk, measuring about fifteen by eight by two centimetres, he judged. "I understand your need for something concrete to analyze, Maggie, but next time, ask me before you disturb anything. This oval may be a vital component of the whole thing." He passed the oval across to Ratana.

"Sorry, Dr Hay. Okay, the obelisk is basically polished and smoothed, with the top a truncated six-sided pyramid. There are carvings in it--very low relief, that are hard to see. I took a number of digital photos and some rubbings." Maggie passed over a bundle of paper with patterns of white lines amid the silvery grey sheen of graphite. James stared blankly at one, then turned it upside-down and smiled at the figure of an elephant with a huge domed head and massive curved tusks.

"I don't recognise all of the figures," Maggie continued, "But I'm sure that one's a mammoth. There's also what looks like a lion, wolves, bison, deer and people. The mammoths and things are down near the bottom of the obelisk and higher up are more familiar things, even a kangaroo and a koala. The top ten centimetres are blank and smooth--like an unwritten tablet."

"Interesting choice of phrase," James said. "Do you have any reason to think more carvings will be added?"

Maggie grinned self-consciously. "No, not really. It's just that the animals seem to be getting more modern as you rise up the obelisk. I just thought that there's room for something else."

James nodded. "Thank you, Maggie. Any thoughts anyone?"

"Are you sure it's quartz?" Ed asked. He fingered the oval disc and only reluctantly gave it back to James. "I mean, black quartz can't be common. Could it be obsidian?"

"Black or smoky quartz is fairly rare but certainly not unknown," Maggie said. "Obsidian is made of silica like quartz but obsidian is a glass, non-crystalline, whereas quartz has a definite crystal structure--six-sided."

"And the obelisk?" Robbie asked.

"Is very slightly six-sided and the pyramid on top is the give-away. It's quartz all right."

"Okay, Robbie, let's hear from you. What have you found out about the electromagnetic feature?"

"Actually very little. I won't bore everyone with figures--they're all in the data I've uploaded to the study page, but basically there is a very low level hum associated with the obelisk. You can't hear it without instruments but it's there. Ultra-low frequency, rather like an elephant's tummy rumble..."

"Communication?" Ratana asked.

"Could be, but I've no idea how you'd find out. Anyway, that low level rumble is a constant, but every now and then, like when that last flock of lorikeets flew into the circle, there's a sharp spike, a pulse of electro-magnetic energy. Unfortunately, I can't measure it as it knocks out my recording instruments."

"You've made recordings of everything you can? Okay, any questions?" James looked round the group but the others shook their heads. "I have one," he said. "You get a pulse whenever animals enter the circle and the guy who found it, Rick what's-his-name, said his watch stopped immediately and his camera battery drained quickly, but does it react when we enter?"

Robbie shook his head. "No-oo, not exactly."

"But?"

"Well, there's no reaction to any of us, Dr Hay, but when you come close, there's...well...sort of an expectant surge of interest...I'm sorry, that sounds daft and a tad unscientific."

"It does rather," James said with a grin, "But what do you mean by an 'expectant surge of interest'? Are you implying it's aware of my presence in some way?"

"Shit, I'm putting this badly. Not aware, but like a motion detector that switches on when somebody moves, but then doesn't sound the alarm."

"And you have recordings of this 'expectant surge of interest'?"

Robbie flushed. "No. There's no change in the background hum. It's just...just a sort of...well, feeling."

James grunted. "Unfortunately, feelings are hard to quantify. We'll leave this for the time being. Ed, you were looking at the life in the soil."

Ed turned from his amused regard of Robbie and addressed James self-importantly. "Yes, I have full records of everything. I have taken samples of soil, subsoil and air in several transects out from the obelisk and recorded every organism found."

"You did find organisms then? It's not as sterile as it looks?"

"Yes, I did, and no, it's not," Ed said smugly. "There is plenty of life on a cellular level or less--unicellular algae; a few fungi, especially spores; and bacteria. However, nothing mobile, nothing that can move of its own accord. The closer you get to the edge of the circle, the more normal the soil flora and fauna becomes, though it's only in the last metre or two that you find insects and earthworms."

"Interesting."

"Yes, very, and when Robbie can get his act together and identify the frequency of the obelisk's hum; I'm going to make a mint manufacturing pest repellants."

James laughed. "Well, if you do, remember to talk to the University's legal department. Remember we're on university time and anything that results from this expedition is strictly university property, intellectual or otherwise."

"That's stretching it a bit, isn't it, Dr Hay?" Ed said slyly. "Professor Howard says that he never gave permission for this trip. He says..."

"Just shut up, Ed," Ratana said forcefully. "I've told you before that I have no interest in what your uncle says. He wouldn't know his ass from..."

"Cool it, guys," James cut in. "Ed, I don't answer to you..."

"Thank God," Maggie muttered.

"But in case you hadn't noticed, this is lecture break, and the Head of Department has no control over my free time--or yours, for that matter. Now, does anyone have any questions for Ed?"

"Just one," Maggie said. "If he thinks this is all so useless, why does he bother to volunteer for all our trips?"

"Because he's a spy," Robbie growled. "He's reporting back to his uncle."

"So what if I am?" Ed pouted. "I thought this was supposed to be university property anyway. What does it matter who knows?"

"It doesn't," James said. "I just wish you'd be honest and up-front about it. It makes it harder to trust if people have hidden agendas. Now let's say no more about this. Ratana, do you have anything to report?"

"I was looking at the relationship between this black obelisk and other references to black stones or black places in the literature."

"I can think of one black place," Ed muttered under his breath.

Ratana shot him a hostile glance, and then ignored him. "The obvious connection is the Black Mountain near Cooktown, but while it is a mysterious place in its own right, the blackness is from basalt rocks rather than quartz. There's a place called Blackrock in Ireland, with an obelisk, no less, but they aren't black and are certainly not mysterious. Then you have a handful of Heavy Metal bands and fantasy games that incorporate a black rock or obelisk in some way, but nothing relevant. Turning to history, a black quartz crystal was found in a Cro-Magnon grave in southern France, a handful in the Middle Ages in Europe and one in Australia about sixty years ago. Of course, seeing as quartz crystals figure in Aboriginal folk-lore, perhaps you should ask a practitioner."

James smiled. "I already have. As soon as I heard about this I sent word to Mick."

Ratana gaped. "Grandfather Mick? Do you think he'll come?"

"Mick's a law unto himself, but I wouldn't be surprised."

"Er, sorry, Dr Hay," Maggie interposed. "Who's Mick?"

"A very old Aboriginal...medicine man, I suppose you'd call him. What is sometimes referred to as a Karadji man. He is my grandfather." James grinned at the expression on Robbie's face. "My adoptive grandfather, but that's another story. Anyway, a Karadji man talks to the spirits by means of crystals, usually quartz, so when I heard about this thing," he gestured towards the clearing, "I sent him a message."

"No kidding?" Maggie asked, grinning in turn. "How did you send it? Drums? Carrier pigeon? In a dream?"

"No, by e-mail. He's quite modern despite his age and his learning."

"Where does he live?"

James shrugged. "Wherever he happens to be. He moves around a fair bit."

"And you believe he's some sort of witch doctor, talking to spirits and everything?" Ed sneered. "I thought you were supposed to be a scientist."

"I am," James replied seriously. "But not everything I've seen can be neatly pigeon-holed. I try to keep an open mind." He shook his head at the young man's open disbelief. "It doesn't actually matter what you or I believe. Facts tend not to pay any attention to belief..."

A distant crack broke the relative quiet of the rainforest, interrupting James. As everyone turned toward the sound, the sound came again, followed by a crackle of what sounded like automatic fire.

Ratana leapt to her feet. "That's coming from the road head. Nathan's there."

"What should we do?" Robbie asked. "Should we go look for him?"

"Stay here, all of you," James ordered. "I'll go." He grabbed his hat and water bottle and started toward the track that led to the road. He was only a few metres down it when he heard running footsteps and stopped, staring into the bushes.

A young Aboriginal man burst out of the undergrowth, closely followed by another. Both were dressed in camouflaged army fatigues and the front one carried an old Lee Enfield rifle. He stopped and raised his weapon when he caught sight of James, but the man behind caught at his arm and pushed the barrel down.

"It's all right, Burnum, that's Dr Hay. He's Kalti's uncle." The second man pushed past his gun-carrying friend. "Hi, Dr Hay, I'm Miro, a friend of Kalti...Nathan Wambiri."

James nodded. "I recognise you, but I thought your name was John."

The man shrugged. "That's my European name. My Aboriginal name is Miro, the throwing stick."

"What was that shooting we heard? Was that you?"

"The Army's here. We fired a few shots and ran for it. We're well outnumbered so we'll fall back and try again." Miro tapped Burnum on the arm. "Come on." They ran off into the forest.

"Wait!" James called after them. "What about Nathan?"

"He's coming..."

James hesitated, wondering whether to continue to the road and risk running into soldiers with their adrenalin running or head back to the camp. Nathan knew where they were so maybe that was the safest course. He headed back and found Nathan had arrived ahead of him and was busy changing into jeans and a tee shirt.

"Hi, uncle," Nathan said as James arrived. "I've been here all along, okay?"

"Was anyone hurt?"

"Nah...heads up." Nathan sat down and started scribbling in a notebook, managing to look surprised as several Australian Army diggers burst into the camp, their weapons at the ready.

An alert captain led them, sending his men off to secure the perimeter before turning to stare at the four men and two women in the camp. He scrutinised Nathan and Ratana carefully before turning his attention to James. "You'd be Dr James Hay of James Cook University?" When James nodded, he went on. "I'm Captain Kevin Mason, Tenth Queensland Regiment. You will please all consider yourselves guests of the Australian Army. We'll be flying men in soon to secure this whole area..."

"This is a National Park, Captain Mason, not Defence Force territory. You have no jurisdiction, whereas I have written permission from the National Parks Authority..."

"Superseded, I'm afraid, Dr Hay." Mason pulled out a folded letter from the top pocket of his camouflage jacket and handed it across. "You'll see that a ten kilometre radius from that map reference cited is under Army Authority until further notice."

James recognised the map reference. "How did you find out about this so fast?"

"Not for me to say, sir." The radio at the captain's belt crackled into life and Mason listened for a moment before acknowledging the message. He gestured toward the circle which could be seen through the trees. "Perhaps you'd better show me the circle and the stone, the Black Hawk's two minutes out."

"What? You're flying them right in to the circle? You can't." James turned and ran out into the circle, staring into the sky from whence he could hear the rapidly approaching helicopter.

Mason ran after him, drawing his Browning pistol as he burst out into the open. "Dr Hay, stop immediately. I will fire."

James whirled to face the captain. "You don't understand. Any intrusion into the circle sets off..." he searched his memory for a phrase that might convey urgency, the whoop of the rotor blades growing ever louder. "It's booby trapped, Captain. If anything intrudes on the circle, a pulse of electromagnetic radiation will knock out any electrical circuit...you've got to stop them."

Mason stared at James, indecision rampant on his face. Abruptly, he snapped on his radio and yelled into it, "Bravo Leader to Bravo One, abort. Repeat, abort. Pull back. Do you copy?" He stared at his radio and tapped it. "Odd, it's not working."

"Back under the trees," James snapped. "Hurry, man."

The two men stepped back across the border and Captain Mason tried his radio again. It crackled into life while the tops of the trees around the southern perimeter of the circle started whipping into life. Mason yelled into it again, "Bravo Leader to Bravo One, abort. Repeat, abort. Pull back."

The Black Hawk slipped over the circle boundary descending toward the ground. Dust rose in a swirling storm. "Say again, Bravo Lea..." The radio and the twin engines cut out simultaneously. The Black Hawk lurched in flight, but the safety devices controlling the engines and rotors could not prevent the helicopter from nosing toward the baked earth of the circle. The jar of the landing snapped wheels off and rocked the helicopter sideways. Rotor blades heaved uncontrollably, slashing into the earth. Metal screeched and buckled under the hacking force, and the helicopter twisted and spun, slamming heavily to the ground. The whine of dying engines arresting all other sound. Abruptly, the doors of the Black Hawk flew open to release the pilot and crew. Yells of command filled the air. Soldiers poured out, weapons at the ready as injured men were helped out of the tangled mess and into the shade of the forest. The self-sealing fuel lines held, so there was no immediate danger of fire. Captain Mason stared aghast for a few moments before raising his pistol again.

"Dr Hay, you are under arrest for sabotage and possible terrorism. If you resist, I will be obliged to use all necessary force."

3

Collinsville is a town of about thirty thousand people in western Illinois, just across the Mississippi River from St Louis, Missouri, known as the 'Gateway to the West'. The town's main claim to fame is as the Horseradish Capital of the World and hosts a small festival each year. A lesser known claim to fame is as the home town of Samantha Louis, freelance journalist and sometime International Geographic correspondent. She owned a small apartment on the south side of town where on her tiny back balcony she could glimpse the town's other main attraction, the World's largest Catsup bottle. Samantha, or Sam as she liked to be called, had not bought the apartment for its view, but solely as a place where she could crash between assignments. Elegantly furnished, the heavily insulated apartment provided freedom from the noisy world and an equitable temperature year round without having to use much in the way of heaters or air conditioning.

On this particular morning, she was sitting in front of her computer downloading emails and sifting through half a dozen offers of employment, none of which particularly attracted her. Now in her mid-thirties she had carved out a reputation and a comfortable bank balance and could afford to select her assignments. She sipped on her mug of freshly brewed coffee and read each email carefully, then either flagged it for further consideration or deleted it. She reached the end of her short list of messages and was just about to push back her chair when another message came in. Sighing, she opened it, read for a few seconds and moved her cursor toward the delete button...and stopped. *James Hay*, she thought. *Why does that name ring a bell?* She minimised her screen and Googled the name. A few moments later she laughed and pushed back her chair grinning, remembering.

The previous summer she had covered a conference in San Francisco on the unlikely subject of Cryptozoology. Her research beforehand had led her to believe it was the habitation of kooks and weirdos, but she was between assignments in 'Frisco, so she decided to wander along for a laugh. There certainly were strange people in attendance--it was San Francisco after all-- but she was surprised to find some of the speakers showed a high level of education and erudition. By lunch-time she was prepared to think that cryptozoology, the science of hidden or unknown animals, might be a valid area of research. One speaker in particular attracted her. Dr James Hay from Townsville, Australia, was a tall, broad-shouldered academic with twinkling eyes and an adorable British accent. She estimated his age as about forty. His hair was thinning slightly, but otherwise he was definitely hunky and in the break, she sought him out.

"Hi! You must be Dr Hay. I heard you talk this morning on...what was it...Yowies?" She brushed her shoulder length red hair aside and found that despite her own height of close to six feet, she still had to look up to meet his dark brown eyes. *Very nice*, she thought.

"Er, hello. Yes, James Hay. Pleased to meet you...er, Ms..."

He stuck out his hand and she took it, noting the firm strength, the long artistic fingers and the calluses. *A man who works with his hands, not just an armchair academic.*

"Samantha Louis. My friends call me Sam." She saw with amusement that his eyes strayed to the ring finger of her left hand, then back to her eyes with only a cursory detour to her chest. Most men spent considerably longer checking out her form. "Did I understand you correctly when you said that a Yowie was the same as our Bigfoot?"

"Er, yes...Sam. Basically, the sightings of Australian primates match those of the Pacific Northwest, though there are some local differences. You are familiar with the phenomenon?"

Her research, plus her enquiring mind meant she probably knew more than the average layperson, but she felt a definite attraction to this man and settled down into the old game of playing him like a seven pound trout on a quarter-pound line--carefully and with finesse. Professing ignorance, she persuaded him to talk and as he swam within familiar waters he lost his shyness and hesitancy, revealing a mind that staggered her with its breadth and openness, yet at the same time critical and orderly. They sat together during the afternoon sessions and he took her to dinner that evening. She was aware of his interest but intrigued that he made no effort to invite himself up to her room, or her to his. A brief kiss on his cheek in her hotel lobby lit a spark in his eyes and she could feel him stood watching her until she was out of sight.

They sat together at the conference the next day, but now she impressed him with her open-mindedness, her perspicacity and knowledge, revealing that she was a journalist but between assignments. Everything they said was off the record. They lunched again and in the afternoon walked along the waterfront, oblivious to the scenery as they again explored each other's worlds. Sam listened in fascination to his descriptions of Australia and its wonders.

"I've never been there," she said. "I've always meant to but never got around to it."

"You should," James replied. "I'd be happy to offer you a bed if you came for a visit."

Sam's eyebrows rose, then she realised James had not been aware of the entendre. "Thanks," she said. "I'd like that."

They made a date for dinner again and Sam spent a long time getting ready. She intended to invite him to her room for a coffee afterward, and wanted everything to be just right. As she stood barefoot in her bath robe, trying to decide on her shoes, a knock came on her door. It was the bellhop with a note from the lobby. Sam slipped him a dollar and closed the door, opening up the note as she turned away.

"Sam," it read, "sorry I won't be able to make it tonight. I'm at the airport and flying home tonight. Family emergency. Please call me or email if you feel inclined. I had a marvellous time. James."

His telephone number and email address were at the bottom of the note. She crumpled it and tossed it on the table.

Damn him, she thought. *Couldn't he at least call me if he wanted to brush me off?* She phoned the conference organisers and learned that Dr Hay had in fact left that evening but did not know the reason. Sam hung up and threw herself down on the bed, feeling unaccountably lonely.

Sam grimaced as she came out of her reverie back in Collinsville. By the time she had gotten home, she realised that the only contact detail James had had was for the lobby of her hotel. There was no way he could have phoned her. She immediately decided to call him but then found she had left the note behind. Normally, that would be no problem thanks to the wonders of the internet, but his telephone number was unlisted and there was no answer on his university one. An email to the head of his department at the university elicited no reply after three days, so Sam pushed aside what might have been and got on with her work. The next few months had her scurrying after a story on the Great Lakes and James' name and face drifted out of her memory. Until now.

The email was a short message from her sister Andi with a link to a newspaper in Australia.

"Hi Sam," the message read, "I'll call you soon but didn't you meet this James Hay guy in SF? See ya, Andi."

Sam clicked on the link and found an article from the Townsville Bulletin about a strange black rock found in the jungles of northern Australia. One of the local lecturers at the university, Dr James Hay, was investigating. She peered at a grainy picture of a nondescript rock standing in a clearing, then at the picture of the man. Sam found herself smiling and wondered whether she should try calling him again.

Instead, she launched a search on the internet and reacquainted herself with the topic of cryptozoology, James' frustratingly short biography, and a few more references to black rocks and their significance. Sam sat back and gave the matter some thought, sipping on her coffee, only to find it was cold. She got up and made herself a fresh pot, waiting in her kitchen until it was brewed. Carrying the fresh cup back to her desk she put the cup down to cool a fraction and called up a picture of the black rock again, staring at the grainy pixelated image...she picked up her coffee cup and was astounded to find it was stone cold. *What the hell?* she thought. *I made myself a fresh cup.* Sam got up and went through into the kitchen, only to stop dead at the sight of the coffee urn, almost boiled dry. *I...I left at least two more mugs in there, didn't I?* The wall clock read ten minutes of seven...*but it's afternoon*...she checked outside, staring into the dusk, and feeling disoriented. *I fell asleep. I never do that.* Frowning, she sat down at her desk again, absently rubbing a sore spot on her right shoulder.

After a few minutes she came to a decision and picked up the telephone and put through a call to a Science Fiction and Fantasy magazine in Milwaukee. Half an eloquent hour later, she had sold the editor on the idea that she would write an article on 'The Black Rock of Australia and its Yowies'. The magazine agreed on a small advance and she started thinking about photographers. Sam had worked with many over the years and after a disastrous affair at the start of her career, had learned to keep business and pleasure separate. Now she had a small stable of reliable photographic artists who could be relied upon to keep their pants on, even when sharing accommodation. The problem was that she only worked with the best and they were in great demand. She consulted her notebook and started calling.

The first two on her list were in the field and the third was nursing a severe head cold, so she tried the fourth, Marc Lachlan. His agent said he was on assignment but gave her a number at which he could be reached.

"Hello, Marc...Sam here. I've got something interesting...where's Tasmania?...You're kidding?...It's right in your back yard then. Townsville." Sam listened for a few moments. "That far? Okay, where do you fly home from?...Sydney. Okay, how about I meet you there in three days; we do a quick jaunt up to Townsville, take a few photos and be home within the week?...Well, you've got your fare home already but I'll spring for your fare to Townsville and back, and your food...no, you'll be getting some great pics out of it...have you heard of the Yowie? No? Look it up...okay, I'll call you tomorrow when I have my flight booked."

The next twenty four hours was hectic, booking a flight from St Louis to LAX, then through to Sydney, Australia. She decided to leave the last hop up the coast until she got there. It might be more convenient to drive if it wasn't too far. Her neighbour agreed to water her pot plants and collect her mail, she selected items from her wardrobe and went out to buy some more, and she set up an automated answering service for her telephone and email address. Then she called Marc back and let him know her flight number and time.

The flight out of St Louis left at noon so she was out of her apartment just after eight, suffering through heavy traffic on Highway 70 across the Mississippi and through the city to Lambert Field by taxi. It cost her an arm and a leg but at least she didn't have to worry about long term parking at the airport. Another two hours in queues and working her way slowly through the security procedures and she could relax in the departure lounge for half an hour with a book. She had found a copy of Tony Healy and Paul Cropper's 'The Yowie--In Search of Australia's Bigfoot'. The cover put her off with its lurid representation of a fierce, obviously fictitious monster, but she persevered and by the time the boarding call sounded, she was lost in the wilds of Australia, face to face with dozens of carefully chronicled reports.

The United flight to LA was cramped and crowded and a bawling kid in the seat next to her prevented reading, so she put her book away and stared out of the window at the monotonous cloud cover and glimpses of land far below. She thought again about James and wondered if she was making a fool of herself. Perhaps she had misread the situation months before and he had in reality felt nothing for her. Well, if that was the case it was no loss. She'd just write her story, spend a couple of weeks seeing as much of the country as possible and head home. As a result she was miserable by the time she got to LA and had to negotiate her way from the domestic terminal to the international. To make it worse, one of the handles on her suitcases snapped and she was forced to carry it instead of wheeling it along.

By the time she checked her luggage in and boarded the Qantas flight to Sydney, she was in a foul mood and downed several glasses of a mediocre Chardonnay in an attempt to escape her thoughts. Somewhere over the eastern Pacific her mood mellowed and she slept as the jet chased the setting sun across the ocean.

When she awoke, she gulped some analgesics and plenty of water, ate a rather delicious meal of braised steak and salad, then put her earphones on and returned to her book, whiling away the long hours with the wild man-apes of Australia. She found the problem was not a simple one as no one could agree as to what the Yowie was. Some people saw it as a cryptid, an animal that was so rare or secretive that it successfully hid itself away in remote areas. Others saw it as a paranormal phenomenon, existing only in people's minds or as some exotic construct more akin to a poltergeist or a haunting. Muddying the waters were the connections between the Yowie and alien big cats and UFOs. *James believes all this?* she thought incredulously. *What am I getting myself into?* She took out her notebook and started roughing out an article that poked fun at the whole idea. By the time the jet started losing height for its descent into Sydney, she had the bare bones written. *All it needs now is a little local colour and a few decent pictures of the black rock, the mad scientist and...I wonder if I could get someone to dress up in a monkey suit?* She read it over again and felt a little niggling itch of guilt. *Am I condemning James out of hand? No, I'll give him his chance, then I'll finish the article.*

Sam picked up her bags at the baggage carousel and moved through customs before making her way over to the Virgin Airlines counter. She had agreed with Marc that this was a delightfully funny place to meet and...there he was. Marc was a tall, thin man in his late twenties, not bad looking, with a wispy black beard obscuring an otherwise strong face and what Sam knew to be a deceptively mild manner. Marc was passionate about environmental issues and had won many awards for his in-your-face style. When he saw something happening, he was often the first one there and he brooked no opposition.

Marc pushed himself upright from a lounging position against the Avis rental car booth and sauntered to meet her.

"Sam, good to see you again. You have a good flight?"

Sam hugged him, something Marc obviously enjoyed. "Not bad. How about you? Rarin' to go?"

Marc looked around at the crowded concourse and lowered his voice. "You don't really think we'll get to see one of these things, do you? A yowie?"

Sam grinned. "You never know. From what I've been reading, they should be as thick on the ground as kangaroos. Now, have you priced air tickets against a rental car? I'd rather drive a few hours and get the feel of the country."

Marc laughed. "Australia's the size of the Lower Forty-eight. We may only be moving between two adjoining States but it's about the same distance as New York to Miami. We gotta fly."

Sam looked sceptical but allowed herself to be persuaded and she bought two tickets on a Virgin Blue flight from Sydney to Brisbane, then on another an hour later from Brisbane to Townsville. She stared at the tickets and the flight times. "What are these planes, puddle-jumpers? It's going to take us all day to get there."

The 737 climbed swiftly and Sam soon came to terms with the size of Australia as the brown and thirsty land spread out underneath her, rolling for hour after hour beneath a patchy cloud cover. Sunset overtook them an hour out of Townsville and Sam was amazed and a little disturbed at how few lights showed from the ground. Then they were descending through warm air and clear skies to a welcoming patch of light along the shores of a large bay. The wheels screeched on the tarmac and reverse thrust slowed the jet quickly. Once they had collected their bags they walked out of the tiny airport terminal--only six departure/arrival gates--into a balmy evening and took a taxi to a hotel on the Strand.

Sam and Marc took a taxi up to the university the next morning, calling at the great grey concrete block that housed the School of Biology. They found Dr Hay's room locked, so they made their way up to the second floor to see the departmental secretary and were shown, after a slight delay, into the office of the Head of Department, Professor Peter Howard.

Howard rose from behind his desk as Sam and Marc entered the room. He was a medium sized man, about a hundred and seventy two centimetres tall, but of stocky build. His florid face sported a closely trimmed but full black beard beneath a thick thatch of similar coloured hair. Deep-set eyes scanned Sam's chest avidly as she advanced across the carpeted room to take the proffered hand, only rising to meet her eyes at the last moment.

"Ms Louis," Howard said in a high-pitched, rather breathless voice. "I am delighted to meet you. Won't you take a seat?" He waved his hand toward one of two chairs set in front of his desk.

"Thank you, professor," Sam said. "This is Marc Lachlan, my photographer."

Howard tore his gaze away from another deep consideration of Sam's mammary development and glanced at Marc, shaking his hand perfunctorily and letting him find his own chair. "Now," he said, turning back to Sam, "What can I do for you?"

Sam handed Howard a business card. "I'm a freelance journalist based in the States, professor, and I'm following up the story reported in the Townsville Bulletin concerning the black rock. I understand one of your department members, Dr James Hay, is investigating it?"

Howard scowled. "Dr Hay does not have the support of this department."

"So you are against him investigating this rock?"

"Personally, yes. I think it a complete waste of time, especially for an eco-biologist. I would have thought a geologist the most obvious candidate...or maybe an anthropologist, if it is in fact carved. However, as long as Dr Hays completes his departmental duties, I cannot prevent him wandering off into the bush chasing wild geese on his own time." He smiled toothily at his own joke.

"I see," Sam nodded. "Would you have any objection to my talking to Dr Hay?"

Howard shrugged. "None whatsoever, if you can see any point to it." He hesitated, and then leaned forward, lowering his voice confidentially. "Strictly between you and me, the man's lost it." He tapped his temple. "It's only a matter of time before the university dismisses him."

"Really?" Sam leaned forward herself, well aware of the effect the motion had on her anatomy. She was all for equality, but also saw no point in denying whatever weapons nature had given her. Judging by Howard's reaction, she'd just blasted him with both barrels. "Lost it in what way?"

"The man's as mad as a hatter. Oh, he's competent enough when he sticks to academic matters, but this obsession he has with the paranormal and what he calls 'mystery animals' is intellectually obscene."

Sam had a good idea that wasn't the only obscene thing floating around in the professor's mind. "So I take it you do not believe in cryptozoology?" She leaned back in her chair and made a few notes on her stenographer's pad.

"What's cryptozoology?" Marc asked.

Howard glanced at Marc briefly before transferring his hungry gaze back to Sam. "Cryptozoology is defined as the study or search for animals that are hypothesised to exist but for which there is no proof. It is also the search for animals thought to be extinct. I have no objection to the study of this latter aspect, for instance, following up sightings of the Thylacine in Tasmania..."

"The only Tassie tigers I saw down there were on bottles of beer," Marc murmured.

"Quite." Howard pursed his lips as if he had bitten into a lemon. "Dr Hay goes far beyond the acceptable limits of science with his pursuit of nonsense animals like this yowie of his, or bunyips, or ghosts. If that was not enough, his pursuit of this black rock compounds his error. I think he has left the realm of fantasy for that of deception."

"Deception, Professor Howard?" Sam asked. "Those are strong words. How is he deceiving people?"

"I have it on good authority--a member of his research team is loyal to the good name of this department--that the black stone is very probably a hoax. An elaborate one, no doubt, but Dr Hay has many friends among the Aboriginal communities..." Howard made the idea sound unwholesome. "...and they would do anything to aid him in his deceit."

"Why would they do that?"

"You don't know the Australian Aborigine, Ms Louis," Howard said. "There are some good ones, I'm sure, but by and large they are shiftless and lazy and will do anything for enough money to buy alcohol."

"Not in my experience," Marc said sharply. "I've been here before and..."

"I think perhaps we have discussed this enough," Howard said stiffly. "If *you* wish to discuss other matters at another time, I am happy to do so Ms Louis." He audibly accented the second-person personal pronoun.

Sam rose to her feet and shook hands, smiling pleasantly. Professor Howard did not offer to shake hands with Marc or show them to the door but instead, stared at Sam's posterior. She turned at the door and caught him but he showed no embarrassment, treating her instead to another toothy grin.

"Creep!" she said as she closed the door behind her.

Marc grinned. "I was watching and waiting for you to deck him."

"I considered it, but then I thought, 'hell, a little ogling ain't gonna hurt me', so I played it up to see how much he'd tell us."

"So are you going to see him again? Who knows what you may find out?"

"Hell no. Let's go see if we can find that student who first saw the rock."

A few enquiries in the student tea-room led them to Rick Jennings but he was disappointingly vague about the whole thing. He had even wiped all record of the stone from his computer and camera. The only interesting thing he had to say concerned the notion that it was all a hoax.

"Uh-uh. As far as I'm concerned, the rock was, well, ordinary. The circle was the most amazing thing. Every single living thing gone for a hundred metres. The rock was just a lump of glass or something. Perhaps just a painted rock."

Rick's supervisor was away, so Sam and Marc took a taxi into the city and saw the reporter, Jenny Bolton, at the Townsville Bulletin who had written the story.

"Sorry, I can't tell you any more than what was in the paper," Jenny said in a friendly enough manner. She tossed her head, throwing her long blond hair back and smiled sweetly, her eyes lingering for a moment on Marc.

"Where did you get your information?" Sam asked.

Jenny looked solemn. "I can't reveal my sources." Then she spoiled it all by giggling. "I've always wanted to say that. But seriously, I don't think it's any great secret it came from Ed Sanders."

"Who's he?" Marc asked. "We're from out of town, remember."

"Mmm, yes," Jenny eyed Marc appreciatively. "Are you doing anything this evening?"

"Probably working. Ed Sanders?"

"Pity. He's Peter Howard's nephew, up at the uni. He's also a volunteer on the Dr Hay's Black Rock Expedition. He sent me the reports and the pictures."

"How do you know him?"

"Well, I don't really. Aside from being a part-time student myself, I don't know why he'd send them to me."

"You said there are other pictures?" Sam asked. "We only saw the one in the paper."

Jenny opened a folder on her desktop and spread half a dozen thumbnails out. "These are the only ones I have. Want to see them?"

Rick Jennings had been right. In the pictures spread out on the computer screen, the black rock looked fairly ordinary, a black bollard out of place in a tropical jungle. What really took their breath away was the hundred metre diameter circle neatly excised from the rainforest, the edges sharp and clean.

"Jeez," Marc breathed. "It looks like God's own cookie cutter took a chunk out of it."

"Could we get a copy of these?" Sam asked. "I'd be happy to give you credit if I use them."

Jenny hesitated. "I shouldn't really." She smiled coyly at Marc. "I'll be having a drink tonight at seven in the Australian Bar on Palmer Street. If you're not working I could give them to you then--if you're good."

Marc looked sideways at Sam, arching an eyebrow.

Sam shrugged. "Don't look at me. You're old enough to know what you're doing. I'm feeling a bit jet-lagged anyway, so I'll be having an early night."

"Okay then, Jenny. I'll see you at seven."

"Try not to be too late tonight, lover-boy," Sam said with a grin as they emerged onto the hot streets of Townsville. "I want to be up at the university again tomorrow and I want you bushy-tailed. And make sure you get those pictures."

"She might not want to give them up," Marc said with a smile. "She said only if I'm good."

"Then you'd better be very good, Marc. We need those pictures."

4

There were only minor injuries sustained on the Army Blackhawk personnel, largely because the aircraft had been no more than a few feet off the ground when its systems died. Captain Mason immediately commandeered James' camp and had his injured men attended to. The other soldiers spread out under the supervision of their sergeant and secured the area, though their numbers were stretched thin by the extended perimeter.

Once all was secure, Captain Mason came over to where James sat alone with an armed soldier guarding him. He dismissed the guard and sat down on a log a metre or so from James.

"How did you do it, Dr Hay?"

"Do what?" James asked cautiously.

"Bring down the Blackhawk. It's lucky for you there were no serious injuries."

James' lips quirked into a wry smile. "That would be some trick, wouldn't it? Just how am I supposed to have generated an electromagnetic pulse strong enough to take out every electrical system in the vicinity? Is your watch working, by the way?"

Mason looked at his watch, raised it to his ear, and then tapped it a few times. "Everything?" he asked.

James nodded. "Everything electrical, but it's only temporary. It'll come on again in about half an hour, so you'd better have your pilot make sure everything is switched off."

"So how did you do it?"

"I didn't. It was the black rock."

"A chunk of stone?" Mason stared at the university lecturer in disbelief.

"It would seem to me that you are looking at things backwards, Captain. It emitted an e-m pulse; therefore it cannot just be a chunk of rock. And before you ask, I don't know what it is. I've been here twenty-four hours and while I've noted a few things, I'm no nearer deciphering its function or mode of operation."

"You said earlier it was booby-trapped."

"I said that to get you to react fast without arguing. I'm inclined to think it is not just an automated system but there is intelligence involved."

"In a rock?"

"No, but in whoever or whatever put the rock here in the first place. Look, it knocks out electrical signals in machinery, but only mildly interferes with animal nervous tissue, which is also electrical in nature. Anything crossing the boundary into the circle is affected. The man who discovered the circle said he felt uncomfortable and noticed his watch, cell-phone and camera stopped working. When we arrived, none of us felt anything, but any animal that crosses the boundary, turns back immediately. What does that tell you?"

Captain Mason shook his head.

"It tells me that it learns. The first person to find it set off the e-m pulse, but we didn't. Animals continue to set it off. It appears to want people close to it but not animals."

"Then why did it knock out the Blackhawk and my people?"

"I don't know. Perhaps a large machine arriving with a great many people alarmed it."

"Yet you have machinery here that is unaffected."

"Yes, I'm not sure why that should be. Maybe there's a size threshold or something. The machinery is affected once an animal sets it off."

Captain Mason chewed his lip for a few moments and adjusted his floppy camouflage hat. "Okay, I'm going to take a chance that you weren't responsible, Dr Hay. Will you show me what you know?" When James said nothing, he hurried on. "Anything you can tell me might save lives. When we don't report in, there'll be someone coming to look for us, and they may not be quite so willing to listen."

James smiled. "Oh, I'm not raising any objections; I'm just not sure what I can tell you."

"Anything you can."

James took him out into the circle again and together, he and the captain walked across to the black rock. He put his hand on it. "It's quite safe to touch. We analysed a fragment of what we think is similar material found at its base and it appears to be ordinary quartz. As you can see from the top pyramid, it is a six-sided crystal, apparently natural, but the sides have been carved and polished. It should be quite warm from standing in the sun but in fact it is cold. As near as we can determine it remains a constant fifteen degrees Celsius."

26

Captain Mason ran his hand over it tentatively. "Are those carvings of animals on it? They're a bit hard to make out."

"Yes, prehistoric ones at the bottom, modern ones toward the top and...hello, that's new." James peered closely at a carving near the top of the quartz cylinder. "It's a brumby. I'd swear that wasn't there before."

Mason raised his eyebrows but made no comment, and after a few moments, James continued. "There's a subsonic hum associated with the rock that rises sharply when the alarm is set off. We don't know what the endpoint is as our instruments go dead."

Mason looked around at the huge open circle and at the black crystal at its centre. "It's obviously been placed here deliberately. Any hints as to its function?"

"Only one."

"Which is?"

"To attract attention," James said simply. "And it's accomplished that. Now that it's got us here, it'll be making the next move."

"Sounds ominous."

"If it had bad intentions, I think we'd know about it by now."

Mason grunted. "Reconnaissance first, then the strike."

"I think you're wrong."

"Well, hopefully we'll be ready for it if it is hostile. I'm going to go and check on my men now. Will you let me know if anything untoward happens?"

James wandered back to the campsite, where he was immediately quizzed about what was happening. As a couple of soldiers stood close by, their automatic weapons at the ready, he kept the discussion upbeat, trying to sound positive about the presence of the military. There were a few grumbles but Nathan caught on quickly, as James thought he would, and talked only of inconsequential things. When everybody broke up to get some rest, or eat or play cards, James managed to have a few words individually.

"Ratana, gather together all the data and send it to everyone on the team, even Ed. Include home as well as JCU addresses. The captain hasn't said anything yet, but it's in the nature of the military to be secretive. I don't want this event to disappear from sight."

"Robbie's got a website too. Shall I get him to upload it there?"

James nodded. "If he can, yes." He crossed to where Ed Sanders was sitting reading a book, and sat cross-legged next to him. "Who have you sent the data to, Ed?"

"What...what do you mean?" Ed stammered. "I haven't..."

"Of course you have. I'd guess just to Professor Howard, but I'm hoping other people too."

"Uh...other people?"

"Yes." James smiled sadly. "I know you're the spy in my camp, Ed, feeding information about what I do, what I say, to your uncle. Normally, I'd just kick your sorry butt off the team, but this time you've done us a favour. I need as many people to know of it as possible, so fire up your computer again and...do you know any newspaper or television reporters?"

Ed nodded, not trusting himself to speak.

"Okay, do it, and quickly."

James beckoned to Nathan and together they sauntered out into the circle again, seemingly just chatting casually. "Are your friends likely to cause trouble?"

"We don't cause trouble, uncle," Nathan replied. "We take a stand for Aboriginal rights. What the white man does is cause trouble."

"Then are your friends likely to take a stand right here that might cause the army to make trouble?"

Nathan grinned. "Nicely put, uncle. No, I told them to scarper soon as we knew the chopper was on its way."

"How did you know that?"

"We heard them on the walkie-talkies up at the road. I reckon there'll be more coming."

James nodded. "The Captain intimated as much."

"Are we just going to sit around and wait for something to happen?"

"I'm open to suggestions."

"We could ask Grandfather Mick."

James turned and stared at the young Aboriginal man. "You know where he is?"

"Nope. Not a clue."

"Then how do you propose we talk to him?"

Nathan chuckled. "Uncle, have you really forgotten everything you learned at the Settlement? Has too much science destroyed your faith?"

"No, Nathan. I'm well aware of Mick's reputation as a Karadji man and I have heard him say he communes with the spirit world and believes he can run like the emu, but..."

"There you have it, uncle. You know of his reputation, you have heard him say, he believes he can...What of your belief, Dr James Hay of James Cook University? Are you just humouring an old man or do you believe him, here?" Nathan struck his chest with his open palm.

James was about to answer and then thought better of it. He remained deep in thought for several minutes, staring across the open circle toward the far edge of the jungle and a stand of emergent gums now hosting another flock of raucous lorikeets.

"It's not that I don't believe him," James said slowly, trying to be precise in his choice of words. "It's just that I have been trained as a scientist and I try to look at things logically. Something like this black quartz rock excites me, but it also disturbs me. It represents a logical and ordered world that has become frayed around the edges."

"But you've spent all your adult life pursuing things like yowies and ghosts and UFOs. How do they reflect a logical and ordered world?"

"They don't, obviously. But in the pursuit, in the scientific investigation, I strip away the dross, the hoaxes and the imaginings and reduce a phenomenon down to a tiny core of solid data. I'm hoping that one day I can find the scientific basis behind them."

"Can't you do that with Grandfather Mick's stories?" Nathan asked.

James scratched his head. "What? That he can sleep beside a waterhole and visit the spirit Tjakkan who lives underwater, exchanging crystals and cords from within his body for knowledge? That he can run like an emu all day and night? Or that he can control the weather? Which of those sounds like it might have a scientific basis?"

"You've seen him call up a storm."

"It was the rainy season, for God's sake."

"Ask him," Nathan said. "Just put away your scientific narrow-mindedness for a few minutes, and ask him for help."

James shook his head wearily. "I thought I'd taught you better than that, Nathan. Has none of your scientific training had any effect?"

Nathan smiled. "I thought Grandfather Mick taught you better than that, uncle," he said, mimicking his closest non-blood relative. "Have none of his words stayed in your mind."

"Oh, I can remember what he said, and he said to listen to my heart."

"Then do it."

"I am. I know my methods..."

"Your heart, uncle, not your head."

James was silent again for several minutes, thinking. "I feel...foolish. It's like I'm praying to him." He scanned the clearing and the cleanly cut edges of the rainforest, but he and Nathan were alone. "Okay, you win," he grumbled. He cleared his throat and spoke to the heat-shimmered air. "Grandfather Mick, I have need of your wisdom so that I can understand this black rock.

29

Please help me." He waited for thirty seconds before turning back to Nathan. "There, you've got me to make a fool of myself. I don't know why I let you talk me into this."

"I wonder 'ow long 'fore you ask for my 'elp," said a deep, heavily accented voice behind him.

James swung round and stared in utter disbelief at the ancient Aboriginal man standing before him. The man only came up to his chest, but his personality towered over James', overpowering him. "Mick," he said in a strangled voice. He felt suddenly faint and sat down on the hard earth and put his head between his knees, taking rapid breaths.

"Whas wrong wit 'im, Kalti Wambiri," the old man asked, concern tingeing his voice.

"I think you startled him, Grandfather."

"I'll be okay," James muttered. "Just let me catch my breath."

The old man looked down on the sitting white man, concern mingled with amusement glinting in his deep-set dark eyes. He was dressed in a pair of grubby red shorts, his deep chest bare and liberally patterned with scars. A faded red bandanna was fastened around his head, making a vain attempt to control his wild hair which, curly and greying, covered his head. His feet were bare also, large and callused and covered with a patina of fine dust.

A chorus of shouts broke out along the far wall of vegetation and half a dozen men armed with assault rifles raced across the open ground toward them. James struggled to his feet with Nathan's help and managed to interpose himself between the soldiers and the old man. Captain Mason holstered his pistol and faced James while his sergeant and men surrounded the trio with weapons raised.

"Who is he, Dr Hay, and why is he here?" Mason asked belligerently.

"He's my adoptive grandfather, Mick Wambiri. He's here because I asked him to come, days ago when I first heard about this site."

"And how in hell did he get here? I have this place surrounded."

"I would imagine he walked, but you can ask him if you like."

Mason pushed James aside and stalked over to the old man. "Okay, you'd better start talking, old man. This is a restricted area and I want to know how you got in."

"I apologise for this man, Grandfather," James said softly. "He is upset and says things that on mature reflection I'm sure he would not say."

"Thas okay, Aparrerinja, 'e is in a 'urry, like mos' white men."

"What did he call you?" Mason rounded on James.

30

"It's my nickname from when I was first adopted into the tribe. Aparrerinja is a Central Desert word for the ghost gum. It's relevant on several levels."

Mason swung back to Mick again. "Why are you here?"

"Aparrerinja, did you no' tell 'im I was ask to come?"

"I told him, Grandfather."

Mason exploded. "Will you two stop talking as if I wasn't here and answer me straight?" he yelled.

"Whys 'e turnin' red, Aparrerinja?"

"Because he has no patience, Grandfather." James moved in between Mason and Mick. "Captain, please calm down. You are upsetting my grandfather and it really would be better if that didn't happen."

"I only want my questions answered," Mason snapped. He took a few deep breaths. "Okay," he said in a softer tone, "Please ask your grandfather how he got through my men without being seen."

"Can you tell him, Grandfather?"

"I walk t'rough. They don' see me."

Mason shot a vicious look at his sergeant. "Ask him where on the circle he came in."

"I hear you plurry well, bileela," Mick said. He pointed across the circle, past the wreckage of the Blackhawk. "T'ey make plen'y noise. I walk close, dis close," Mick indicated arm's length, "T'ey no hear--I walk t'rough, no see me."

"What did he call me?"

"He was referring to the fact that you are somewhat...ah, noisy."

Captain Mason grunted and walked over to his sergeant. "Get these men back in position. Then you and I are going to get to the bottom of this. I want to know how an old man can get past your men so easily."

The sergeant snapped to attention and saluted. "Yes, sir." He barked orders at his men, who immediately turned and raced across the open until they disappeared into the trees.

Mason looked back at the three men and grimaced. "I'll leave the old...your grandfather in your care then Dr Hay. Please see to it that he behaves himself." He beckoned to his sergeant and together they trotted away toward the wreckage and beyond to interrogate the luckless soldiers who had let Mick through unchallenged.

James smiled ruefully. "Poor guys. I suppose you pulled that same trick on them as you did on me, sneaking up like that."

"I don' sneak. I walk in open, 'ide nothin'."

"He's right, uncle," Nathan said. "You had your back to him but he was right in front of me when he appeared." The young Aboriginal man grinned. "Popped right out of thin air."

"And how is that walking in the open?"

"I can' 'elp it if pe'ple don' see me." Mike grinned broadly and tugged at his straggly grey beard. "We go see dis black rock now?"

"Sure." He led the way over to the obelisk, detouring slightly so Mike could admire the wreckage of the downed helicopter. "Ratana's here too, by the way, Grandfather."

"Thas good. Kalti, you marry dis girl soon. Gi' me lots gran'chil'en."

"Yes, Grandfather," Nathan said meekly. He stared back questioningly at James when he smiled and raised an eyebrow at the answer.

Mick stopped a few paces away from the obelisk and contemplated it for several long minutes. "Is a crysta'," he said at last. "I t'ink Tjakkan send it."

"The sky spirit?" Nathan asked. "Why?"

"Nex' time I see 'im, I ask."

"How do you know it's from Tjakkan?" James asked.

Mick shrugged. "I feel. Also, Tjakkan like carvin' of an'mals. See?" He pointed at the carvings on the black pillar. "Old. Many an'mals dead, gone 'fore Aboriginal man made from mud. Tjakkan have ot'er pe'ple then, mebbe still do. You see?"

James squatted and peered closely at the carvings near the bottom. Though in low relief and polished, the images were recognisable. Mammoths, a great bear, an eagle, a wolf...and what looked like an ape. *No, that's a man.* James frowned, for surely such men had died out long ago? The image had a heavy brow ridge, receding chin and rounded shoulders, but a barrel chest and muscular arms and legs. *Neanderthal man?*

Mick moved closer and ran his hands over the cool surface of the crystal. "It speak," he murmured.

James looked up in surprise. "You can hear it? What does it say?"

Mick listened, and then hummed in a low, monotonous tone. "No' much," he grinned. "I ask Tjakkan when I see 'im."

James smiled but looked disappointed. "So you can't tell us anything?"

"I sit an' talk wit' it, mebbe Tjakkan speak."

"Yeah, sorry to have dragged you all the way here. Where were you when you got my email?"

Mick was already settling himself into a cross-legged pose about a metre from the obelisk. "Bamaga," he said without looking up.

"All the way up the Torres Strait? That was only three days ago. How did you get down here so fast? Fly into Cairns?"

"Aparrerinja," he said reprovingly. "You know I can' fly. I run--like emu." Mick turned back to the quartz column and started to hum, the drone gradually forming words. He would chant for a few moments, and then lean forward as if listening.

Nathan plucked at James' sleeve and beckoned him away, so the two retired to a bit of shade near the forest edge, not far from where the stream crossed the circle. This close to the edge, a few flies braved the emanations from the obelisk, drawn by the scent of sweat, and James flapped at them ineffectually as he sat down.

"I love him dearly," James said, looking at the sitting figure of the old man fifty metres away, "But sometimes he drives me to distraction."

"I noticed that. You think like a white man too much, uncle."

"You mean I should suspend my disbelief and take what he says at face value? How can I, Nathan? You heard him; he claims to have run from Bamaga to here in three days--like an emu, he says."

"So?"

"So even if he was an athlete he couldn't do it. How's an old man going to do more than walk? He must be, what, close on a hundred?"

"Twenty years ago, when I was a kid, I saw him for the first time," Nathan said. "He looked exactly the same then."

"Well, once you're really old you don't change much."

"My grandfather saw him when he came home from the war in the islands," Nathan said slowly. "In nineteen forty-five. He said Mick was an old man then." Nathan looked at James. "How old does that make him?"

"I thought Mick was your grandfather?"

"He is my grandfather like he is your grandfather, Aparrerinja. A matter of courtesy. He is Wambiri, so my family took the name."

James sat and digested this information for a while with Mick's droning song sounding like a distant swarm of bees. "And the emu business?" he asked at last.

"You know he is Karadji, but do you really know what that means?"

"I've read the books, I've talked to tribal elders, even to Mick when I was a kid," James said, nodding.

"Then you know some of it. A man who would be a Karadji goes to a deep waterhole where he knows a spirit lives and falls asleep beside it. If he is chosen, the spirit kills him and takes him down into the water, there giving him gifts in exchange for the magic crystals and cords inside him. The spirit tests him and if he passes, the man is brought back to life on the edge of the waterhole. Thereafter, the Karadji man can travel through water or up into the sky. He can talk with animals and birds and he can control the weather. He can run like the emu."

"This is Dreamtime magic," James said carefully. "The Dreamtime has a reality of its own for its people."

Nathan smiled. "But not for the white man?" James said nothing. "Let me tell you a story," Nathan went on. "When I was ten, I was playing by myself in the scrub, pretending I was a valiant hunter with my spear and my throwing stick, when I was bitten by a brown snake. Now, as you know, the venom of the brown snake kills quickly, within an hour, faster if the victim is a child as I was. I was alone in the scrub, over an hour's walk from the Settlement and three hours walk from the nearest doctor. I was dead. When the pain became fierce I cried for my parents and I cried for Mick to help me. Five minutes later, he was there, I swear it. He stepped out from behind a tree that could not hide a rat. He picked me up and ran, carrying me to the doctor. I told myself at the time that I was dreaming, for the scrub flowed about us like water and the sun stood still. He ran those fifteen kilometres, carrying a ten-year-old child, in twenty minutes. He put me down outside the clinic and stepped behind a fence post, vanishing in an eye blink. That is the emu man."

"That's a hell of a story, Nathan."

"But you don't believe me?"

"You could have been mistaken as to where you were. Perhaps you were really playing near the doctor's clinic and when you found yourself there, your mind played a trick and you thought Mick had helped you."

Nathan smiled sadly. "Forgive me if I'm blunt, uncle, but like many white men, you can be an arrogant sod at times. You think your world view is the only one and you blind yourself to the greater reality out there."

"The truth is out there?"

"Now you are mocking me, but yes." Nathan turned away and looked into the distance, sorrowing for his friend. He felt a hand on his shoulder.

"I'm sorry, Nathan. That was unconscionable. I have spent long enough with you and your tribe to know that you do not lie. I may not know how a thing works but I would be a fool to deny it does when I can see the evidence in front of me. Please forgive me."

Nathan hesitated a moment before turning and embracing James. At that moment, Mick let out a yell of surprise and pleasure and leapt to his feet. Nathan and James did likewise, running across to him. As they did so, Ratana and the other members of the research team appeared and Captain Mason emerged from the forest at the far side of the circle.

"What is it, Grandfather?" Nathan asked. "What have you found?"

"A big wrong is to be made righ'," Mick said, a great smile enveloping his face. "Tjakkan speak t'rough stone."

"What wrong?" James asked.

"How is it to be made right? Nathan inquired.

"Who the hell's this Jack-An person?" Mason said as he arrived.

"Big wrong," Mick repeated. "Made lon' 'go, in Dreamtime, by quinkan. You fix, Aparrerinja, it has you brumby sign on it."

"Me? How can I fix something from the Dreamtime?" James said.

"Will somebody please tell me what's going on?" Captain Mason was starting to turn red again. "Who is Jack-An and who is Quin-can?"

Ratana took him aside and explained. "Tjakkan is a spirit, sort of like a god, and Aboriginal Karadji men like Grandfather Mick, who are witch-doctors I suppose you could say, can talk to them. The Quinkan are dark figures, like the shadows of men, which live in crevices and holes and cause trouble."

"Shit," Mason said sourly. "I thought for a moment some of this might be real. This whole thing is turning into a nightmare."

"Oh, it's real enough," Ratana said. "Not being Karadji I haven't met Tjakkan, but I believe Mick when he says he has. The nightmare part is the Quinkan. I've met them once and I hope never to again."

Mason regarded the tall Torres Strait Islander girl in disbelief. "Barmy, the lot of them," he muttered. He walked back and stood near James, where he could overhear the conversation.

Maggie and Robbie stood close to James, looking worried. Ed stood a lot further back, his expression reflecting distrust and apprehension.

"What's going on, Dr Hay?" Maggie asked. "Who is this?"

"He's a very high ranking Aboriginal elder. I asked him to come and look at the stone and he now says he knows its purpose."

"Cool," Robbie grinned. "What's it do?"

James ignored him. "What did Tjakkan say, Grandfather?"

"'e calls for you by name, Aparrerinja. You mus' go south, to Tunbubudla."

"Where's Tunbu-whatever, Dr Hay?" Maggie asked.

"It's one of the peaks in the Glasshouse Mountains," Nathan replied when James said nothing. "Actually, two peaks close together that are called 'The Twins'."

James took Mick to one side, warning off Captain Mason with a glare. "Grandfather, explain to me exactly what you were told," he said in a low voice. "Why do I have to go to Tunbubudla? What else did he say?"

Mick stared hard at his adopted white grandson, as if deciding what he could safely be told. "Is difficul', Aparrerinja. Tjakkan no use words, mos'ly picshures, feelings. You go Tunbubudla, take Kalti, Ratana, o'ders. You pick, but mus' take woman in Townsville. She wai' for you."

"What woman?" James asked sharply. "What's her name? And why?"

"Don' know why, but she 'Merican, red hair, ver' nice." Mick grinned and made suggestive motions with his hands. "You like her, Tjakkan say."

"I haven't the faintest idea who you're talking about," James said with some asperity. "And I have no intention of lugging along somebody I don't even know..." He frowned as a stray memory flitted across his forebrain. Shaking his head, he dismissed the idea. "Anyway, I'm not even sure I can go, Grandfather. Lectures start again next week. Maybe in about three months..."

"No, mus' go now, Tjakkan say. Mus' be at Tunbubudla in five days."

"That's cutting it fine, even if I could go." James eyes sparkled as a thought occurred to him. "Unless Tjakkan's going to help me--make me run like the emu or something."

"It woul' take many years t' make you Karadji, Aparrerinja. I t'ink you take car, 'stead."

James laughed. "Well, I'm not making any promises until I find out whether I can take time off, but what am I supposed to do down there?"

Mick shrugged. "Don' know. Tjakkan don' say, just say you go five days."

"Then we'd better leave immediately." James turned back to his little group. "Right, we're finished here, guys. Pack up and we'll head back to the vehicles. I take it that is allowed, Captain?"

Mason nodded uncertainly. "I suppose so. As long as you're not taking the black rock with you. I got a call from HQ a few minutes ago saying they were bringing in a Chinook to airlift the stone out of here. Don't worry," he added, "We're not bringing it into the circle."

"That's not what I was worried about," James said. "Are you sure the people who put it here will let you take it away?"

"I think I have the firepower. Certainly I will have when the Chinook arrives."

"Tjakkan will no' le' you take it," Mick said softly. He cocked his head on one side as if listening. "'E says to stan' clear. 'e take it 'ome." He stepped back quickly.

The other people in the group scattered, Ed retreating all the way to the tree line, Maggie and Robbie a few paces braver than him. Ratana, Nathan and James stayed near Mick, confident that, being in contact with Tjakkan, he knew what was safe.

Captain Mason looked worried, but stayed where he was, a few paces from the obelisk. He drew his pistol again and tried to look determined. "Nobody's taking it," he said firmly.

The black quartz started to hum audibly, the pitch rising rapidly.

"I think you'd better stand clear, Captain," James said. "I don't know what's going to happen but..."

There was a sharp cracking noise and the crystal column split up its length. The humming rose to a scream and Ratana put her hands over her ears and stepped back. Abruptly, the screaming shut off as if a switch had been thrown and the quartz rock exploded, blossoming outward in a soundless tornado of fine black dust. Captain Mason was thrown back and the others were enveloped in a choking, gritty cloud for a few moments. Then the particles settled and spread out in a gentle zephyr that invaded the circle. Rubbing the grit from their eyes, they stared at the empty spot where the rock had stood.

"I don' t'ink dat s'pose teh 'appen," Mick said, breaking the silence. "It s'pose teh dis'pear."

"Where's it gone?" Mason demanded. He brushed at the coating of dust on his clothes. "Is this all that's left?"

Mick poked around in the dirt near the indentation in the clay that marked the site of the obelisk. He uncovered a flat oval of quartz that fell apart as the sunlight gleamed on it. Advancing a few steps, he uncovered another one, then another, and each well apart, disintegrating, until eleven patches of dust were all that remained.

"Where o'der one?" Mick asked. "Tjakkan say shou' be twelve."

Maggie blushed and dug into the pocket of her bush jacket. She pulled out a sealed plastic bag containing the disc she had dug up earlier. "I'm sorry. I just wanted a sample. I showed everyone earlier, remember?"

"Tha's why it no work," Mick said. "S'pose dis'pear but bit missin'."

"Does that mean this Tjakkan fellow's gonna be pissed?" Robbie asked, squinting nervously at the sky.

Mick grinned. "'E say it okay."

"I'll take that, Miss." Captain Mason held out his hand to Maggie. When she hesitated, he drew his pistol and held it not quite aimed at anyone. "Miss, I have complete authority in this area. You will hand that disc to me now."

Maggie looked at James and he nodded. She gave the disc in its bag to Mason and backed away, looking discomforted.

"Good girl," Mason said. "At least this exercise will not have been a total waste." He holstered his pistol and grinned, becoming chatty as he relaxed. "I was a bit worried what the Colonel would say, crashing a helicopter and not having anything to show for it. This will help." He held up the gleaming disc, then tucked it into his tunic pocket.

"Do you mind if we leave now, Captain?" James asked. "You have something of what you want, at least."

Mason considered for a moment before turning to the forest and yelling, "Sergeant!"

The non-commissioned officer burst from cover and ran to his captain, his assault rifle at the ready. "Sir?"

"Call the men in."

The sergeant barked out a series of orders with parade ground gusto and within minutes, the eleven men from the Blackhawk and the dozen who'd arrived on foot were assembled.

"Sergeant, escort these people to their camp and supervise them as they pack up. They will surrender their computers and other recording equipment to you. Give them a receipt and take them to their vehicles." Mason nodded to James. "You will leave now, Dr Hay. You will get your equipment back once we have removed all reference to this incident. The old Aboriginal man will remain with me. I will have him questioned."

"Is okay, Aparrerinja," Mick said. "I be okay."

Fifteen minutes later, the research team was on its way back to the road and its transport, under army escort. Captain Mason watched a flight of cockatoos screech noisily across the circle and he smiled to see his watch still working.

"The Chinook will be able to land in the circle," he said happily.

Mick yawned. "I go now, cap'n."

"Oh no you don't. Williams, Ross, hold him," he snapped to the two soldiers remaining with him.

Mick muttered something and gestured, before smiling at Mason and taking a sideways step, vanishing between one step and the next as completely as if he had opened a door and stepped through, which in a way he had.

5

The trip down from the Daintree, through Cairns and along the coast road was uneventful. James wrestled the university long-wheelbase Toyota Landcruiser along the rutted and pitted back roads with skill and then onto the paved but still potholed Bruce Highway that connected the whole of the East coast. He drove fast, right on the speed limit, knowing time was of the essence. He dropped his research students off on the way through to the university, continuing over the Ross River to the sprawling mass of the university nestled in the lee of the brown hills. It was evening by the time they got there, so Nathan had to go and find keys to let them into the padlocked Biology Department courtyard to unload the vehicle. An hour later they were finished and they all separated, Ratana and Nathan heading off for a drink at the Student Union club and James headed home for a shower, a meal and an early night.

The next morning he was in the department by seven o'clock, and immediately set about re-organising his schedule. He answered emails, wrote several more, and set up a meeting with Peter Howard for nine. Then he went in search of students and staff who might have seen this mysterious woman who was looking for him. James grunted in surprise when he heard her name and went back to his tiny office to sit and think. After a few moments, he took a piece of paper and constructed a note for her. "Ms Louis," it read, "I will be at my research lab between eight and nine. Please come and see me. There are things we must talk about. James." He added a sketch map of the university ring road and the placement of the Biology building and his out-of-the-way research lab, then stuck it at eye-level on the outside of his door after locking it.

James was sitting at his desk in the little office off his research lab, talking on the telephone to the Dean of Science when he heard a commotion out in the laboratory. He cut short his conversation, having covered the essential points already, and hung up just as the door to his office was flung open. A tall red-haired woman in a black pantsuit and white blouse stood framed in the doorway.

"James Hay, you are a hard man to find," said the woman.

James got to his feet and smiled. "Samantha Louis. It's been a while but it's a pleasure to see you."

Ratana craned her neck to see past the tall woman, something she rarely had to do. "Are you okay, uncle? She just barged in before I could stop her."

"It's fine, Ratana. This is Samantha Louis, a journalist from the States. Samantha, Ratana Allira, my research assistant."

"Uncle?" Sam asked.

"It's a long story, but Ratana's family. What are you doing over here?"

"Well, you did say to give you a call, remember?"

James gaped, and then suddenly grinned. "So I did. Look, I'm sorry to have run out on you like that..." He saw Ratana's interested face and stopped his chatter. "Ratana, could you rustle Sam up a cup of coffee?"

"Hmph, you never ask me if I want one," Ratana said. "You watch Dr Hay," she confided to Sam, "He'll have you running errands for him in no time." She disappeared back into the lab.

"Ah, yes, as I was saying," James said, not meeting Sam's eyes. "I left a message at your hotel. I had a bit of a family emergency...and I sort of hoped you might..."

"I hope it wasn't too serious."

"What?"

"The family emergency. That is, supposing there really was one."

James looked at Sam uncertainly and frowned. "Serious enough," he said. "Did you come all the way out here just to see me?"

"Don't flatter yourself. I came because I'm doing a story on this black rock in the jungle."

"Oh." James knew nobody would travel halfway around the world on such a casual acquaintance, but her words still managed to hurt him. "Well, I'm afraid you're too late. It's gone."

"What do you mean, gone?"

Even Sam's sharp tone sounded lyrical to James and he groaned inwardly. *I don't want complications...do I?* Aloud, he said, "Just that. It disintegrated. It's not there anymore." He glanced at his watch. "Look, I've got an appointment in ten minutes. Why don't you stay here and have your cup of coffee and I'll be back soon. We can talk some more then." He edged around Sam and out the door. "Ratana," he called. "Keep Samantha company, will you? I have to see Howard."

"Okay, uncle."

Sam walked back out into the lab as Ratana approached carrying two mugs of coffee. "Don't let me put you out. I can amuse myself."

Ratana placed one of the mugs on the bench near Sam. "I hope you like it black, because we don't have any milk."

"Yeah, look, don't bother. I'll come back another time." Sam turned to go.

"What's wrong with you Yanks? You're in such a great hurry you can't be pleasant?"

"What?" Sam turned and stared at the tall Islander woman. "What did you just say?"

"You heard me, and I heard you just now, in there. Maybe not the words but I heard the tone. And let me tell you, nothing Dr Hay could possibly do allows you to speak like that to him."

"What the hell would you know about it? Or has he gone running to you telling tales out of school?"

"If you hurt him, I'll hurt you, seriously," Ratana said softly.

Sam stared, and then her lip curled. "My god, I should have known. You're in love with him and you're jealous." To her great astonishment, the Islander woman burst out laughing. Her teeth flashed whitely and her bosom heaved, and she had to put her coffee mug down to prevent it spilling. "What?" Sam grated, "What's so damn funny?"

"Have you ever got the wrong end of the stick, sister," Ratana chuckled, wiping her eyes with a tissue. "I'm not in love with him. He's my uncle."

"He told me he had never married. Was he lying?"

"No, but neither is he a blood relative."

There was a pause of over a minute but finally Sam asked, "Are you going to tell me?"

"I don't know. I'm not sure you're worth it. I only tell my friends and my friends all like James."

Sam stared at Ratana for another minute. "He must be quite a man to bring out such fanatical loyalty," she said softly.

"He is," Ratana said simply.

"So I'm not allowed to hurt him, but it's okay for him to hurt me?"

"I didn't say that." Ratana cocked her head to one side and studied the tall, red-headed American. "You like him, don't you?"

"I hardly know the man...yes."

"What happened over in San Francisco?" Ratana asked. "I assume that's where you know him from. He came back from that conference all moody and distracted. It was weeks before we could get any useful work out of him." The Islander woman perched herself on a lab stool and sipped her mug of coffee. "I knew he was hurting but I couldn't just ask him."

"He was the one who hurt me. He stood me up and left without a word of explanation except a note about a family emergency...if that really existed."

"It did. His aunt died in the Settlement."

"Shit. I thought it was just an excuse."

Ratana shook her head. "James wouldn't do that. He'd tell you to his face if he was breaking up. What happened in San Francisco?"

"Nothing."

"I don't believe...no, scrap that. What might have happened if he had stayed?"

Sam said nothing but tried without success to stop her cheeks colouring.

"James has always been a good judge of character," Ratana said. "If he thought that much of you..." She reached a decision. "Sit down and drink your coffee. We need to get to know one another."

Sam sat and sipped her coffee, grateful for the silence. After a few minutes, she had relaxed enough to notice the aroma and flavour of the brew.

"It's good. What is it?"

"Goroka coffee from the Papua New Guinea highlands. James did some research up there a few years back and developed a taste for it. A friend sends him a bag of beans every now and then."

They talked of inconsequential things for nearly half an hour, carefully avoiding any topic that might lead them back into the minefield.

Ratana looked out of the window to where a tall man with a camera was taking pictures of a small mob of wallabies across the dry creek that ran behind the building. "Is he yours?"

"He came with me, if that's what you mean. His name's Marc, Marc Lachlan. He does photographic work for a lot of big magazines."

"Is...is he your boyfriend? Is that why you..."

Sam shook her head. "No, he isn't, I thought I'd made it plain I wasn't here to cause James any pain, so why would I bring a boyfriend?"

"Okay, I'm sorry." Ratana smiled tentatively. "I've been watching too many American 'soaps' on TV."

An uncomfortable silence descended on the laboratory. After a few minutes, Sam sighed. "Can we start again, Ratana?" she asked in a small voice. "I'm not normally this defensive; I don't know why I should be now."

Ratana nodded. "Sure. I'm willing to trust James' judgment."

"We're friends?"

"Let's say, willing to make friends."

"Oh."

Sam looked so dejected, Ratana relented. "In a spirit of friendship I'll answer one personal question about James or myself, but only one. The rest will have to wait until I know you better."

"Thank you. The 'uncle' thing then."

"I thought that might be your question." Ratana sighed. "Bear with me, it's a rather complex story." She sat and thought for a moment. "I'm a Torres Strait Islander, as you can see, or at least my father was. My mother was Aboriginal, from a small tribe near the Queensland--Northern Territory border. We lived on Ngurupai Island in the Strait and when I was five a cyclone came along and wiped out my whole village, including my family. I was sent down to my mother's people and was adopted into the Wambiri family. You haven't met him yet, but Nathan Wambiri is another of James' research assistants. He's also my fiancé." Ratana smiled. "I know, you're wondering where James comes into this."

Sam shook her head. "No, I'm thinking of a five year old girl orphaned by a storm. Ratana, that is so...so awful. I'm sorry, that sounds inadequate."

"At least I found a loving family to raise me," Ratana went on. "James' parents had been involved in an education program designed to help Aboriginal communities and often journeyed round the communities and James tagged along, getting his schooling where he could. When he was twelve, he was sick and his parents left him with the Wambiri family while they flew down to Cunnamulla. The plane crashed and his parents were killed. Grandfather Mick never thought to tell the authorities James hadn't been on the plane and everyone thought he'd died with his parents."

"Surely the absence of a body..."

"The plane broke up and wreckage was scattered widely. They only found fragments of bodies." Ratana grimaced. "Dingos."

"Ugh, how dreadful." Sam frowned. "Who is Mick?"

"That's another question, but..." Ratana shrugged. "Mick is...well, I suppose you could call him a medicine man or witch doctor...shaman maybe...none of the terms really describe the man, but it'll do. Mick Wambiri, one of the most powerful and influential elders I know of. Nobody really knows who he is. The stories say he wandered in from the desert fifty years ago. He was an old man when I first met him twenty years ago and he doesn't look a day older now."

"When did you last see him?"

"Early yesterday morning. He was at the black rock site."

"What was he doing there?"

"As I said, he's a shaman. We call them Karadji men here--Aboriginal men of high degree. He came because James asked him to."

"And he's related to you?"

Ratana laughed, a little uneasily. "I don't know of anyone actually related to him. It feels sort of wrong saying one could really be related..."

"So how...?"

"Mick adopted James and reared him, along with me and Nathan. That's why we all refer to Mick as our grandfather. It is a term of great respect among the tribes."

"And 'uncle'? Why do you call James your uncle?"

"Same thing really. Despite being schooled along with the rest of us kids in community schools that got the bare minimum of resources, he shone. He got into university, first here at JCU, then in Canada for his PhD. Then he came back and harried politicians and businessmen until he got funding to upgrade education for us, and brought the brightest of us to university. We all look up to him as our hero and again, to show our respect, he is called 'Uncle'."

"That's quite a story. How did he get involved in things like yowies?"

Ratana looked surprised. "You've heard of them? I didn't think anyone outside of Australia had."

"You forget he came over to the States to talk about them at the conference."

"You're right, I was forgetting. Well, that's because Mick is a Karadji and can talk to spirits. The yowie is a spirit too."

"Really? I got the distinct impression from James' talk that he thought they were real flesh and blood critters."

"That's the white man in him," Ratana said with a laugh. "I hate to generalise, but where the Aboriginal sees a spirit, the white man sees an object. James is very good at seeing the spirit side, perhaps better than most white men, but he still has his blind spots."

"What else does he believe in?"

Ratana hesitated. "I think he should tell you himself, but possibly 'believe' is the wrong word. He investigates a great many odd things, as often as not with a view to finding rational explanations. I mean, you could say he believes in yowies, but what he's doing is investigating everything he can to determine whether they exist in the first place, and if they do, to identify them. I honestly think he'd be equally happy showing they were unknown primates or spirit creatures or hallucinations."

"And what do you think?" Sam asked. "Sorry, but I'm writing a story on all this and I'd like to get different points of view."

"Who's the article for?"

"Science and Fantasy magazine in Wisconsin."

"Never heard of it. I think they're spirits." Ratana said. "Not just because I'm TSI, but from some of James' investigations. For instance, there was a series of sightings in the Blue Mountains behind Sydney last year. An eight foot man-like creature seen repeatedly along a river bank but despite crossing sandbanks, it never left a trail. To me, that's not a flesh and blood creature."

"I can see I'm going to have to have a long chat with you sometime."

"Sure, but it'll have to wait a while. James is off on another expedition today and Nathan and I are going with him."

"Where to?"

"Down south," Ratana said evasively. "Sorry, but I'll have to leave it to James to tell you. I'm not sure if it's a secret or not."

"Okay," Sam said equably, making a mental note to ask James about the trip at the first opportunity.

An uneasy silence descended again and both women almost sighed audibly with relief when Marc knocked on the lab door and entered. Sam sprang to her feet and introduced Ratana to Marc, babbling a little in relief.

"Did you get some good shots, Marc? I saw you out there with the kangaroos. Do you want a cup of coffee?"

"Whoa, Sam," Marc grinned and he carefully put his camera down on a bench. "What have you girls been talking about?" He did not wait for an answer but started wandering around the laboratory, poking at jars with preserved plants or animals with one finger, scanning the names on drawers. "Is this Dr Hay an entomologist?" he asked, pointing at a set of drawers.

"Among other things," Ratana replied, moving over to forestall any attempt to open the drawers. "That's a research collection." She leaned against the drawers, denying Marc access.

"Hey, so sweat. I was just curious." Marc held his hands up and backed away, feigning fear.

"What's entomology?" Sam asked.

"The study of insects," Marc replied. "Our good doctor is a bug collector."

"Not bugs," Ratana said. "Butterflies and moths. He's doing work on Townsville butterfly communities at the moment. And strictly, he doesn't collect them. He has examples of every species, but only as a teaching aid for his classes. All his research work is done with photographs."

Marc nodded approvingly. "My kind of man. Can we see?"

"I suppose so." Ratana bent over and pulled out one of the drawers. "The Papilionidae," she said. "Swallowtails."

Sam gasped at the beauty of the perfect specimens in ranks on the white floor of the drawer. Marc whistled in appreciation.

"He has four of every species mounted," Ratana explained. "Male and female, upper and lower surface. These big ones here are Cairns birdwings, the female is the black one and the male the green one. Here we have the Ulysses or Dunk Island Blue, here the four and five bar swallowtails, *Graphium* species, *Papilio*, *Pachliopta*, and *Cressida*." She pushed the drawer in and pulled another out. "This one is the family Nymphalidae, in particular the species *Hypolimnas bolina*. This row are males, the rest of them are females."

"Why not just four like the others?" Sam asked. "And some of these are damaged."

"This species is quite plastic--it varies in patterning quite remarkably. Some of them are quite rare genetic variants, so he collected them."

"Seems a pity to kill so many," Marc said. "Sacrifices on the altar of Science."

"It seems that way, doesn't it," Ratana replied calmly, "But you should talk to James about that sometime. He has all the facts at his fingertips."

"And what is it that you and Nathan study?" Sam asked. "Butterflies as well?"

"Nathan's looking at the distribution and ecology of wolf spiders in the wet tropics and I'm studying the mango shield scale."

Sam smiled. "I'm afraid you've lost me."

The door banged open and James stamped in, swearing under his breath. In his wake strode a heavyset young Aboriginal man, who looked enquiringly at Ratana as he closed the door behind them, shutting off the blast of hot air from outside.

James stopped short at the sight of the little group in the lab. "Sorry to be so long. We'd better get going."

"Uncle, you haven't met this young man," Ratana said. "He's Marc Lachlan, a photographer and friend of Sam."

James nodded and extended his hand. "Hello. I'm James Hay. Did you er, come up here with Sam or were you up here, er already?"

"He's my photographer," Sam said. "He came with me to cover the story about the black rock."

"Ah, I see. Well, it's a pity you've had a wasted trip, but the black rock has gone."

"Yeah? Damn." Marc turned to Sam. "What are we going to do? Interview the witnesses and maybe get some shots of where it was?"

Sam raised a hand. "Hold your horses, Marc. James, can I talk to you alone?"

James nodded. "Oh, yes, by the way, this is Nathan, my other research assistant. Nathan, Samantha Louis the journalist and er, Marc." He opened the door to his office for Sam but turned back in the doorway. "Nathan, I want to leave in fifteen minutes. Would you just check the Landcruiser is packed properly? You know what we need."

"Sure, Uncle."

"Hey, I'll give you a hand with that," Marc said. He clapped Nathan on the shoulder and ushered him outside. As the door closed they could hear him say, "So what's with these wolf spiders?"

James shut the door behind him and gestured to Sam to take a seat. She crossed her legs and regarded him solemnly as he sat on the corner of the desk facing her.

"You're heading south," she said. "I want to come."

"Why on earth would you want to do that?"

"I came to do a story on the black rock. Seeing as how you've got rid of that, I want to do one on you. You're a fascinating man, James Hay."

"Ratana's been rabbiting on again, has she?" James said sourly. "I'm going to have to have a word with her about that."

"It wasn't her fault. I'm a trained journalist and I wormed it out of her."

"Ms Louis, I think I know my own research assistant better than you. If Ratana put her mind to it, thumbscrews wouldn't make her talk." James stood up. "Now, if you'll excuse me, I have to be somewhere else."

Sam had cringed inside at his continued use of her surname, and now he was set to walk out of her life, perhaps forever. The Sam of old would have shrugged and got on with her life, but ever since that evening in her apartment in Collinsville, when she had received the email from her sister, and then apparently sat unmoving for hours in front of her computer, she had felt a bond with a man she hardly knew. A feeling of panic gripped her. "I...I'm coming with you."

"I don't remember inviting you, Ms Louis."

"Why not? James, what have you got against me? Why have you suddenly..."

"Look, Ms Louis...Sam...this has nothing to do with...with...I'm a scientist and I have a research project that frankly I'm not ready to share with the public yet."

"I ain't the public, buster. I'm the press."

"All the more reason."

Sam tried a smile and softened her voice. "James, as soon as I heard about the black rock and saw your name again, I knew I had to come to Australia. My sister sent me the newspaper clipping and I got so wrapped up in it hours passed without my knowing it. That's never happened to me before and I...I just knew I had to see you. It was like I was being told to come--I can't explain it. The black rock was a good excuse."

James opened his mouth to refuse again, and remembered Mick's words about the red-haired American woman waiting for him who had to accompany him to the Glass House Mountains. He sighed and capitulated.

"We are headed into the bush, Sam." James looked critically at Sam's pantsuit and shoes. "I don't think you're dressed for it. Maybe Ratana has something; you're about the same size."

"Are you saying I can come?"

James nodded. "If we can find something functional for you to wear."

"I have outdoor gear back at my hotel. I knew the black rock was in the jungle so I brought jeans, shorts and hiking boots."

"We'll stop and get them on the way." James chewed his lip and hesitated before continuing. "Look, I have to make a couple of things clear before we start, Sam. First is, we are venturing into an unknown situation. If I tell you to do something, I want you to do it, immediately. I need your utmost cooperation, without argument."

"And the second thing?"

"You don't write about what we find without clearing it with me first."

"You don't want much, do you? Total obedience and total subservience."

James nodded. "You're an intelligent woman Sam. Think about it. We are heading into possible danger and I may be the resident expert. It makes sense to listen to me. Whatever we find is likely to be controversial and something totally new to you. I need to be sure that your take on it is accurate. A lurid piece may sell well to the newspapers, but it may also damage my standing as a serious researcher."

"I don't write lurid pieces," Sam said. "But I take your point. I won't cause trouble."

"Then I guess we'd better go and break the news to your photographer Marc. I suppose he'll be coming too." James held the door open and locked it behind them. "You know," he said, as they walked down the concrete path to the parking lot, "My Grandfather Mick said you'd be coming with us, but I thought he must be mistaken."

"Your grandfather? The Karadji? He doesn't even know me."

"Ratana did tell you a lot. But Mick knew of you even if he'd never met you. He claims to have higher sources of information."

"Spirits, you mean?" Sam stopped dead and looked at James with a slightly outraged expression. "You mean you'd have left me behind, despite Mick and his spirits saying I should go?"

James shrugged. "I don't know. I doubt it though. I think I was hoping you or Mick would provide me with a good reason to take you." He smiled and took Sam by the arm, starting them toward the waiting vehicle once more. "Don't knock it, it worked."

6

"We're going where?" Marc Lachlan stopped fiddling with his camera gear and stared at Nathan.

"Tunbubudla," Nathan said again. He folded the creased map and passed it over, stabbing a finger at a point apparently crisscrossed by roads.

Marc studied the map for a few minutes. "Jeez," he muttered. "Doesn't anyone speak English around here? Look at these names. Hey, there's even a couple with 'Beer' in them. Do they have decent taverns?"

"Beerwah and Beerburrum," James said with a grin.

"Come on Marc," Sam said. "You've come across worse in other countries."

"Yeah, but they weren't pretending to speak English there."

"I don't hear you speaking the Queen's English," Nathan shot back.

"Behave children."

After stopping off at Sam and Marc's hotel on the Strand to pick up their luggage, James had taken the inland road out of Townsville toward Charters Towers instead of the coast road south.

"There's a bit of a blow brewing in the Coral Sea," James explained. "I don't want to risk any major delays if there's a storm. Besides, the inland route will show you a less traveled part of Queensland."

They had a quick lunch at a pub in the Towers before turning south along the Gregory Development Road, a two-lane highway. The road was in good condition, better even than the main highway north of Townsville. After a while, though, the flat landscape proved monotonous and even the infrequent flocks of galahs or small mobs of 'roos failed to elicit more than a polite look from Sam or Marc. They dozed off, lulled by the low roar of the tires on the sealed gravel surface, only to be awakened by a sudden deceleration and a swerve.

Sam came awake suddenly, gripping the door handle tightly in expectation of a collision. A door slammed behind her and she saw Nathan and Marc running back along the road, Marc busy trying to set his camera up as he ran.

"Come on, you'll like this," James said.

Sam followed them back along the deserted road for nearly a hundred yards to where the two men were bent over something on the road.

"You haven't dragged me out here to show me road kill, have you?" she groaned.

"Much better than that, sister," Ratana said.

The first time Ratana had called her 'sister', Sam had assumed it was by mistake but she had repeated it, adding, "You don't mind, do you?"

Sam felt strangely pleased but felt moved to reply, "As long as you don't expect me to address James as 'uncle'."

Ratana had chuckled. "I don't think there's much danger of that."

The object on the road was not moving and Sam felt sure that, despite assurances to the contrary, it was the remains of some poor creature that had tangled with an automobile.

"What was it?" she asked. "It looks like a porcupine."

"It's an echidna," Nathan said, "And still very much alive." He nudged it with the tip of his boot and it picked itself up and shuffled off down the road.

"Guide it to the edge of the road before a car comes along," James said. "It just needs a patch of soil." Working together, they herded the spiny animal toward the shoulder and from there into a region of bare earth. The echidna hesitated then its clawed feet started moving and it sank into the earth until just its spiny back showed above the surface. "It'll probably stay like that now," James laughed. "It works on the old principle of 'if I can't see you, you can't see me'."

The sighting of the echidna led to a discussion of Australia's native animals and the pressures on them from the modern world. Sam sat quietly and listened, asking a question only when the talk slackened, becoming increasingly impressed by the breadth of James' knowledge. Nathan and Ratana added their experiences and the unique perspective of the Australian Aborigine and Torres Strait Islander. Sam told some stories from her journalistic life and Marc talked of his assignments around the world.

Sam yawned at length and looked out at the monotonously undulating land with its covering of scrubby vegetation, the setting sun turning the heavy cloud along the western horizon an ominous red. "I hate to quote a cliché, but are we there yet?"

James laughed. "Not even close. We've just passed through Clermont and we've about another hour to Emerald, where we'll stay for the night. Then about the same again tomorrow, but we'll head to Rocky first. We're meeting someone."

Sam groaned. "I need to stretch my legs, use the little girls' room and have a hot shower. Then a decent meal and a glass or two of a good white wine, if you have such a thing."

"Oh, I think we can manage that," James smiled. "But make the most of it because we'll be going 'bush' soon and there are no mod cons out there."

Marc looked up from the map. "Where's Rocky, and who are we meeting?"

"Rocky's Rockhampton--on the coast, and we're meeting an old friend of mine called Spence," James explained.

"Really?" Nathan exclaimed. "You didn't tell us, Uncle."

"Thought I'd make it a surprise." James switched the headlights on just as the first spatters of rain hit the windscreen. Gusts of wind rocked the Landcruiser and he slowed, increasing the rate of the wipers. "This is a bit sudden," he said. "The bad weather's supposed to be northeast of here."

The rain got steadily harder, drumming like hail on the roof of the cruiser, and James slowed to a crawl. There was no other traffic on the Developmental Road, so they were able to inch along with their lights on high beam. After about twenty minutes the rain eased considerably and another ten minutes later shut off completely, leaving the road awash with muddy water that proved difficult to negotiate in the fading light.

South of Capella the road was blocked by a muddy landslide from an adjoining hill, a loose and water-soaked mass of clay and rock spilling out across the road. James stopped about twenty yards short of the slip and they all examined it as best they could through the windscreen.

"Not good," James said. "The Works teams won't even be coming out until daylight, which means a cramped, uncomfortable..."

"And hungry..." Marc interposed.

"...and hungry night. Plus we lose the better part of tomorrow as well."

"Can we backtrack and take another road?"

"The only one is the Clermont to Mackay Peak Downs Road. I wouldn't want to try that in the dark and it'll deliver us straight into that blow offshore."

"Is this a four-wheel drive vehicle?" Marc asked. "You could drive us over the slip."

James shook his head. "Too dangerous. If it started to move it'd carry us into a ravine over there on our right."

"Is it likely to move?" Marc persisted. "It looks stable to me."

"I think we should try, Uncle," Nathan said. "Mick gave us a timeline to get to Tunbubudla. If we delay here a day we'll miss it."

"He's right, Uncle," Ratana agreed. "I don't like it either, but I don't see we have any choice under the circumstances."

James sat and stared at the offending landslip. "Sam?"

"Hell, I'm game. If we get stopped right at the gitgo, we might as well give up."

James sighed raggedly. "All right, but everyone out of the car. I'll take it through empty."

Marc opened a back door and closed it again hurriedly. "Starting to rain again."

"That's it, then," James said. "The rain will make it even more slippery. We'll just have to wait here for the grader."

"Not if we go now, Uncle."

The others joined in with a chorus of agreement. James nodded. "Hold tight then." He engaged the four-wheel drive and inched forward. The wheels slid on the slippery surface, and then gripped, pulling the vehicle across the sloping surface. The headlights picked out a confused jumble of rocks, logs and earth, the rain lancing down in the yellow beams. A gust of wind caught them and blew them sideways in a skid down the shallow slope. James instinctively turned into the skid, straightening the vehicle, gently feeding more torque to the wheels. They gripped again and hauled the Landcruiser onward toward safety.

"What the fuck's that?" Marc yelled suddenly, pointing to the left. "Something moved."

"Probably just a 'roo or something, caught by the slip," Nathan said.

"It was human, or...or...shit, there it is again."

"I saw that," Sam said excitedly. "Well, not the thing itself, but I saw its shadow. A man, definitely."

"Shadow from what?" James asked. "What light source is throwing shadows?" He took his eyes off the route through the mud and glanced sideways, feeling the wheels slip as he did so. "Bugger!" He wrestled with the steering wheel, resisting the urge to floor the accelerator.

"Quinkan," hissed Ratana. "I see them."

"What the hell are...Jesus!" Marc yelled and jumped back from the door, knocking into Ratana. "It was...it had...eyes in a...a black mask. What the fuck is it?"

"Quinkan," James said grimly. "Look."

At the limits of the headlights, where the yellow wash of light faded into the rain-streaked darkness, several man-shaped shadows stood facing them. Sam stared at them, feeling a prickle of unease at the sight but uncertain as to why. She had seen shadows before and these were...she gasped. They were shadows without a source. A man-shaped shadow standing upright in a beam of light needs a solid man-shaped object to cast it and a vertical surface on which to be cast. These man-shadows had neither, being disembodied shapes of emptiness, holes punched into the widening light beams.

"What are they doing here?" James grated. "Quinkan are associated with tribal areas like Laura in Cape York, they shouldn't be haunting a landslip down here."

As he spoke the shadows moved, surging forward, their blackness unaffected by the increasing intensity of the headlights as they approached. Sam instinctively shrank back in her seat, feeling the urge to throw open her door and flee as far and fast as she could.

"Lock the doors, wind up the windows," James urged. "They can enter through a crack."

"Won't do any good, Uncle," Ratana said calmly. "They can come through the air vents."

"Jesus. There's gotta be something we can do," Marc said, his voice rising toward panic. "Are they ghosts? Can we exorcise them?"

"Nothing that'll work that quickly," Nathan said. "Stay strong, refuse to cooperate, and refuse to let them into your mind. That might work."

The shadows enveloped the vehicle in a cocoon of darkness, slithering over the metal and glass with a dry rustling sound despite the rain pelting down. A few moments later, the scale-slithers sounded within the Landcruiser's hood and an inky blackness seeped out of the air-conditioning. Sam waved at it frantically but it slipped past her hand and congealed around James' head.

"No, damn it," James groaned. He stabbed at the accelerator with his foot and jerked the steering wheel to the right, sending the vehicle into a spin, sliding over the slippery surface toward the edge of the road and the ravine beyond. "I can't fight it," he howled.

Ratana screamed and grabbed at the steering wheel, while Nathan and Marc clawed ineffectually at the miasma surrounding James. Sam snatched at the hand brake, jerking it on. The vehicle lurched and the shadow flowed again, over Sam's arm and up toward her head. She pulled back sharply, the shadow surging with her and for an instant, its hold on James weakened. He turned the ignition off, pulled the keys out, and dropped then onto the floor at his feet.

The motor cut immediately and in the silence, a sibilant rustling like the rush of myriad clawed insect legs, filled the cabin. The sound rose and fell, like a great beast breathing, and a feeling of triumph gripped them all. Although the forward motion of the vehicle ceased, it continued a slow slip to the side, heading for the unseen ravine hidden in the darkness.

"We've got to get out," Nathan yelled. He tried the door but the central locking system was engaged. James tried to move his hand to switch it off, but could not. The slow slide continued.

"Oh, god," Marc groaned. "Now what?" He pointed off into the darkness to the left, where the remnants of the water-slipped hill still stood.

A large white glowing light appeared, though whether in the sky or on the crest of the hill was impossible to say. The light was bright, almost dazzling, but failed to illuminate the ground. It grew larger, rushing closer, and Marc stared at it, as transfixed as any rabbit caught in the headlights. As it came closer, he jerked spasmodically and lifted his camera to his eye. The figure's approach was soundless, but the rustling like dead leaves within the vehicle grew to a crescendo and waves of anger and fear washed over the occupants.

A man appeared in the light, almost as if stepping through a doorway from a brightly lit room, tall and thin and dark, Aboriginal, wielding a long spear. He was naked save for a red cloth around his head and his eyes glowed with the same white light that surrounded him. The muddy ground did not slow the approach of the apparition, for it seemed to glide over the surface, closing rapidly with the slowly sliding vehicle. The figure gestured, and shards of brightness, like a shattered mirror in an arc light, sped out from his hand, arrowing through steel and glass and flesh as if they were not there, leaving them unharmed. The shadows, though, fled from the vehicle into the night, dissipating into the darkness even as the shards seemed to slice into their insubstantial bodies.

James felt the sideways slide stop. He held his breath, waiting for it to start again, and when it did not, slumped in his seat with relief. The figure of the Aboriginal man looked through the front window, first at Sam and then past her at James. A slight nod and he was gone, the darkness of the night crashing in again.

"Who or what the fuck was that?" Marc breathed.

"Language, Marc," James chided gently. "There are ladies present."

"Don't mind me," Sam laughed nervously. "I was wondering the same thing."

"It was a spirit," Nathan said. "It scattered the Quinkan."

"Wandjina," Ratana stated.

"Well," James temporized. "I guess it's possible, but I thought Wandjinas were creator spirits from the Dreamtime. Tall and almost featureless, with no mouths. I never heard of one that looked just like a man."

"It was a Wandjina," Ratana repeated.

"Okay, but we're still in trouble." James peered out of the side window toward the invisible ravine now very close at hand. "I think we'd better, very carefully, abandon the vehicle before it starts moving again."

Nathan wound down his window and peered out. "I can't be sure, but I think there's a ridge or a rock by our right-hand wheels."

James cracked the door open and looked out, using the backwash from the headlights and the glow from the cabin light. "You're right. We are reasonably safe where we are, I think, but if we start moving the car again, all bets are off. We have to abandon ship."

Sam and Marc opened their left-hand doors and gingerly stepped out, sinking to their ankles in the gluey mix. Ratana followed and Nathan and James started inching cautiously across the seats.

A rumble cut through the sound of steadily falling rain and the ground beneath their feet began to tremble.

"Earthquake!" Sam yelled.

"Landslip," James corrected, throwing himself out of the cruiser. He fell to his knees in the shaking mud and looked around wildly for the direction the new flow was coming from. "There," he pointed ahead of them where the headlights illuminated the earth moving sideways. "Back the way we came..."

A loud crack cut him off, a sound like a rock snapping under immense pressure. A fissure opened up across the front wheels of the vehicle and snaked away into the darkness. The rumble grew, rising rapidly in scale to the roar of a 747 taking off. The ground ahead of them quaked, liquefying under the vibrations and suddenly, like a plug pulled from a bath, poured past them like a river. The sight froze them in their tracks as a seemingly endless river of mud swept by them, threatening at any moment to carry them away to their deaths. The surge ceased as abruptly as it began, the mud and stones pulling away down the slope as the supply uphill eased.

Sam gulped and dug her fingers into James' arm. "Is...is it...it...over?" she stuttered.

"I think I've wet myself," Marc muttered.

"You and...and me both," Nathan replied shakily.

"Wandjina saved us," Ratana said calmly.

"Well, even if someone or something kept the mudflow from engulfing us, we might not be so lucky next time," James said. He pried Sam's fingers from his jacket and slipped his arm around her. "Come on now, back the way we came, but tread carefully."

"Uncle." Ratana pointed to the road in front of them. "I think the Wandjina is leading us."

Ahead, barely visible in the attenuated headlights, the naked Aboriginal man stood looking at them. He stood in a typical pose, on one leg and resting on his spear, the other bent and the sole of the foot resting against his thigh. In front of him, rivulets of water from the hillside were washing the mud clear of the road seal. Though pitted and scarred from the passage of the mud, the grey road surface showed through the sheet of water.

James stared for a long moment, and then nodded, reaching a decision. "Back in the car. We're driving out."

The Landcruiser inched forward, still in four-wheel drive, and after a few metres of uneven surface, they drove slowly through the devastated landscape, following the thin, winding strip of clear road in the darkness toward the waiting man.

After a few seconds, Sam noticed something incredible. The Aboriginal man was not moving, yet as they advanced they seemed to get no nearer. He remained standing where the headlights faded into the darkness. Sam brought James' notice to it. "Is he real?"

"I'd noticed that," James replied quietly. He flicked the high beam on but the figure now seemed further off, still at the point where the light faded. When he dipped the lights again, the man drew closer, though still standing, resting on his spear. "I'm not sure he is real," James said, "Except perhaps in our minds."

Sam had a sudden idea. "Marc, take a picture."

"Sure, why not, I've already taken some of the shadows and light...shit! I've still got the effing lens cap on. I haven't made a rookie mistake like that for years."

"Marc, never mind that, quickly now. I think he's fading."

The mud and debris slipped away behind them and the road showed up dark and black in the headlights with the centre line showing up brightly white. The man faded back and evaporated as Marc snapped off a series of pictures on his digital camera.

"I think I got him." Marc bent over the screen, pulling up shot after shot of an empty road. Only in one picture was there a hint of something, a shape that might have been a body, or equally likely a reflection of the headlights off a glistening wet road. He swore colourfully before apologising.

"Sorry guys, I thought I had him."

James looked thoughtful. "It's an odd thing about paranormal phenomena, but it is very common for cameras to fail or the photographer, even an experienced one, to make an elementary mistake."

"What are you saying?" Sam asked. "The spirit or ghost or whatever, somehow reaches out to sabotage the evidence?"

"Or perhaps the subconscious mind, knowing it is a hallucination, deliberately sabotages its own efforts at gathering information."

"What would be the point of that?" Marc asked.

"Self-deception," James replied. "Something humans are very good at. Crisp, clear photographic evidence might contradict what the eye sees. With no evidence to the contrary, you can continue in your comfortable delusion."

"I'm not sure I appreciate being called deluded," Marc grumbled.

"It wasn't a delusion," Ratana said firmly. "It was a Wandjina."

James grunted. "Well, I don't want to get into a debate about subjective perception and objective reality. Suffice it to say we all saw something, though we have to classify it as anecdotal, lacking any concrete evidence."

"What about the landslip?" Marc asked. "It would be a hell of a coincidence for the slip to clear the road ahead of us like that."

"Yes, but it could be just a coincidence."

"Then what about the shadow attack?" Sam asked. "Those things surrounded you and forced you to try and crash us. Surely you know what happened to you wasn't just imagination?"

"Perhaps I was just buying into your collective delusion..."

"Now you are acting like a narrow-minded scientist, Uncle," Nathan chided. "Why can't you just admit that something happened that cannot be explained by science? We all saw it, we all experienced it--an attack by Quinkan and a rescue by a Wandjina."

"Ockham's Razor," James retorted.

"What?" Sam looked mystified.

"The scientific law of parsimony, as voiced by the fourteenth century English logician, William of Ockham. Basically, it says that all things being equal, the simplest solution tends to be the right one."

"Jeez, that really clears things up," Marc complained.

"In this case, all it means is that the simpler solution is to say we all had some sort of collective hallucination brought on by tiredness or something, rather than invoke a whole parcel of supernatural creatures out to get us."

"Well, whether or not there are supernatural beings out there trying to get us, I know of one very natural being making itself known to me right now," Sam said firmly. "My stomach is about to eat the rest of me, I'm so hungry. Can we please head for the nearest restaurant?"

James laughed, and put the Landcruiser back into Drive. "At least that is easily solved. We are about twenty minutes from Emerald, a decent meal and a good night's kip."

7

J ames was right in two out of three points. Emerald lay only seventeen minutes away, and a good meal was enjoyed at the local pub, but the accommodation left a lot to be desired. Only two units were available at the Emerald Fields Motel so Sam and Ratana shared one, while James, Nathan and Marc crammed themselves into the other one. The women emerged rested the next morning, but the men were grumpy and short tempered.

"Marc snores like a buzz saw," Nathan complained.

"And when he wasn't ripping up planks, Nathan was talking in his sleep," James added.

"I've slept in some nasty places on assignment but that bed kept me awake all night." Marc muttered, ignoring Nathan's complaint.

Sam pulled Marc aside and quizzed him about the previous evening. "That was quite a scary experience with those shadow things. You didn't have nightmares about them, did you?"

"Nah, I've hardly thought about them. What about you?"

Sam shook her head. "For some reason, the vision of that old Aboriginal man calmed me right down. I just remember the shadow things like an old horror movie or something. Scary at the time but not in the light of day."

Sam moved away to join the others and Marc watched her, his bottom lip trembling a little. "It didn't happen," he muttered. "It was a hallucination." He took a series of deep breaths, calming himself before hurrying on down Opal Street.

By nine o'clock, they had breakfasted at the pub restaurant, packed up the vehicle and checked its levels of gas, oil, water and air. The day was sunny, without a hint of the rain of the day before, and James drove out onto the Capricorn Highway that lead east toward the coast and the City of Rockhampton. They talked mostly of inconsequential things, their minds steering away from the events of the previous evening. Marc regaled them with stories of his photographic assignments and Sam fed them juicy tidbits about the lives of the rich and famous in the States. Ratana and Nathan returned the favour with descriptions of tribal life and custom, together with anecdotes about the places they'd been and people they'd met. After one story which Nathan told about one of the elders of his tribe, 'that old man', and his hunting exploits, Sam had a question.

"That's the sort of story I'd love to write about," she said, "But I can't just call him 'that old man'. What's his name?"

Nathan hesitated. "He has passed on, Sam. We just call him 'that old man' now."

"Yes, but he must have had a name. I need it if I'm going to write the story down."

Nathan remained silent.

"What?" Sam asked, perplexed.

"In Aboriginal culture, a dead man's name is not mentioned out of respect," James explained quietly. "Now Nathan here is trained in science and is conversant with white man's views, but he still, quite rightly, holds his own culture in high regard. So he not only won't tell you 'that old man's name', but he is reluctant even to tell you why."

"Sorry, Ms Louis," Nathan muttered.

"No, it's I who should apologise, Nathan. I did not realise the importance you laid on such a thing. I will not mention it again."

"That's all right. You were not to know."

There was silence in the vehicle for many kilometres until Marc cleared his throat and asked a tentative question. "What's at this Tunbubudla place anyway? Or is that also taboo?"

"No taboo, Marc," Nathan said with a smile. "It's just a peak--well, two actually--in the Glass House Mountains."

"What an interesting name," Sam exclaimed. "Why are they called that?"

"Let me guess," Marc said. "There's a lot of horticultural production in the area."

"Nice one, Marc." James laughed. "It was actually named by the explorer James Cook when he sailed by. He saw these strange looking hills or mountains inland from the coast and thought they resembled the glass furnaces from his native Yorkshire in shape."

"Are they high mountains?"

"No. The highest is Beerwah and it's only about five hundred and fifty metres--that's eighteen hundred feet to you non-metric Americans. They are rather spectacular though, as they consist of steep-sided eroded volcanic plugs. They were ancient volcanoes that stopped erupting. The soft ash and rock of the slopes washed away, leaving the hard lava of the throat intact."

"I'm guessing there's an Aboriginal story too," Sam said.

"Yes," replied Ratana, "But it's nothing to do with glasshouses or eroded volcanic plugs. Tibrogargan is the father and Beerwah the mother. Their children are Coonowrin, Tunbubudla, Ngungun, Coochin, Tibberoowuccum, Elimbah and...there's a couple of others, but I can't remember them."

"Miketeebumulgrai was one," Nathan murmured.

"One day, Tibrogargan noticed the sea rising," Ratana went on. "He told his eldest son Coonowrin to help his mother while he rounded up the other children. Coonowrin ran for it though, leaving his pregnant mother behind, so Tibrogargan chased after him and hit him with a club, dislocating his neck. When the seas went down again, Coonowrin was ashamed and asked forgiveness of Tibrogargan, but his father wept with shame. He approached his mother, but Beerwah also wept with shame. He went to all his brothers and sisters but they wept too, which is why there are so many little streams in the area. Tibrogargan turned his back on his son and now just sits there gazing out to sea. Coonowrin hangs his crooked neck and cries, while his mother, Beerwah, is still pregnant, because," Ratana said mischievously, "It takes a long time for a mountain to give birth."

Sam clapped her hands with delight. "I love it, though it is a bit tough on poor old Coonowrin. Will we get to see him?"

"Probably," James said, "But possibly not up close. I'm not sure yet exactly where we're going."

"I thought you said Tunbubudla."

"I did, but there's damn all at the twins," James said. "They are two small mountains, about a thousand feet high each, with forestry plantations around them. There is some thick bush around the base of them, but nothing mysterious. I really don't know what we're looking for."

"Another black rock maybe?"

Marc started humming 'Also Sprach Zarathustra', the theme to the movie 2001: a Space Odyssey.

"Well, who knows?" James laughed. "Though I didn't feel any surge in knowledge at the first rock. Anyway, I'd rather not discuss our plans just now. I'd rather do it when our team is complete, so we'll wait for Spence to join us first."

"You mentioned him before," Sam said. "Who is he?"

"A real pain in the arse," Nathan said loudly.

James grinned. "He only says that because Spence used to give him hell when he was a youngster. Nathan was a typical teenager, rebellious..."

"Which he still is, Uncle," Ratana added.

"... and questioning all the tribal values. Spence set him straight."

"He's an Aboriginal elder?"

"No, he's from over the ditch..."

"The Tasman Sea," Ratana explained. "New Zealand."

"... and he's a Maori, or at least half-Maori. His mother was a pakeha..."

"White woman," Ratana murmured.

"... but his father was a Tohunga, a healer of the Tuhoe tribe. They're called the 'Children of the Mist' and I'll let Spence tell you more if he wants to. A gentle word of warning though. Spence may come across as a rambunctious in-your-face sort of fellow, but inside he's sensitive and very spiritual. He's a Tohunga himself, which is a highly respected position in Maori society. He's also a very private person, so don't ask too many questions. Let him volunteer information."

"Can I ask when you met him?"

"About ten...no, twelve years ago now. I was investigating a report of an ABC in the New England hinterland between Tenterfield and Glen Innes..."

"What's an ABC?" Marc interrupted. "It sounds like something out of 'Sesame Street'."

"It stands for 'Alien Big Cat'. Those are large, usually black cats, seen in places where big cats have no right to be."

"I've read about those," Sam said. "There was a report of a black panther in a town in Illinois a couple of years ago. They said it was a leopard that had escaped from a circus."

"That's a common explanation, but judging by the number of sightings, all over the world, there must be hundreds of circuses losing beasts every day. It's an interesting fact that when you try to find out exactly which circus has lost a cat, nobody knows. Anyway, I was in the Currys Gap State Conservation Area outside of Tenterfield, following some large pug marks along the stream that runs through it when I chanced on this scrawny old man doing the same thing. That was the first time I met Spence, or Spencer Tuhua to give him his full name. Since then we've investigated a range of paranormal phenomena together."

"So what are these big cats?" Marc asked. "Escaped panthers or something more exotic?"

"Take out the hoaxes, the misidentifications and the imagination and there is definitely something more exotic there."

"What about the Tenterfield cat?" Sam asked. "What did that one turn out to be?"

"I don't know, I never saw it, and the tracks stopped in the middle of a muddy field."

Marc whistled. "No shit? And you've followed these things again?"

James nodded. He eased up on the accelerator and nudged the brake pedal to drop their speed below eighty kilometres per hour and a minute later to sixty. "We're coming into Duaringa. Does anyone need a loo break?" Nobody did, so he turned to bypass the town and a little later accelerated back up to the open road speed of one hundred.

"To answer your question, Marc, I have investigated cats since then, but Spence seems to be fascinated by them. I prefer looking for Yowies."

The traffic was light on the Capricorn Highway and James continued his informal lecture on paranormal phenomena as he drove. Nathan and Ratana had heard most of it before, but listened happily, interested in the reactions of their new American friends. He talked about the unknown fauna of the Great Southern Land, and then moved on to the existing animals, telling stories about beasts he had encountered.

"Don't forget to warn them about 'Drop Bears'," Nathan said with a grin.

James made a rude sound. "Save that for your university field trips. It's only funny in that context."

"Drop bears?" Marc frowned. "You don't get bears in Australia, do you? Or do you mean the Koala?"

"Koalas aren't bears," James said. "They're marsupials."

"They're carnivorous cousins of the Koala," Nathan said. "They hang out on branches over paths and drop on unwary passers-by, usually Americans. Sometimes, if the group is very gullible, you can get them to smear Vegemite on their faces as a deterrent."

"And you find that funny?" Marc growled. "I've tasted that shit."

"I have to admit to being moderately amused by it in the past," Nathan murmured.

"I apologise on his behalf," Ratana said. "Unfortunately little boys don't always grow up."

"Here too?" Sam laughed. "Still, sometimes that playful aspect can be quite appealing."

They entered the outskirts of Rockhampton a little after noon, but instead of turning left at the roundabout intersection with the Bruce Highway, James turned south, away from the city. "I told Spence we'd meet him at the Capricorn Café," he said. "We're running a little late, but he should still be there."

They pulled into the parking lot of the Café a few minutes later. It was a flashy structure that obviously catered to the tourist trade, with several people snapping pictures of a plaque that purported to mark the exact position of the Tropic of Capricorn. Sam raised her eyebrows as they pulled up in the shade of a jacaranda tree, but said nothing.

James noticed her look and smiled. "It's not as trashy as it looks. They have a little beer garden tucked away in the back that serves good food. Best of all, they have some secluded tables. Nathan, why don't you take everyone in and get some drinks ordered while I find Spence?"

James waited until the others had entered the café before scanning the car park for Spence's battered old Jeep. It was not out the front, so he walked around the side and spotted it in the heavy shade of an old *Ficus* tree on the parkland next door to the café. He walked over and smiled when he heard the rhythmic snores emanating from the cab. He peered in through the open side window at the old man behind the steering wheel. A shock of white hair topped a thin, unshaven face with a protruding nose. His mouth hung open as he snored, revealing yellowing but regular teeth. The thin body beneath the khaki shirt and patched blue jeans shook with the vigour of his stertorous breathing. He reached through the open window and shook the sleeping man's shoulder.

"Eh? What?" The sleeping man opened his eyes and shut his mouth, turning a bleary gaze toward James. "Oh, it's you, you old bugger, you got here then?"

"How are you keeping, Spence? It's been a while."

"Too long." Spence yawned and stretched. "I was glad to get your email." He pushed open the door of Jeep with a protesting screech from the hinges and clambered out, slamming it behind him hard enough to rock the vehicle. "Let's go get something to eat. I'm starving and you're paying." He strode off across the grass toward the café.

"Shouldn't you lock your car?" James called after him.

"Nah, nothin' worth stealing in there."

James shrugged and hurried after Spence, catching him up only as the sprightly old man darted through the doorway with its strips of brightly coloured fly screen into the dim, cool interior of the café.

Spence pushed through the throng of tourists to the counter before turning to James. "Whatcha havin'?"

James pointed through to the rear of the building where a small restaurant opened out into a shaded courtyard with discretely placed tables

65

under large umbrellas. "There are a couple of people I want you to meet. We can order out there."

"Fair enough. Lead on MacDuff." Immediately contradicting himself, Spence led the way out into the courtyard. He looked around expectantly and saw Nathan sitting at a secluded table at the far end.

"Nathan!" Spence bellowed. "Nathan, you old black bugger, it's your Uncle Spence." He rushed across the courtyard, oblivious of a variety of stares from other customers ranging from curious to downright hostile. The old man clasped the sturdy body of the young Aborigine firmly and slapped him on the back repeatedly. After a few moments, he pushed away and stood looking at Nathan critically. "You've put on weight, Nate." He turned to Ratana who was sitting regarding him with an amused smile. Holding out his scrawny arms, he roared, "Come to my arms, you ebony beauty."

Laughing, Ratana rose to her feet and embraced Spence. "Welcome, Uncle," she said. "We have some visitors." She gripped his arm tightly in one hand and held on as she leaned close, whispering into his ear, "Be nice now."

"Aren't I always?" Spence complained. "So who's this delectable lady?"

Sam got up, towering over the old man and extended a hand. "I'm Samantha Louis. I've heard a lot about you, Spence."

Spence grinned. "None of it good, I hope." He roared with laughter and shook Sam's hand vigorously.

"And this is Marc Lachlan," Ratana said, deflecting Spence's appreciative gaze from Sam's figure.

Spence tore his eyes away from Sam and regarded the tall man in front of him. "Blimey, you're a tall one." He shook hands a little less enthusiastically and turned to James as he approached the table. "Are these the ones you wanted me to meet? Bloody good. When do we eat?"

James attracted the attention of a waitress and after a few minutes discussion, ordered a variety of dishes and drinks. The service was prompt and friendly and Sam commented that the waitress would be getting a decent tip after the meal.

"We don't actually tip in Australia," James said. "I mean, you can if you like, but it's not expected."

For a while there was little conversation as everyone made inroads into the generous portions on the plates. At length, the eating slowed and Spence leaned back, stifled a belch and patted his belly as if his cadaverous physique had transformed itself into rounded proportions.

"So, what's this all about, Jimmy? Your email was bloody uncommunicative."

"The black rock."

"Ah, I thought it might be." Spence dropped his outgoing, loud persona and took up a thoughtful, introspective one. "I read a bit in that rag you call a local paper. Was it quartz?"

"Yes, but why do you say 'was'?" James asked.

"I'm assuming it disappeared."

"Actually, no. it disintegrated."

Spence's bushy white eyebrows lifted. "Really? I didn't expect that." He thought for a moment. "What was carved on it--the last figure, I mean? Possibly it appeared after you arrived."

"A brumby."

"Figures. You've been called personally, James."

"Excuse me," Sam interrupted, "But what's a brumby and why should it be important?"

"Delighted to excuse you, lovely lady," Spence said, slipping back to his former self for a few moments. "A brumby is a wild horse and it's significant because it's James' totem."

"Totem? Like in a totem pole?"

"Not unlike, Marc," Nathan replied. "But in this case an animal sacred to one man, rather than a whole tribe. It's a spirit guide assigned by the holy men to men of worth. James' was a surprise as spirit guides are always native animals, but in this case, perhaps because he's a white Australian, the brumby chose him. Yes, and before you ask, the totem chooses the man."

"Do you have a totem, Nathan?" Marc asked.

"He does," James said quietly, "But he's not allowed to tell anyone."

"But everyone knows yours..."

"Ah." James smiled wryly and refused to meet Nathan's eyes. "That's because I'm a white man and I don't know any better."

"Nobody holds it against you, Uncle," Nathan murmured.

"Getting back to what you said earlier, Spence," Sam asked. "You said James had been called personally. What did you mean by that?"

"A black quartz rock, particularly one that appears suddenly, is viewed by some as a symbol of a task, a challenge by the spirit world. If one can interpret the signs correctly, one can find out who the message is for, and what the task is. We now know the who, we just need the where and the what."

"Tunbubudla," James said.

Spence shivered, despite the heat of the day. "What makes you say that?"

"Mick was there. He said Tjakkan told him 'Tunbubudla'."

Spence was silent a long time, drawing into himself while he thought through the implications. "Send them all home, Jimmy," he said at last, his voice shaking. "I'll accompany you to that place."

"Can't do it Spence. Mick said Sam was to come too."

"Why, for God's sake? The others then. I wouldn't want them on my conscience."

"Mick said I could choose my companions, with the exception of Marc. No offence, but you are here because of Sam."

"None taken," Marc replied, "But I'm having second thoughts now. Is this going to be dangerous?"

"I don't know, I certainly didn't think so. What about it Spence? What do you know?"

Spence thought for a moment. "Well, you have a right to know, I guess. But first a bit of background. Strange things can happen anywhere, but if you are looking for high levels of strangeness in Australia, you'd look in certain areas. By far the most famous of these are the Blue Mountains behind Sydney. Others are the far south coast of New South Wales, Springbrook on the Queensland--New South Wales border, the Glass House Mountains, and the Daintree area.

"Now these areas have a much higher incidence of reports of strange animals, manimals, alien big cats, aerial lights, disappearances, and right down to just plain uncomfortable feelings of being watched...have you heard of these things?" Spence looked at Sam, and then at Marc.

"We discussed ABC's briefly," James said.

"The other things are fairly self-explanatory, I think," Sam replied, "With the exception of 'manimals'. I have no idea what those might be."

"Man-animals. You may have heard of ones like Sasquatch, Bigfoot and the Yeti, but they also include our own yowie and the smaller Junjadee or Winambuu, also found in Australia. Then there are a host of other manlike animals around the world, like Almas in Mongolia, Ebu Gogo in Indonesia, Hibagon in Japan, the Orang Pendek of Sumatra and the Orang Mawas of Malaysia. Everywhere you look; there are native tales of strange creatures, even from places that can't possibly harbour them. We could imagine a primitive Gigantopithecus-like creature island hopping through Indonesia, but it's a lot harder to think of him surviving an ocean voyage to get to New Zealand. Yet we have the Moehau, a man-like being in a land with no other native mammals."

"And there are manimals in Glass House?" Marc asked.

"Yes, there are reports of Yowie and other things from the Glass House Mountains."

"Is that really a matter for concern?" Sam asked. "From what I've heard, both Bigfoot and Yowie are generally shy creatures and non-violent."

"By and large, that's true, though there are a few disturbing exceptions. Also, if ABCs are involved, all bets are off--they can be vicious."

James looked troubled. "I've known the Glass House Mountains are a hot spot for years, and I've been there several times, but I've never come across any dangerous sightings associated with the area. What have you heard, Spence?"

"Have you got a map of the area?"

Nathan nodded. "There's one in the Landcruiser." He pushed back his chair and got to his feet. "I'll get it if you promise not to talk until I get back."

"Just get it, Nate," Spence said. He watched the young Aboriginal man head off across the courtyard and rubbed his bristly jaw with one hand. "While we're waiting, lovely lady," he leaned toward Sam with a twinkle in his eye. "Why don't you tell me about yourself? Are you married? Are you liberated? Are you free?"

Sam laughed. "I'm a journalist," she said. "No, I'm not married; yes, I am liberated; and no, I'm not free--but very reasonable."

Spence gaped for a moment before breaking into great guffaws of laughter. He slapped the table, setting the crockery rattling and took out a large grubby handkerchief with which he proceeded to wipe his streaming eyes. "I like you, Sam," he wheezed. "Any time you want, just throw this old stick-in-the-mud over..." he jerked at thumb at James, "...and come and shack up with me. I'll treat you right."

"I would be honoured, Spence," Sam replied with a smile, "But..." She let the sentence hang.

Spence blew his nose loudly. "Ah well, what might have been, eh?" He glanced across at James, who was trying to ignore the word play. "I'm not getting to you, am I, Jimmy? You've gone all pink around the back of your neck."

"Hey, what am I missing?" Nathan threaded his way through the tables and sat down with a folded topographic map in his hand. He looked around at the broad smiles and grins and James' discomforted look with perplexity. "Why do all the good jokes get told when I'm out of the room?"

"Because you're a bit young to understand the complexities of adult conversation," Spence told him. "Let's have a look at that map." He unfolded it and spread it out on the table, Ratana and Marc piling up some of the dishes and moving them to a nearby table. "Pity, it's too small scale for what we need, but it'll do for now. I've got a larger scale one in the Jeep. Now, one set of coordinates is twenty-seven degrees south and a hundred and fifty-two, fifty-five east--would you care to plot that Sam?"

Sam quickly oriented herself and placed a manicured fingertip on the map. "Here," she said. "Near Tunbubudla."

"What do the coordinates refer to?" James asked quietly.

"That one was a sighting of a Yowie on a forestry road three weeks ago. A forest worker saw what he described as a very big man in a gorilla suit who threatened him."

"And you said you had two others?"

"Yes. Two other sets of coordinates with no more than a minute or two's difference between all three. Another yowie sighting five days ago, and a UFO sighting three nights ago."

"You think they are connected? The yowie and the UFO?" Sam looked startled.

"Yes, I do. What's more, all three are near Tunbubudla, which is not a site I would have selected for investigation. A little further north, around Coonowrin or Beerwah maybe, but these are the first around Tunbubudla. In fact," Spence added, "If it wasn't for James' instruction to head for 'The Twins', I'd dismiss the sightings as aberrations."

"So, what's our plan of attack?" James asked.

Spence consulted a battered digital watch. "If we get moving, we can be down in the town of Beerwah by tonight. I'll do a dreaming there and see what we come up with. I would imagine we'll just walk in the front entrance and knock." He stabbed his finger on Woodford Road, which led from the highway past 'The Twins'.

"Dreaming?" Marc shook his head. "I'm almost afraid to ask."

"Dreaming is a way of contacting the spirit world," Ratana explained. "Believe it or not but Spence is good at it."

"Then that's settled," Spence said, standing up. "Jimmy, your shout, I believe? Okay, so who's going to ride with me down to Beerwah? I feel like a chat."

"I'd like to, if I may," Sam said.

Spence beamed. "Delighted, my dear." He offered his arm to Sam and they walked from the restaurant, the thin old man almost scurrying to keep up with Sam's long stride.

James scowled and went to pay the bill, a bit perplexed by his sudden feeling of loss.

8

The next day dawned bright and still, with the promise of a hot afternoon. James' expedition had found a comfortable motel in the little town of Beerwah, in the shadow of the northern end of the Glass House Mountains the night before and emerged into the fresh air and bright light rejuvenated after a good night's sleep. Spence had not joined them, preferring to sleep out of doors. Despite the late hour he had dropped Sam off at the motel before coaxing his battered Jeep along the back roads to Mount Coochin. A track led across fields to light scrub at the base of the volcanic plug, and Spence took with him only a torch and a sleeping bag. He explained his actions to James before he left.

"It doesn't seem right to be doing a dreaming in a town. The Glass House Mountains are important somehow, so I'll go and sleep on one of them."

Spence turned up early the next morning and sat outside the motel in his Jeep until the others emerged to track down some breakfast. Sam was concerned at his appearance and urged him to use her unit for a shower and freshen up. He accepted quietly, without any of his usual banter, and twenty minutes later rejoined them at a café up the road, looking no tidier, though at least his hair looked clean. James had ordered breakfast, so he sat and ate quietly, answering questions monosyllabically until they gave up and left him to finish his bacon and eggs in peace.

James waited until Spence had finished his first cup of coffee before breaking into his train of thought. "What happened, Spence? Did you have your dreaming?" Spence nodded. "Can you tell us about it? We need to know what to expect."

Spence sighed and visibly gathered his thoughts before speaking. "I saw the rays of the setting sun light up the peaks of Tunbubudla. All was peaceful and quiet, birds were singing and the first stars hung in the evening sky. The sun disappeared and the creatures vanished, then a star fell from the sky onto the...the left peak of Tunbubudla. It sank into the ground, not crashing down in destruction like a meteorite, but gently, and it lit up the ground as if the earth was transparent. Things moved under the ground, monsters and people that looked mutated, and there were shadows who looked like men but weren't." Spence drained his coffee and stared at the bottom of his empty cup.

"You want another?" James asked. The old man nodded.

"I'll get it, Uncle," Ratana said quietly. "Go on, Spence."

"The party was divided and some went beneath the ground, though whether in death or not I wasn't shown. Death was there, though. Death and violence; fear and wonder." Spence looked up and focused his eyes on James. "You are definitely called. And you Sam. I fear the rest of us are just cannon fodder." A grimace quirked his lips. "Oh, and one other thing; an Aboriginal man will lead you, but it's not you, Nathan. It's an old man, but one who knows you."

"Mick?"

Spence shook his head. "No, I know Mick, and while I didn't see his face, I know it wasn't him."

James frowned. "I know many Aboriginal elders, but only Mick knows of this quest. I suppose we'll just have to wait and see."

"Probably the best thing," Spence agreed. "Ah, thank you, Ratana." He sipped on his fresh cup of coffee. "I think in view of the dreaming our essential plan of attack is unchanged. We basically march up to the left peak of Tunbubudla and knock." A faint smile, the first of the day, crossed Spence's face.

Marc was studying the map. "Which peak is the left one? Doesn't it depend on which way you approach them?"

"The dream," Nathan said. "Spence said the peaks were lit by the setting sun." He pointed to the map. "The sun sets about here. The only way you can approach them and have the mountains lit is from the northwest. Come in from this other direction and they're in shadow."

"Very good, Nate," Spence said with a smile. "You were listening for once. Perhaps my chastisement paid off all those years ago."

James pored over the map. He pointed out the features to the others. "Here's where we are in Beerwah. We take the road down to Beerburrum, then turn right onto the Woodford Road. A little before the seal ends we can pull off the road and cut across to the peaks."

"What's the country like up there?" Sam asked. "Should I put on my boots or will walking shoes be enough?"

"It's mostly State Forest," James replied. "Managed pine plantations, but an area around the peaks themselves is dry sclerophyll forest--mostly gums, box trees, acacias, and long grass. Don't be fooled by the small size on the map, the plentiful roads and seemingly built-up nature of the surrounds. There are places in there that are wild and seldom visited by man. So in answer to your question, definitely boots. Also jeans, long-sleeved shirts and a hat, sunscreen and insect repellent. Bring a water bottle and snacks too. If you don't have any of these and can't find them in the local shops, see me. I already have a medical kit, enough food, sleeping bags and tents."

"Jeez! It sounds like a major expedition to darkest Africa," Marc said with a grin. "Where do we find the porters, big white bwana?"

"Don't bring anything you're not prepared to carry yourself. Sleeping bag, change of clothes. We'll probably only be away from the cars for a day or two and at a pinch we could probably make it back to them in say six hours, but I like to be prepared. Now, go to it guys." James checked his watch. "It's eight-thirty. I want to be packed up and ready to go by ten. We don't have far to go, but I think in view of the dream we should be at the base of the mountains by sunset."

They drove slowly down to Beerburrum, giving Sam and Marc ample opportunity to view the spectacular views of the Glass House Mountains. The road passed close to Tibrogargan, the father of the tribes, so they stopped to admire the steep-sided rock with the thick eucalypt forest surging around its base like an ocean swell. Marc took several pictures and examined the results critically before packing his camera away again.

"I think I can appreciate how things could be hidden in this forest. The mountain's only a half mile away, and there are houses here, but that looks impenetrable and mysterious."

Ten minutes later, James turned off onto Woodford Road. The right side of the road comprised the lower slopes of Mount Beerburrum, covered in open scrub and forest, while the left was a subdivision with rows of neat houses. After a few minutes, the houses finished and pine trees took over, marching away in ranks toward the south and west.

"Over there," James pointed almost due west, "Is Tunbubudla, only about three kilometres away. The road curves round so we will be approaching...hello, what's this?" He slowed the vehicle and glanced in his rear-vision mirror to check Spence's Jeep was also slowing. Across the road, about a hundred metres ahead, was a barricade and what appeared to be an unmarked police car. As the Landcruiser approached, a policeman got out of the car and waved them to a stop.

James wound down the window as the policeman walked over. "What's the trouble, officer?"

"Just routine, sir." The policeman leaned on the car and peered in, scrutinising the occupants. "What is your business here, sir?"

"Research. I'm with the Biology Department of James Cook University and these are my research assistants." James took his driver's license out and handed it across. "There's another one in the car behind us. What's this all about?"

The officer glanced at the license and handed it back. "There's an escaped prisoner loose in the area. The Woodford Road and other roads around The Twins are closed unless you live in the area. Please return the way you came."

"How long is it closed for? I have research that must be completed."

"Forty-eight hours, sir. Now, please, turn your cars and go back to Beerburrum."

James nodded and as the policeman walked back to his car, made a u-turn and pulled alongside Spence's Jeep. "Back toward Beerburrum," he said. "Something's going on but I can't quite put my finger on it."

Five minutes later they pulled into a public rest area on the main road and everyone got out and gathered around one of the picnic tables. "Okay, here's the thing," James said. "On the face of it, an escaped prisoner is loose in the Tunbubudla area, though where he escaped from and why he should head there is anyone's guess. There was something not quite right about our encounter but I'm not sure what. Any ideas?"

"Does this mean we have to give up on our expedition?" Sam asked.

"No, but we may have to rethink our strategy."

"Why was there only one policeman?" Ratana asked. "I thought that they were required to move around in pairs."

"Normally," Spence replied, "But if they are stretched thin in rural areas, you could just have a single officer."

"On a manhunt, when the escapee could be trying to break out?" Ratana said.

"Okay, valid point but maybe resources really are stretched," James said.

"There's an easy way to find out," Nathan said. "Ring up the local cop shop and ask them."

James scowled. "Now why didn't I think of that?" He flipped out his mobile phone and called directory service. "Beerburrum police station please." He listened then hung up and called again. "Hello, I have information about the escaped prisoner on Tunbubudla...yes, that's right...are you sure...no, sorry, my mistake." James cut the connection. "That's interesting. There is no escaped prisoner."

"So who's that joker out on the Woodford Road?" Spence demanded, turning toward his Jeep. "By God, I'll have a piece of him."

"Hang on, Spence. Don't go off half-cocked. Let's think this through first."

"What's to think through? He's not a policeman so let's kick him up the arse and be done with it. We have to get going."

"All the same, take a few minutes and cool down. Ask yourself why anyone would do that?"

Spence looked at James with a calculating expression. "You think this was deliberate? Aimed against us?"

"It's a possibility. Look, what could it be? He's a nutter who just happened to pick the road we want; or it's one of these reality shows with somebody inconveniencing the public and filming their reactions. I didn't see any cameras, did you?"

"You're saying this is personal?" Sam asked. "Somebody is out to stop us from doing whatever it is we are doing?"

James nodded. "I guess that is what I'm saying, but who is it? There are not many people who know where we are going."

"Actually, there are a few, Uncle," Ratana said. "Maggie, Robbie, Ed, the army Major, anyone they may have talked to..."

"And you can bet Ed will have talked to his uncle, Prof Howard," Nathan added.

"Somebody may have overheard us at the café," Marc said with a grimace. "We didn't exactly keep it quiet."

"Okay, I was wrong," James grumbled. "It seems every man and his dog knows about us. The question remains, what do we do about it?"

"Go and kick some arse," Spence said promptly. He emphasized the point by smacking his fist into his palm.

"We could report him to the police, couldn't we?" Sam asked. "Impersonating a policeman must be a crime."

"I'm tempted--by both suggestions. The only problem I can see is that is we expose that joker on the barricade, whoever controls him knows we are onto them. They may try something else--something more effective."

"So we make them think their ploy has worked?" Nathan nodded. "We can get to The Twins by another road."

"Exactly. They can't have them all manned by phony policemen."

James was right. They met no more phony policemen, but every road they tried was blocked, one way or another. Eaton Road, just to the south, was closed for road works, and several dirt and gravel roads into the State Forest ended at padlocked gates or where trees had fallen across the roads.

"I can't believe any guy has this much power. We're just unlucky," Marc grumbled.

"Why don't we just park here and walk," Sam asked when they pulled up at another barred and locked Forestry gate. "We were going to do that anyway, so why not just start a bit earlier?"

"Unfortunately, we are on the wrong side of the mountains and it's too far to tramp through to the other side. We need to get to the Woodford side."

"So let's just drive there and be done with it," Spence said. "If we take the D'Aguilar Highway, we could be in Woodford by two o'clock. Here, look at the map. They can't have blocked the road to the Woodford Forest Station; Forestry would be on their backs at once. The road gets bad after that but there is a fire tower here, and here." He pointed out the features on the map. "They can't interfere with those either. Follow the road through and it joins up with the main Beerburrum-Woodford road where we were stopped. Now, if anyone is watching for us, they'll probably watch the Forestry roads so we ought to go cross-country. Right here is a lay by, and here is a creek running more or less toward the peaks. I estimate we can be in that creek and within sight of the mountains by six."

The drive through to the Woodford Forest Station was uneventful. They filled up petrol tanks at Woodford itself and bought fast food to eat as they drove. Dust lay thick on the relatively unused road past the station and Spence and Ratana, following in the Jeep, fell back to avoid being choked by the clouds thrown up by the Landcruiser. Presently the road divided and James waited for Spence to catch up before starting off down the left-hand fork. To their right, the land fell away steeply and through gaps in the dense forest they could make out the dark green of the pine forests and the lighter blue-green of eucalyptus scrub surrounding The Twins, which from this angle, appeared as a single mountain. The road curved eastward and descended, passing from tangled vegetation with the trees set close together to open grassland with tall trees within the space of a hundred metres.

"Why the sudden change in the plants?" Sam asked. "Is it because this is a managed forest?"

"It's an ecotone," James explained. "You have relatively damp air in the upland portion and dryer air on this eastern slope. The humidity favours two different types of vegetation, and often the boundary is quite sharp. This one is a natural ecotone, but shortly we'll cross an artificial one into managed pine forest."

Blasts on the horn from Spence's Jeep made James pull over. Spence pulled alongside, the leaned over Ratana and shouted across the gap between the vehicles.

"I'd better take the lead. I know the place I'm looking for."

Another three kilometres on, Spence turned right onto what appeared to be another Forestry road through the pine trees and almost immediately left into an overgrown, potholed track that led back into tangled re-growth paralleling the Woodford road. The track came to a dead end in huge piles of rough earth fill and the grassed remnants of a turning bay. Just beyond the weathered piles of earth, the land dropped away into a steep-sided creek choked with gums and long grass.

They parked the cars and removed all their equipment, James supervising an equitable division of the supplies into each backpack. He inspected each person, some, like Spence and Nathan, cursorily; others, like Sam and Marc, with more care.

"Tuck your jeans into your socks," James instructed. "And apply liberal quantities of repellent. The bush is fairly dry at the moment, but there will be biting flies and mosquitoes. Don't shake any trees in case there are wasp nests or stinging ants and keep an eye out for leeches."

"Leeches?" exclaimed Marc. "I thought you said it was dry."

"They don't need water, only a moist place and they're always on the lookout for their next meal." James looked around at his little group. "One last warning concerns snakes. There are a few quite deadly species around but generally they are more afraid of you than you are of them. Just be careful where you put your feet and don't go wandering off into any long grass. In fact, don't wander off at all. I'll be in the lead, followed by Spence, then Sam, Marc and Ratana. Nathan will come last to make sure there are no stragglers."

"I really don't like snakes," Marc said, scanning the undergrowth. "Or spiders. Is it going to be safe?"

James considered Marc's anxious face. "It'll be safer than walking the streets of any American city and a number of Australian ones too. Nothing is ever completely safe, Marc, but I doubt you'll even see a snake in the next couple of days." He pursed his lips. "I don't honestly know what's going to happen in the next day or so, but if anyone feels they'd rather sit this one out, they can stay here with cars."

Marc licked his lips and glanced at Sam, but noting her resolute stance, said nothing.

"Okay, let's move out. We're probably no more than a kilometre or two away as the proverbial Corvid flies, but we'll be taking a slightly longer route and we can't walk fast through this." James scrambled up the earth pile and scanned the vegetation below him for a moment before selecting a likely entry point.

The next hour was spent forcing their way along a dry and overgrown creek bed choked with long grass and weeds. Hordes of little yellow butterflies flitted above the grass and large brown ones burst from under their feet, winging ahead a few paces before vanishing the instant they alighted. Flies gathered, drawn by the sweat that soon soaked tee shirts, seemingly not bothered at all by the insect repellent. Mosquitoes whined and thorny vines clung to the clothing or raised welts on exposed skin.

"Uncle," Nathan called from the rear of the little column. "I don't like to complain, but we're making bloody awful time in this gully. Don't you think we would be better off in the forest?"

James called a halt and consulted with Spence and Nathan, examining the map again. The others sat and inspected their feet and clothing for unwanted guests.

"Shit," Marc muttered. "I've gone and cut myself on something." He gingerly poked at a blood-soaked sock. Peeling it back he uttered a small cry of disgust and brushed the squashed remnants of a leech from his leg. Further looking found two more still feeding and Ratana dabbed a spot of disinfectant on them to make them let go, before applying more to the welling wounds. "Can I change my mind about going?" he asked.

"Sorry, Marc, too late for that, I'm afraid. You'll be fine." James tapped the map. "The good news is we are almost clear of this gully. It opens out into a shallow valley in another hundred paces or so. A little after that we should be in sight of The Twins." He reached out and helped Sam to her feet. "How are you holding up?"

Sam fanned herself with her hat, mopping at her damp face with a tissue. "I'm okay."

"Remember to drink plenty of water. Dehydration is your biggest enemy out here."

The gully widened into open eucalypt forest interspersed with patches of vine thicket and stands of grass that blew in the warm breeze. Ahead, through the trees, occasional glimpses of Tunbubudla could be seen, though the vegetation was still dense enough to necessitate walking close together.

Then the forest dwindled to scrub and the land started to rise. The twin spires of exposed rock stood clear above the low trees and bushes, backlit by the rays of the setting sun.

"The dream," Spence murmured. "This was the place."

"You're sure?"

Spence nodded. He eased his pack off his shoulders and stood looking up at the mountains while he stretched his limbs. "This is it exactly."

"Okay, then we camp here. Tomorrow is the day we were supposed to be here, so maybe we'll get a sign tonight."

"A sign?" Marc queried. "You mean a UFO like in the dream?"

"Who said it was a UFO?" Spence smiled at Marc's eager expression. "All I described was a light from the sky."

"Just remember that the dream was almost certainly metaphorical rather than a statement of things to come," James cautioned. "Don't be expecting anything."

Sam had been unpacking her backpack. "I don't seem to have a tent," she said. "Only this roll of plastic and a rope."

"I thought tents would be too heavy," James explained. "Besides, the forecast is fine over the next few days, so we'll only need lean-tos. You tie the rope between two trees and sling the plastic over it, anchoring it at one end."

"I'll show her how it's done, Uncle," Ratana said. "Perhaps you'd like to share, Sam? With two sheets of plastic we can be really cozy." She led Sam off to select a good site for their lean-to.

Marc watched them for a few minutes before starting his own. Nathan cleared a small circle of grass and set up the gas bottle and burner in the middle of the bare earth, putting a pan on to boil some water for tea. He also removed a Tilley lantern from his pack and added kerosene from a plastic bottle. Several torches were laid out, ready for use.

"No fire?" Marc queried. "I thought all camps had a fire."

"It's a National Park," Nathan explained. "No fires are allowed. This'll be all we need."

"Latrines are in those clumps of bushes," James said, pointing. "Left for ladies, right for gents. I don't want to seem paranoid but either go in pairs or at the very least tell someone when you go."

Night fell swiftly and Nathan lit the kerosene lantern. It threw a small pool of yellow light over the ring of lean-tos and the six people sitting around it. The light also cast shadows out in a ring toward the surrounding darkness and the flicker of the flame as the breeze caught it made the shadows move, keeping them on edge. Darkness brought fresh swarms of mosquitoes and more repellent was applied to keep them at bay. Supper was a frugal affair of bread, cheese, some tinned fish and dried fruit, washed down with draughts of black tea sweetened with sugar.

"I'd have been a little more adventurous with the rations if we were going to be out here longer than a couple of days," James said.

"Do we have to have tea?" Marc complained. "I'd kill for a cup of coffee."

"I have a bit of instant, if you want it."

Marc grimaced. "Where's a Starbuck's when you need one?" He took a sip of the black tea and made a face. "Perhaps more sugar?" he said, stirring in another spoon. "Nope, not doing anything for me."

The night sounds of the Australian bush were both comfortable and worrying. Insects called incessantly and from deeper in the gully when they'd come, small frogs 'tinked' metallically. Overhead, unseen, bats flitted across the night sky, diving low between the trees to catch moths and other small insects attracted to the light of the kerosene lantern. Fruit bats screeched and squabbled in the distance and the hoarse coughing bark of the possum sounded from the denser scrub toward the black pinnacles of rock.

"Are we likely to see any animals?" Sam asked nervously as some small creature screamed in the undergrowth.

"You never know," James replied, "But it's more likely you'll just see eye shine."

"Like cats and dogs, you mean?"

James nodded. "Except in this case it'll be possums and wallabies."

The stars shone clearly in the night sky, which remained cloudless. Sam and Ratana retired to their lean-to after a quick visit to the trees on the left. Nathan took Marc out beyond the circle of light with a couple of torches and a camera to try and spot some animals by their eye shine, and the two older men reminisced about old camping trips. Marc and Nathan returned, the former quite excited at what he'd seen.

"Possums," crowed Marc, "And I got a decent picture of one."

Nathan was fiddling with his torch, thumping it against the heel of his hand. "Damn thing must have a loose connection. It keeps flickering and dimming."

"Here's another." James tossed another torch to Nathan who caught it and put the faulty one down.

"This one's doing it too. Are the batteries flat?"

"Shouldn't be," James replied, looking across at Nathan. "I put fresh ones in from the university store before we left."

"What's the time?" Sam called out from her lean-to. "My watch has stopped."

"Well, it's about moonrise, if that's any help," Marc called back. "I can just see its glow behind the mountains."

Sam laughed. "Great! Now all I need to know is the time of moonrise."

Spence was on his feet staring toward Tunbubudla. "It can't be much past nine or ten and moonrise isn't scheduled until about three in the morning. Plus it's in the wrong direction. That's not the moon."

9

The twin peaks of Tunbubudla were limned in a pearly glow that strengthened as they watched. Everyone now stood in the open, their eyes fixed on the mountains, watching the unfolding spectacle with feelings that ranged from awe to profound disquiet. Without speaking, they moved forward, past the light of the Tilley lantern, so nothing interfered with their view.

"Are you sure it's not the moon?" Marc asked, a faint tremor in his voice. "Perhaps we are mistaken about what time it is."

"Not a chance," Spence murmured. "That glow is to the southwest."

As the glow rose behind the peaks it grew smaller, concentrating its light into brilliant blue-white lights that dazzled, far larger and brighter than any celestial object. The lights lifted above Tunbubudla which now lay in darkness, a black shadow that remained unaffected by actinic display above it.

"They must be very high up," James commented quietly. "The light isn't reaching the ground."

The lights moved, changing from line abreast into a triangular or arrowhead formation and moving slowly toward the mountains. The night sounds around them dropped off, hushed as if waiting for something to happen.

"I think I can see something solid between the lights," Nathan said. "It looks triangular with lights at the apices. Are you getting this, Marc?"

"My damn camera has shut down," Marc replied disgustedly. "Don't let it get away, I'm going to get my film camera." He backed away slowly, almost tripping over the lantern as he went.

"I disagree," Spence said. "It's circular with the lights around the perimeter. I can see light gleaming off metal."

"There's nothing there," James disputed. "Your eyes must be playing tricks. Those are three separate lights."

"Four," Sam corrected.

"Where are these lights?" Ratana asked. "Are they in that luminous cloud or somewhere else?"

The lights moved over the higher of the peaks and started circling, slowly, looking equally as if they were separate objects chasing each other or a single solid object turning ponderously on its axis. Gradually the lights grew in size as they descended over the western peak of Tunbubudla. They descended so low that the light washed over the bare rock and scrub, revealing the peak as if bathed in the midday sun. Things moved amid the rocks of the mountain top, small and black that hopped and hid quickly.

Sam shuddered. "Are those the dreadful shadows we saw at Emerald? I don't think I could stand another visit by those things."

Without thinking, James put his arm around Sam and held her tightly. "I think they are just wallabies," he said. He remained transfixed by the sight, his mind working rapidly over possible identifications. Remotely, he was aware of Sam's warm body nestled against his, and of Marc a few paces back, snapping off a series of pictures.

The lights moved eastward, over the gap between the mountains, the brilliantly lambent objects circling rapidly now, as if eager to achieve their goal. They centred on the lower, eastward peak and a beam of white fire dropped, lashing the rocky peak in a coruscating flood of brilliance. Everyone drew back on a reflex except Marc, who remained glued to the viewfinder of his camera. The flood of fire poured down the mountain side towards the watchers, as if the ancient volcanic plug of Tunbubudla was once more in furious magmatic eruption. Then, as if a tap was turned, the light shut off, plunging the peak and surrounding countryside into stygian darkness. Eyes were left blinking as a glow of complementary colour tinged the mountainside, but as their eyes reaccustomed themselves to the night once more, they saw that a thin strip of the mountain, from the base to a point about a third of the way up the steep slope, remained glowing, as if heated from within.

The torches, discarded on the grass, flickered back into life, and Sam's watch started up again. James called over to Marc. "Is your digital camera working again?"

Marc switched it on and nodded. "Doesn't matter though, I've taken plenty with my other camera."

"Uh-huh. I'd still like you to take a few of that glowing strip before it fades. It looks as if it's marking something and I'd like to be able to examine its position tomorrow. I'll need a digital image for that."

"Gotcha." Mark put away his film camera and set up his digital again, snapping off a dozen shots of the already fading track of light on the left peak of Tunbubudla.

Sam felt a strange desire to remain where she was, with James' arm around her. She hesitated, and then slipped her own arm around his waist. "Thank you for being concerned," she murmured.

James smiled awkwardly. "Er, my pleasure." He knew he should be getting statements from the observers but he felt reluctant to let Sam go.

"That was quite a light show," Spence said, "And it fit the dream reasonably well. All that was missing was the light underground and strange people walking around in it."

"The night is young," Nathan said, grinning. "Bloody hell, that was incredible. Were they UFOs? Flying saucers?"

"What, little green men and all that?" Marc asked with a laugh. "What's next? The Loch Ness Monster?"

"Let's just say UFOs in the sense that they were unidentified," Spence replied, a serious expression on his face. "And I don't know if you noticed but from what people were saying, we all saw something different."

"You're kidding? How could you lot see anything different. It was...well, as plain as the nose on your face."

"So what did you see, Marc?" Spence asked.

"A flying saucer...with a dome and three lights underneath of course. What else?"

"And you Nathan?"

"A triangular shaped craft with lights at the corners."

"James?"

"Three lights, unconnected."

"I saw four," Sam said. "I know I did."

"What about you, Ratana?"

"A patch of light, like a cloud lit up by lightning, then that blast of lightning at the end."

"And I saw a circular craft with three lights," Spence concluded. "Now until we examine Marc's pictures, we are left to cling onto our own particular set of beliefs, firm in the knowledge that we are right and everybody else was mistaken."

"That's bullshit," Marc said. "How can something look that different to different people? You're making this up for some obscure reason."

"You're certain of that, Marc?" James asked.

"Fuckin' A. I know what I saw and I have the pictures to prove it."

85

James nodded. "Hold onto that film and don't let it out of your sight. I'm willing to bet you, though, that all it will show is an ill-defined patch of light that could back up any of our beliefs."

Marc laughed. "You believe in that if you want, professor. I'll believe in my own eyes."

"Well, enough said on the subject, I think. We should get some rest; it could be a busy day tomorrow." James reluctantly released Sam and walked back to the Tilley lantern, turning the flame down so the circle of light dimmed and drew in sharply. The darkness of the night, and the silence, was alleviated only by the cold fire-points of the stars and a distant hum that nagged at the mind until one realised it was the sound of traffic on the distant Bruce Highway.

"One more thing, if you would, Marc. Will you download those pictures of the light trail onto my laptop? I'd like to have a closer look at them."

"Sure. Just don't publish them, on the internet or anywhere. Remember what they say about intellectual property."

Sam gave Marc a disgusted look and marched off to her lean-to with Ratana and settled back down into her sleeping bag. She lay awake for a long time, gazing out at the starlit bush, the now-dark mountains as shadows against the star-emblazoned sky, and the faint flicker of a laptop screen as James worked into the night. Despite the beauty of the night, her eyes kept straying back to James' shelter. She smiled and closed her eyes.

Sam awoke with a start and sat up, her ears still ringing from the terrifying roar of the unknown beast that had invaded her dreams. It sounded again and she rubbed her eyes, desperate now to wake up, and yelped in surprise as Ratana touched her shoulder.

"Sam, Sam," Ratana whispered. "Get a hold of yourself."

"What..." The roar came again, closer now, and Sam scrambled to her feet, her face pale and drawn in the bobbing beam of the torch. "What the hell is that?"

Ratana did not answer, but dragged Sam across to where the men were standing. Nathan had relit the kerosene lantern and Marc was fiddling nervously with his camera, while James and Spence held torch beams on the surrounding scrub, their attention focused on the darkness.

"What is it?" Sam asked, nervousness tingeing her voice. "I've never heard anything like it."

"I have," Marc said grimly. "In Rwanda a couple of years back. I heard something like that just before I was charged by a silverback gorilla."

"No gorillas here, chum," Spence said dryly. "What you're hearing is a Yowie."

"No shit? Well, I'm ready for it." Marc lifted his camera.

"A fat lot of good that'll do you," James commented. "But I think we should be all right. Yowies are seldom aggressive and the only thing we might have done to upset it is entering its territory."

"There!" Nathan yelled, swinging his torch to cover a small tree that was shaking violently. Thick shrubs covered its base and they could not make out what was causing the disturbance. Then a roar erupted from another point in the perimeter, and a cacophony of snarls and coughs from several other places.

"They're all around us," Marc shouted. He swung round with his camera and the clearing was lit up by a series of electronic flashes.

"Stop!" James cried. "You'll aggravate them." As if to confirm his words, screaming roars now erupted from several points in the scrub. "Don't make any threatening gesture or noise," he called urgently. He leaned close to Spence. "I'm worried," he whispered. "I've never come across anything in the literature to match this. It sounds like there are half a dozen out there."

"I've heard of one, though it was never reported as a yowie attack," Spence responded in a low voice. "It preceded an attack that led to a fatality. Poor guy was ripped apart."

"That's impossible," James said. "I'd have heard about something like that."

"Not if it was Defence Department in the Top End. Officially it was a croc fatality. I read the original report through a friend of a friend."

"I think it's quietening down," Nathan said. "They sound further off."

"Not over here," Sam called, her voice quavering, though she held her position next to Ratana. "There's something in those bushes." She started to swing her torch toward the disturbance, but Ratana pushed her hand down.

"Careful, Sam," she whispered. "You could set them off again."

Suddenly, as if cut with a knife, the screaming and roaring stopped, leaving the darkness of the night at the feet of Tunbubudla as peaceful as a country churchyard. They waited, senses straining, waiting to see if this truly was the end, or if it was only a lull in the attack.

"Have they gone?" Marc whispered.

James nodded. "I think so."

"Maybe not so much 'gone' as 'quiet'," Spence murmured. "I can still hear something moving out there."

"It's the truth," Marc muttered. Nobody paid any attention except Nathan who laughed.

"I think it's coming closer." Sam swung her torch round toward the bushes where she'd heard something before. The shrubs moved slightly, as if something was trying to force its way through the undergrowth without being seen.

"Oh, shit," Marc muttered. He raised his camera again, almost defensively.

"Do you feel dizzy?" Nathan asked, his attention riveted on the gently swaying bushes. "I did, just now, as if I'd had a few drinks."

"I was wondering about that," Spence said. "But with me it's as if I was so tired my attention was wandering."

"Heads up, guys," Ratana called. "It's coming out."

Several torches and Marc's camera swung toward the bushes. The branches parted and a figure stumbled through and stood swaying in the grass not more than twenty paces from the little group.

"Dear God Almighty," Spence breathed. "It's a woman."

The figure standing in front of them, eyes blinking in the bright light from the torches was a small woman, no more than shoulder height on Spence, who was by no means a tall man. Shoulder length brown hair, matted with sweat and plant debris, framed a delicate well-formed face. She was clad in a brown sweater and long baggy pants of an indeterminate but similar colour. The woman raised a hand to shade her eyes and called out hesitantly.

"Hello. Who...who's there? I...I saw your lights..."

Sam ran across to the woman, her body blocking the dazzle of the torches. Standing a pace or two away, she could see a lot more detail and it shocked her. "You're just a girl," she cried out. "What are you doing out here alone?" Without waiting for an answer, she put her arm around the trembling girl and led her back to the others and introduced them.

The girl nodded at each name, her eyes locking briefly with each person. "I'm Cindy," she said. "Cindy Walsh. Thank you for coming to my aid."

"A pleasure," Spence said, smiling. "But, er...what are you doing out here?"

"I was walking with my boyfriend and we got separated," Cindy said. "Yesterday morning. I've been wandering around those mountains ever since."

"Did you hear those...those things out there?" Marc asked.

Cindy frowned. "I heard you--all of you--shouting and yelling. I...I thought you were a rescue party. You are, aren't you?"

"I'm afraid not," James said. "We're out here..."

"Of course we are, Cindy," Sam interrupted. "Maybe not specifically to rescue you, but certainly a rescue. Now, you look pretty beat-up. Do you need food and drink?"

"Water please."

Sam passed across her water bottle but Cindy just stood holding it, staring blankly. Sam reached over and unscrewed the lid, then tipped the bottle toward the girl's mouth. She drank thirstily and handed the bottle back.

"Thank you."

"I think you need some sleep," Sam said. "Come with Ratana and me and we'll fix you up with a bed for the night." She led the unresisting girl off to their lean-to.

James stood and watched the three women cross the small clearing and prepare their sleeping arrangements. He frowned, and massaged his temples with his hand. "What do you make of that?" he asked.

"Interesting she thought the noise of the yowies was us," Spence said. "Still, after a day lost in the bush she must be feeling disoriented. I wonder where her boyfriend is."

"Who cares?" Marc grinned and stared avidly across at Cindy. "I've always been rather partial to shapely blondes."

James frowned again but couldn't quite identify the thought that skittered through his mind. "I'm feeling bloody tired," he said, yawning. "I'm going to hit the sack."

Spence nodded. "Good idea. I think we've had quite enough excitement for one day, eh Jimmy? Nathan, do you want to walk with me a moment? I'm just going to check the perimeter."

Nathan looked surprised. "Sure." He walked off with Spence, his torch scanning the bushes on the edge of the clearing. "You don't really expect there to be anything out here, do you? All the usual night sounds have started up again."

"I'd be surprised," Spence said, "But I wanted to ask you something." He hesitated, as if trying to find the words. "Do you feel all right? Mentally, I mean."

Nathan scratched his chin. "I guess so. I feel tired, well, exhausted actually, but I put that down to the stress of the last couple of hours."

"Yes, we've been flooded with adrenalin so maybe that's the answer. I'm just finding it hard to focus on anything."

Nathan yawned and stretched. "Can we talk about it tomorrow? I'm bushed."

The two men made their way back to their sleeping bags and within minutes the sounds of multi-toned snoring joined the normal night sounds of the Australian bush.

Sam awoke and lay still, feeling the pressure in her bladder and knowing she would have to get up soon but dreading the prospect of going into the yowie-haunted bushes and squatting defenselessly. *Men have all the breaks*, she thought. She rolled over and retrieved her torch, shielding it with her cupped hands as she switched it on and checked her watch. Four o'clock. She looked up and saw Cindy watching her.

"Hello," Sam whispered. "Couldn't sleep?"

Cindy shook her head.

"Look, I have to visit the little girls' room but James told us not to go alone. Will you come with me?"

Cindy nodded and together they picked their way over to the designated bushes. Sam looked back at the campsite, the lean-tos just visible in the moonlight. She looked suspiciously at the crescent moon, worried it might prove to be something else, but it remained motionless and familiar in the black sky.

"Okay, I'll go first because I really gotta go," Sam said. "When I get back, I'll wait for you." She hesitated, then walked into the bushes, pushing through them into the darkness, the flickering light of her torch her only illumination.

The crescent moon drifted slowly westward, paling as dawn eased over the eastern horizon. Cindy remained sitting on the ground beside the clump of bushes for over an hour, staring into the night sky as if the stars held some great secret. At first light, she got up, and without a backward glance, moved back over the dew-spattered grass to the lean-to she shared with Sam and Ratana, and curled up beside Sam's sleeping bag. Ratana still lay fast asleep, on her back and breathing heavily through her open mouth.

The light strengthened, setting off the dawn chorus as the bird fauna of the area awoke to a new day. The tips of the peaks flushed rosy-gold, the glow slipping downward as the sun rose.

James yawned and stretched, shook Spence awake, and the two of them ambled over to the right-hand cluster of bushes to relieve themselves. As they finished, Marc and Nathan arrived, yawning and stumbling, muttering greetings. Back at the campsite, Spence lit the gas ring and started a pot of water heating for coffee while James dug out some breakfast items.

Marc arrived back, scratching an armpit in a desultory manner and looking around at the surrounding scrub which was now alive with birdsong. "Looks like a great day," he called to James and Spence. "Not a sign of those horrors from last night." He glanced toward the women's lean-to and frowned. "Where's Sam?"

James looked up from laying out the breakfast things, then across to the women's lean-to where he saw Cindy sitting and Ratana standing out in the early morning sun and combing her hair. "Where's Sam?" he called out.

Ratana looked around. "I don't know. She wasn't here when I woke up. I thought she was with you."

"Damn the woman," James muttered. "I told her not to go wandering off alone." He cupped his hands and yelled, "Sam!" A short pause, then again, "Sam! Where are you?" The call was taken up by Marc and Nathan.

Ratana squatted beside Cindy. "Have you seen Sam this morning?"

Cindy shook her head. "Not since last night. We went to the bushes." She pointed toward the ladies' clump.

Ratana immediately called the news across to James. "Cindy says they went to the loo last night."

James and Spence ran across to the women and James stared down at the young woman. Passing a hand over his eyes, he asked, "You say you went to the loo...to the bushes...with Sam last night. Did she come back with you too?"

Cindy shook her head again. "I sat and waited. After a while I came back."

"You didn't think to go and look for her?" James snapped. "After what happened last night..."

"She wasn't here then," Spence interrupted. "How could she know the importance of never being alone?"

"For God's sake! She could be...be hurt somewhere." James leapt to his feet and ran across the clearing to the toilet bushes. "Sam!" he yelled again, and plunged into the shrubbery.

A moment later he staggered back out followed by an irate-looking Sam, her clothing disheveled. She marched toward James and pushed him in the chest again, sending him stumbling back.

"For pity's sake!" Sam shouted. "Can't a gal even take a pee without someone almost knocking her over? What's the matter with you?" She eyed him suspiciously. "Or are you really some sort of pervert?"

"What's the matter with me?" James shouted back. "Where the hell were you? I told you not to go out alone and you turn round and do just that. We've been worried sick."

"What the hell are you talking about? I just came out here not ten minutes..." A horrified look crept over Sam's face as she took in the early morning light. She started trembling and stared at her watch. "It...it's nearly seven," she said unsteadily. "It can't be. I...I came out at four am and that was ten minutes ago."

"Sorry Sam," Marc said, an uncertain grin on his face. "I've been out here the last fifteen, twenty minutes and you certainly haven't..." His smile slipped as he searched for but failed to find the joke.

"Why did you come out alone?" James asked, his annoyance fading fast. "You should have woken one of the others."

"I did," Sam replied. "Or rather, Cindy was already awake so I asked her to come with me."

The others looked at the tiny brunette. "What happened, Cindy?" Spence asked gently.

Cindy shrugged. "I came out with Sam and waited out here while she went in. She did not come out after a long time so I went back to bed."

James frowned. "You didn't think to wait for her? She could have been in trouble."

"Why would she? I thought she had gone back to bed and I did not see her in the dark."

"What about back at the lean-to? Didn't you see she hadn't returned?"

"It was dark."

Nathan nodded. "Sounds reasonable."

Ratana agreed. "You never told her why we went in pairs, so she did not see the importance of it."

"Yup, say what you like about blondes but there was no blonde moment there," Marc quipped.

Spence stared at Marc and frowned. "What exactly do you mean...?"

"Cindy, what time was it when you went to the bushes with Sam?" James interrupted.

"I do not know. I do not have a watch."

"I told you, it was four am, near enough," Sam said, her voice showing a hint of impatience. "I don't take forever to pee, so how can it be seven?"

"Look around you," James said gently. "Sunrise is at six-forty. You must have been out here two and a half hours."

"How can I have been? I can remember...if I'd fallen asleep I'd remember waking up on the ground. I don't. I came out, walked into the bushes, put the torch on the ground, squatted to pee...and next thing is I'm almost knocked off my feet by James barging into me."

"Turn your torch on," Spence said.

Sam stared at him for a moment before flicking the toggle. "Flat," she said. "It was working fine a few...Jesus, what's happening to me?" Tears glistened in her eyes and she looked appealingly at James.

"It's a phenomenon called 'missing time'," James said softly. "It is often reported in conjunction with UFO sightings and involves periods of a few minutes to several days being expunged from a person's memory. Some say it is as a result of alien abduction."

"I was abducted?" Sam looked incredulous. "By whom? Why?"

"If we knew that, we'd understand a lot more about the phenomenon," Spence said. "It's actually commoner than you might think. Missing time happened to me, once."

"You're kidding? What happened?"

"I don't know," Spence replied with a smile. "If I could remember it wouldn't be missing."

"So how do you know it happened?"

"Two parallel scars appeared on my shoulder one morning between washing my face and starting to shave." Spence slipped his shirt off his left shoulder to reveal two lines of white, raised scar tissue.

"Me too," James said. "Though I was apparently out of it for at least two days. I got this for my trouble." He lifted his shirt and pulled the band of his shorts down to reveal a triangular scar on his right hipbone. "In my case, tissue was removed, though for what purpose I don't know."

"Damn, this really is like the X-Files," Marc chortled.

"Except it's not a joke," Spence said. "This is very real and can be totally disorienting. I suggest you go and lie down, Sam. A cup of coffee and a bit of quiet time will help."

Ratana and Cindy helped Sam to the lean-to and made her comfortable. "Spence is right, Sam," Ratana said. "A bit of quiet will calm you."

Sam shook her head helplessly. "I'm not so sure." She shuddered. "What did they do to me? I don't feel anything except a little...well, sore...inside." She put her hand on her belly and smiled uncertainly at Ratana. "A bit like I'm expecting a period," she confided, "But I know I'm not." A panicky laugh bubbled up. "Who is 'they'? I don't even know who did this or why."

Despite her agitation, Sam was asleep by the time James came over with a cup of coffee. He motioned to Ratana to get some breakfast and he sat down beside Sam, sipping at the cup of coffee and trying to get a grip on his emotions. For just a minute there he had felt a real terror that something had happened to Sam.

10

Ratana returned to sit by Sam after breakfast and James wandered over to sit by Spence as he wrote in his notebook. Spence looked across at his friend and saw the troubled look on his face.

"Want to talk about it, Jimmy?"

James laughed. "I sometimes think there are two distinct personalities in that scrawny old body of yours. The guy who's funny and outrageous and calls me Jimmy and the quiet scientist who calls me James."

"And which one suits your mood right now, Jimmy-James?"

James sighed. "Jimmy does, but I think I'm going to have need of your James side."

"Well, let's take it as it comes." Spence gestured toward the mountains. "Are we going up there today?"

"Later. We were definitely being shown something last night, but what the hell was that abduction business? Why go to all this trouble?"

"Ah, Jimmy, if we knew that we could stay in our comfy chairs and never venture out into the wilds. You think Sam really was abducted?"

"Yes." James looked surprised. "Don't you?"

Spence nodded. "I'm almost certain of it."

James nodded. "Do you think the abduction is in any way connected to the black rock? Mick's instructions from Tjakkan were that Sam accompanies us to these mountains. Was that just so she could be abducted? It makes me feel responsible."

"Nah, they could take her anywhere if they wanted to, Jimmy. You know that. They wouldn't need her here specifically. You have no reason to blame yourself."

"I'm a little confused though. When this started, I thought this whole affair was some aspect of Aboriginal Dreamtime mythology, something to do with yowies and the spirit world, but with this UFO intervention, a whole other dimension is opening up--excuse the pun."

Spence laughed, and then became serious again. "Nothing can be viewed in isolation, James. You cannot compartmentalise when it comes to the paranormal. After all, look at how many cases are on record where UFOs and manimals coincide. Well, here's another one."

James looked across the small clearing to where Marc was talking to Cindy, apparently showing her his cameras and explaining how he used them. "What do you make of her?" he asked. "She turns up on our doorstep in the middle of a paranormal event with some story about being lost, separated from her boyfriend, yet she seems quite incredibly calm about it all."

"Yes, and there's another thing that's curious," Spence said. Cindy looked across the clearing at them and waved, so Spence waved back, grinning. "Delightful girl," he chortled.

"What's this curious thing about her?"

"Eh? Oh, I forget. Can't have been very important." Spence frowned. "She is calm, but that may just be a lack of imagination. Or perhaps she's blocking the experience out."

"I guess." James massaged his temples. He fished a foil strip of analgesics out of his pocket and popped the foil cap on two of them, swallowing them dry. "Bloody headache," he complained. "I've been having them off and on since last night."

"What are we going to do about her? It'd be a pain to have to take her out to the authorities, but I'm not sure we have any right to keep her here."

"Today's the fifth day," James said. "We have to be here, so I guess she'll have to stay with us. She'll be okay though; Sam and Ratana will keep an eye on her, and maybe by tomorrow we can take her out."

Sam woke up at midday, feeling refreshed. Her experience of the night before had slipped from the forefront of her mind and now was little more than a bad dream. She got up and dashed for the bushes with Ratana in tow, consumed three cups of black coffee and pronounced herself ready to tackle anything the mountain could throw at them.

James decided to leave the campsite intact as a base camp and take little with them for their exploration of the left peak of Tunbubudla. "It's less than a kilometre to the base," he said, "And the bush isn't particularly thick. We can explore the strip we saw highlighted last night and be back here well before sunset."

They had packed the two packs they were going to take--mostly food and water--and were waiting while James had a last-minute discussion with Spence about procedures, when the sound of bodies moving through the scrub behind them stilled all conversation.

"Not fucking more of them," Marc groaned, but took out his camera anyway. "The digital is still working," he observed.

James and Spence, with Nathan just behind, moved to intercept whatever it was that was approaching the camp. The sound resolved itself into footsteps and a few moments later a man stepped out of the bush and stopped, staring at his reception committee with a supercilious sneer on his face.

"Well, if it isn't Professor Hay and his usually bloody horde of kids," the man said softly. "I thought it might be when I saw the JCU vehicle." He flicked a manicured hand at the crisp seam of his trousers and unselfconsciously struck a nonchalant pose.

"Guilford King." James stared back with a stony expression. "What are you doing here?"

"Same as you, old chap, though as usual I'm a tad more prepared than you." Guilford slapped the stock of the .577 Magnum, under lever, double hammer rifle he cradled in his left arm. "I intend to get me the definitive scientific specimen this time."

"You bloody idiot," Spence growled. "It's people like you who give the rest of us researchers into the paranormal a bad name."

"Ah, the redoubtable Spencer Tuhua. A pity you can't stay in those little backwater islands of yours and leave the serious work to the professionals like me. And for your information, the field is not the paranormal, but cryptozoology. This isn't about spirits and ghosts but about an unknown species of primate. As usual, you've got your head stuck in the clouds again."

"Better than being stuck in shit," Spence retorted. "Why don't you just get the hell out of here, Guilford? You're not wanted."

"This is a National Park, King," James observed. "You are aware that even with a personal gun permit you are prohibited from carrying one here, let alone firing it?"

Guilford shrugged. He took his crisply clean hat from his head and fanned himself. "I'm not worried. If I succeed, nobody's going to quibble about minor infractions of the law." Returning his hat to his head, Guilford turned and shouted behind him. "Ernie, you black bastard. Where are you? I told you to keep up."

"I am here," said a low voice a few paces from Guilford. A slim Aboriginal man of indeterminate but advanced age, his hair grizzled with grey, and dressed only in khaki shorts and a red tee shirt, melted from the bushes, causing James to jump, his appearance was so sudden.

Guilford grunted. "Well, keep up," he snapped. "I can't be worrying where you are all the time. Hand me my water bottle."

Ernie dug into the pack at his feet and passed over a plastic water bottle, waiting until Guilford had finished before repacking it. He smiled at James and Spence and nodded at Nathan, murmuring a few words in dialect.

"What did you say?" Guilford demanded suspiciously. "I've told you before to speak English."

"I was greeting my brother," Ernie said calmly.

"Anyway," James said. "You'd better be moving on, King. There's nothing for you here."

Guilford smiled. "Trying to get rid of me, Hay?" He looked past the three men to where Marc stood with the women. "I'd say there is plenty for me here. Who are the women? I've seen the Islander before but that's a smashing redhead and quite a decent blonde."

"Brunette," James corrected without thinking. "That's none of your business, so just move..."

"Keeping them all for yourself, Hay? That's not very sociable."

"I have no desire to be sociable with you, so I suggest you move on."

"Far be it from me to stay where I'm not wanted..."

"Never stopped you in the past," Spence muttered.

"But my business calls me to the left peak of these mountains. I suppose you saw that lightshow last night? I intend to find out why the peak was all lit up." Guilford's eyes bored into James'. "I don't suppose you're going to tell me what you know?"

James hesitated, thinking furiously, considering the options. "You're welcome to join us, as long as you're prepared to put yourself under my authority."

Spence swung round. "What? No way is this bugger joining us."

Guilford laughed--a high, rather effeminate titter. "Dear me, rebellion in the ranks. I would be delighted to join your little expedition, Professor Hay, for the time being. I'd offer the services of my blackie..." He waved a hand in the general direction of Ernie, "... but I see you have your own."

James turned to Ernie and raised a hand in greeting. He stumbled a bit with the dialect the old man had used in greeting Nathan, but the man's eyes glowed with pleasure at his effort. "Greetings, Uncle," James said. "May I offer the hospitality of my...my people. You are very welcome."

They returned to the others and James introduced Guilford King. Ratana had met him before and was cool toward him, whereas Marc was immediately interested in the gun and by his studied self-confidence. Sam picked up on the tension in James and the anger and contempt oozing from

Spence and was polite but reserved. Cindy seemed frightened and nodded a very quick acknowledgement before retreating behind Sam.

Ernie sparked a lot of interest. Nathan introduced him to his fiancée Ratana, who was deferential, treating him with great respect. Sam was puzzled by the Islander woman's reaction and drew her aside while he greeted Marc.

"I can't exactly say why," Ratana explained, "But he seems to radiate a sense of...of--it sounds silly, I know--of holiness. It's as if he has just stepped off sacred land."

Sam had no time to digest this statement before she found herself shaking Ernie's hand. "So you are Samantha Louis," he said cryptically.

Cindy's reaction to the old Aborigine was odd, given her shyness. The two of them faced each other a pace or two apart, but said nothing. They stared into each other's eyes, as if reading their respective life stories for over a minute, while Guilford King made loud comments about ignorant tongue-tied savages.

Spence pulled James away while this was going on and swung him round to face him, his body tense with anger. "What the hell are you playing at, James? Why have you invited that turd to join us? Have you gone utterly mad?"

James grinned. "It seems that way, I admit, but think about it. King is a gung-ho fanatic with only one aim in life--to prove his little pet theories about Australian myths. Now he turns up here, following those same news reports that first caught your attention, I'll bet. He's armed and determined to kill a yowie. I don't believe he has a snowball's hope in hell of doing so, but imagine him blazing away at everything that moves. I couldn't risk us being on Tunbubudla if he was there with his gun. If he comes with us, we might be able to control his actions."

Spence turned away and scuffed his boot in the dirt. "Damn you, James, you know I hate that man."

"Hate's bad for you, Spence old buddy," James said, putting his hand on the old man's shoulder.

"Ah, Jimmy, you don't know the half of it."

"I know it's hard for you, but for the sake of the..."

Spence grunted. "You needn't be concerned I'll cause trouble," he said. "Just don't expect me to talk to him." He walked off to stand alone on the edge of the bush, studiously avoiding the others.

James called for everyone's attention. "All right, we've wasted enough time, so let's get going. Ernie, would you lead, please? I imagine your bush craft exceeds mine. I'll go next, then Guilford, Sam, Cindy, Marc, Spence, Ratana, and Nathan in the rear. Please stay on the path at all times and stay in sight of the person in front of you. If you need a loo break or to stop for any reason, say so. Tell the person in front of you and pass it along the line. It is essential we do not get separated."

"Being a bit paranoid, aren't you, Hay?" Guilford drawled. "There's nothing up here I can't handle." He patted his rifle again.

"We don't know what we're going to meet," James said patiently. "And half of my concern is you blasting away at a movement in the bushes and having it turn out to be one of us having a pee."

Guilford sniffed. "I'm a damn sight more professional than that."

"Bullshit," Spence muttered.

Ernie nodded to James and set off toward the area James had indicated. He moved confidently and at a slow jog, but after only a few minutes had to stop and wait for the others to catch up. Thereafter he moved more slowly, matching his pace to the slowest in the party.

The sun stood high in the sky, baking their heads and necks and raising a prickle of sweat that rapidly soaked shirts and shorts. Flies were attracted by the sweat, circling and buzzing, covering the shirt backs and making repeated forays to mouth, nose, eyes and ears. Sam was the most affected and quickly dug out insect repellent and liberally applied it to any exposed area. Marc followed suit, but the others contented themselves with just the occasional dab of repellent. Neither Ernie nor Cindy made use of chemicals--Ernie because the flies were not attracted to him and Cindy because she did not seem to like the smell of the repellent. She walked along behind Sam, swatting at the troublesome insects every few seconds.

The smell of the bush was a mixture of acrid dust, the scent of eucalyptus oils with an admixture of various blossoms and a subtle overlay of resin from the surrounding pine forests. The overall effect was to make Sam's heart and spirits lift. She looked past the crisply ironed figure of Guilford King, impossibly free of sweat stains, to where James strode ahead, just behind the flitting form of Ernie the tracker. *A strange man*, she thought. *An academic, but one who is in touch with the real world...and the unreal one*, she added with a smile. *Do I like him? Yes. Do I want it to go further? Yes. Will I let it?* She tucked that question aside to be considered later and turned her attention to her surroundings.

The bush was alive around them. Birds called in the taller shrubs and trees, insects provided an incessant rasp with cicadas bursting into high-pitched whirrs and whines en masse, only to fall silent as they passed. Hawks

100

hung in the still air, riding the thermals above the bare rock of the peaks, following the party below in the hopes of securing a meal from the small wildlife flushed out by their passing. Lizards skittered off the path, racing away and turning to stare at the intruders with fathomless black eyes. Larger animals inhabited the undergrowth and on more than one occasion, Sam jumped as something erupted unseen from near the path and bounded away into the scrub.

Guilford turned and graced Sam with a knowing smile after one such incident. "Wallabies," he said.

"It's quite a place," Sam said, waving her arm to encompass everything. "Everything is so different."

"Where in the States are you from?"

"California, but I've lived the last ten years in Illinois. I'm a journalist and I go where the stories take me. This is the first time I've been to Australia though."

"And what story are you working on at the moment?"

"Yowies and the black..."

"Sam!" James had stopped and was staring hard at her. "I'm sure Mr King has no interest in gossip. Besides, we are coming up on the main area and I need everyone's attention focused."

Sam stared back at James, feeling her cheeks colouring and a biting retort form in her mind. Then she became aware of Guilford's keen interest in her and realised what she had been about to say.

"Yowies and the black what, Ms Louis?" King asked.

"Man," she replied after a moment's hesitation. "Yowies and the black man. As...as part of their mythology."

"Oh?" Guilford smiled knowingly. "Not the black rock?"

"You knew?" Sam gasped, and then rounded on James in a fury. "And you let me make a fool of myself."

Guilford uttered his high-pitched laugh again. "Your Head of Department, Professor Howard, really dislikes you, Dr Hay. He couldn't wait to spread the dirt about you. Of course, most people couldn't care less, but then most people are thick as shit. I recognised the significance immediately and intend to lend my reputation and credibility to our discoveries."

"Very magnanimous of you, King," James growled. "I'm sorry, Sam, I didn't think he knew." He turned back to face the cone of shattered rock in front of him.

For another fifty paces, the land rose steeply, covered in a dense stand of tall *Leptospermum luehmannii*, before shaking itself free of its covering of

101

vegetation. The rock then rose by degrees to precipitous; its plant life reduced to grasses and stunted shrubs clinging to cracks and ledges. There was nothing to distinguish the strip of land that had been illuminated by the UFO the previous evening, or anything that hinted at why it had glowed afterward.

James called the others forward to view the strip, but nobody could see anything different about it. He took a small instrument out of his pack and, switching it on, waved it slowly over the rock and shrubby plants. "Geiger counter," he explained. "In case there is any residual radiation." It clicked loudly, twice.

Marc leapt back. "Shit, it's radioactive!"

James hid a smile. "Relax, that's just background radiation. Nothing at all to worry about." He shouldered his pack again, but kept the counter out and ready. "Okay, we're going to try on either side..." James grimaced and held his head for a moment. "Sorry, another bloody headache. Well, as I was saying, we will move forward slowly, in the same order. I...I want us in two groups...Ernie through to Cindy in one, then a gap to Marc and the rest of you."

"What was that you were going to say about trying either side, Uncle?" Ratana asked. "It might be more efficient to try line abreast across the hillside."

"I...we'll try that later. For now, just form up into two groups behind Ernie and Marc. Keep about ten paces between the groups..."

"Why?" Marc muttered. "I can see the point in going single file, but why the gap?"

James clutched his head again. "Just...do it...Marc."

"Are you okay?" Sam asked, frowning.

James fluttered his hand. "I'll be all right. Come on now, time's a wasting." He signalled to Ernie to lead off and followed as the old Aboriginal man stepped between the bushes and vanished from sight.

Marc watched Guilford, Sam and Cindy follow them into the bushes and for a few moments could hear the noise of their passage. The sound died to silence and Marc frowned, hesitating.

"Come on, Marc, get a move on," Spence snapped. "James said ten paces, not ten minutes."

Reluctantly, Marc moved into the shrubbery and followed the trail of broken and bent leaves and twigs for a dozen paces or so, before being faced with a pristine wall of shrubbery. He stopped in confusion and Spence bumped into him.

"What's wrong?"

"I lost the trail."

"So? This patch of shrubs is only about fifty yards across. Just break through anywhere and we'll find them on the other side."

Marc did as he was told and a few minutes of scrambling up the steep hillside brought him to the top of the shrub line and the steeper but open rock slopes beyond. A wallaby hopped out of right as he emerged, but apart from that, nothing moved on the upper slopes of Tunbubudla. "Okay, where the fuck are they?" he asked as the others followed him into the open.

Ratana looked round. "Perhaps they stopped when they found we weren't following. They might be waiting for us." She called out, "Hello?"

Spence grimaced and took a deep breath, lifting his hands to cup his mouth. "James!" he bellowed. "Where are you? We've reached the top."

The only sound was the faint whistle of a breeze around the shattered rocks of the mountain and the lonely cry of a kite wheeling high above them.

"Where the hell are they?" Nathan asked. He looked down the mountain and could just make out the clearing where they had camped. "Perhaps they went down again when we didn't follow." He looked at Spence, knowing he was clutching at straws. "I'll go look." Nathan turned and ran back into the bushes, scrambling and falling in his haste. They heard him calling, then shouting, and a little later heard him climbing the slope again. He emerged onto the upper slopes looking stricken. "They're not there, Uncle. They've gone, all of them. Disappeared."

11

Ernie led the way into the *Leptospermum luehmannii* scrub, his eyes locked on the trail in front of him. His eyes flicked from left to right, seeking an indication of the presence of a very special type of rock. He found it and smiled, trotting on another dozen paces before coming to a halt and pointing at the path ahead.

"What is it, Ernie?" James asked. He stepped up close behind the Aboriginal tracker and peered over his shoulder. Sitting in full view on the faint path through the scrub was a flat oval of polished black quartz. "My god, we've found it." He beckoned the others up to see, stepping aside so Guilford and Sam could view the object.

Cindy paid no attention to the others but swept the low vegetation on either side of the track with her gaze, found what she was looking for and picked it up. She turned and carefully positioned the oval of black quartz on the path behind her before taking the extra step that brought her to the rear of the little group staring ahead of them.

"Is it another black rock?" Sam was asking.

"Similar," James replied, "But this is one of the ring rocks around the one in the Daintree. It acted, or I guess was supposed to act as some sort of portal."

"What do you mean 'supposed to'?" Guilford sneered. "Did it or didn't it?"

"We had removed one, so the black rock disintegrated instead of disappearing."

"Does that mean we could disappear too, or disintegrate?" Sam asked nervously.

"Not a chance," James said. "I have no intention of entering such a ring and if this stone is part of a ring, it's the first. Now we know where it starts, we can fan out and look for others."

"Shouldn't we bring the others up first?"

"They should be here by now." James turned and saw another shiny oval on the path behind Cindy. "How the hell did we miss that? We've got to get back, quickly." He glanced at Cindy and rocked back on his heels in shock. The girl seemed taller, heavier and her hair longer, golden-brown. A thought came unbidden into his mind, *It's too late, Dr Hay.*

There was an abrupt sound, like cardboard ripping, and the path was empty, even down to the two black quartz ovals, leaving just motes of dust dancing in the bright sunlight. These went unnoticed as moments later; Marc strode up the path and through the bushes at the far end, followed by the other three members of his group.

James felt a jolt, similar to that of a small earth tremor, and heard a soft scream, more of surprise than fear, followed by a particularly foul oath from someone else. His vision swam and he dropped to his knees, registering shock as his hand came down in mud. He stared around at fern-choked undergrowth and the trunks of tall trees near a level path and he felt his pulse start to race. "Where the hell are we?" he whispered. "Sam!" he called out urgently. "Are you all right?"

"You are safe, Aparrerinja," Ernie said quietly, "As are Ms Louis and Mr King. I would, however, advise against any sudden movements. We are being closely watched."

James got to his feet and stared at the old Aboriginal tracker, non-plussed by the sudden change in his voice and accent. Sam was on her feet too, though Guilford King remained sitting on the ground with a stunned look on his face.

"Who are you?" James asked the old Aborigine. "What have you done?"

"Call me Ernie, that will do for now. And I have done nothing except guide you to this point."

"How did you know my native name?"

"Aparrerinja is known to many."

"Where are we?" James looked around, noting the mud on the level track, the lush vegetation and the tall trees. "This is not Tunbubudla, nor, I think, are we in Queensland any longer."

"Very good Aparrerinja," Ernie said with a smile. "We are in fact in a small remote valley in the Blue Mountains."

"And how the fuck did we get here?" Guilford staggered to his feet and thrust his face pugnaciously toward Ernie's. "Did you drug us or something?"

"It was the stones, wasn't it?" Sam said. She still trembled from the shock but she was recovering quickly. "They're a portal, a...a teleportation device."

"Don't be mad," Guilford snarled. "This isn't some science fiction show. He drugged us and brought us here. It's the only logical explanation."

"Both scenarios are possible," James admitted, "But I think I prefer the portal one. I've seen one before, though it did not work then."

"But why?" Sam asked. She looked behind her, down the trail that..."No, we didn't come down there, did we? But where are the others? Cindy was right behind me."

"They were not called, Ms Louis. Only you and Aparrerinja were summoned."

"And me?" Guilford demanded. "Why have you brought me? If you have any stupid ideas about holding me for ransom, forget it. I have powerful friends who even now..."

"You were not summoned, Mr King," Ernie said. "But neither was it judged safe to leave you behind on Tunbubudla. There are still hairy men there."

"Yowies?" Guilford asked.

"You call them that."

"By God, I was right!" Guilford exclaimed. "But shit, I need to be back there. I could bag myself one."

"That is why you are here, Mr King."

"Tell me again, please, Ernie," Sam said. "Ratana and Cindy, Marc, Nathan and Spence are all safe and well back on the mountain?"

"Yes, Ms Louis, all are safe back there except Cindy. She came through the portal with us."

"What? Then where is she?" Sam ran down the muddy path, calling out. "Cindy! Cindy, where are you?"

"Come back, Sam," James yelled. He raced after her and caught her within a few metres. "It's no use. She's gone."

Sam struggled. "What do you mean, gone? If she came through she could be lying dazed and confused somewhere. Cindy!"

"What I mean is, she is not a helpless victim. She sprung the trap that caught us." James led Sam firmly back to rejoin Ernie and Guilford. "That's right, isn't it, Ernie?"

Ernie acknowledged James' conclusion by inclining his head. "The person you know as Cindy is not what she seemed. Please forgive the deception, but it was necessary."

"Necessary to kidnap us? You could not confide in us?"

"It was not my decision."

"Not yours? Then whose?"

"I am...not permitted to say. You will meet them soon and they will explain everything."

"Fuck that!" Guilford exploded. He swung his rifle round at pointed it at the old Aboriginal tracker. "You'd better start talking. These wusses may be cowed by you but I'm not. You wouldn't be the first Abo I've shot."

"Follow the trail please, Aparrerinja. You and Ms Louis. Do not stray from it."

Guilford worked the lever on his rifle, using the action and the metallic sounds to underscore his threat. "Last chance, blackie. Who's in charge?"

Ernie started to fade around the edges, as if he was an image slowly going out of focus. Guilford gaped, then clamped his jaws shut and pulled the trigger. The bullet ripped through the tenuous image of the tracker without having any effect and tore strip of bark off a tree twenty metres behind. He fired again, and again, the foliage beside the track erupting in a blizzard of ripped leaves and wood. The image of Ernie faded from sight, leaving the three humans alone on the muddy path, in an acrid cloud of drifting smoke.

"Fucking bastard," Guilford muttered, reloading his rifle from a small pouch at his belt. "That was some trick though." He stared around at the lush vegetation, his rifle still raised. "How do you think he did it, Hay? Mirrors?"

James shook his head, still shaken by the disappearance. "I don't know."

Sam moved closer to James and took his arm lightly. "We should do as he said."

"All right." James ushered Sam ahead of him and started down the muddy track.

"Where the hell do you think you're going, Hay?" Guilford demanded. "You're not listening to that black bastard, are you?" He pointed the rifle at them and James stopped.

Something growled from the thick vegetation beside the track and Guilford swung round to face it. As he did so, the branches shook violently and something crashed away through the undergrowth parallel to the path, away from Sam and James. Guilford uttered an incoherent cry of triumph and longing and set off up the path at a run, his rifle at high port.

"Come on," James said, starting down the path again.

"What about Cindy?" Sam asked. "We can't leave her if that madman is racing around with a loaded rifle. He's likely to shoot first and look to see what he shot afterward."

James thought about what he had seen just before they passed through the portal. "I think Cindy is able to look after herself."

Sam allowed herself to be persuaded and the two of them set off down the track.

The path sloped gently downward through dense vegetation. James looked through the trees whenever a gap appeared, but all he could see on either side was a steep-sided wall of rock no more than a hundred metres away. A gentle breeze blew up the valley, reducing the heat of the day to manageable proportions and somewhat alleviating the ministrations of plentiful mosquitoes and bush flies. During a lull in the shelter of a large stand of trees, James called a halt and removed his small backpack. He handed Sam a tube of roll-on insect repellent and drank some water while she applied it liberally to every exposed surface. When she finished, the chemical scent reeking the air between them, they swapped, and James dabbed while Sam drank.

"Where are we going?" Sam asked.

James shrugged but smiled. "I guess we'll see when we get there. Don't worry about it, Sam. If they wanted to harm us, they could have done it ages ago."

"Who is 'they'?"

"Again, I don't know, but both Mick and Ernie seem to be tied up with them, and I'd trust Mick with my life."

They continued down the track and soon the forest thinned to open woodland with stands of high grass and eventually to short-cropped grass that led down to a small lake. A large mob of wallabies bounced away from them as they approached, but stopped within a hundred metres and stared at the two interlopers for a few minutes before starting to feed again.

"That explains the short grass," James said with a grin. "I was wondering where they kept the lawnmower."

Sam was looking at the lake. "That water looks inviting. Is it safe to swim, or are there crocodiles?"

James laughed. "There are no crocodiles down this far, and besides, they'd need a river to swim up from the sea. There might be snakes though, so I'd stay away from those reeds over there." He pointed to a swampy region at one end of the little lake. As she started toward the water, he asked, "By the way, what are you going to use as a cossie?"

Sam turned and looked back at him. "A what?"

"A bathing costume. Or were you planning on skinny dipping?" His eyes sparkled and a smile tugged at the corner of his mouth.

"You wish," Sam snorted. "My clothes are all sweaty and mud-stained, so I'm going in like this. I'll wash them too."

"Okay, up to you. I just asked because for some reason it's a lot later in the day than I thought. Maybe that teleport business takes time but I'd say this valley is going to lose the sun very soon."

"So it's late. Why should that concern us?"

"We don't have the wherewithal to light a fire, and if your clothes are all wet, you might have a miserable night. It could get quite cool after dark."

"Damn it, it's a bloody male conspiracy," Sam fumed. "If I didn't know better, I'd say you arranged for the sun to go down early."

"Hey, have your swim," James said mildly. "I'm going to. I reckon my undies are no worse than a pair of bathers. I imagine you've worn bikinis before. I won't look if that's what's troubling you."

"See that you don't," Sam snapped. She marched down to the water's edge where she stripped off her boots and socks, took a quick look around to make sure James was ignoring her before quickly removing her tee shirt and shorts and diving in.

James caught a glimpse of a tall, tanned body in light-coloured underwear, curved in some tantalizing places, before it plunged beneath the surface. He grinned and stripped off to his undies, wading in waist-deep by the time Sam surfaced.

Sam emerged from the water a few metres in front of James, blowing like a grampus. "Bloody hell," she said, "That's cold." Her teeth started chattering and she clamped her jaws shut, eyeing James' serious face for any sign he might be laughing at her.

"It is surprisingly cold," James replied. "I thought a small lake like this would have warmed more from the sun."

Sam rubbed her bare arms vigorously then flushed as she saw James' eyes caught by the effect her movements had on her visible anatomy. She turned and dived, striking out for the far end of the lake, her arms moving in a fast, efficient over arm stroke.

James watched her appreciatively before dipping down into the water and soaking his hair, scrubbing out tangles and dirt with his fingertips. He paddled around a bit before deciding to join Sam at the far end, setting off in a sedate breast-stroke.

Sam watched him approach with a feeling of trepidation. The attraction she had felt for James in San Francisco had re-emerged when they met again in Townsville, and intensified over the last day or two. She had been unprepared though, for the blast of desire that tore through her after surfacing moments earlier. Sam had looked, with eyes suddenly cleared as if by the cold waters of the lake, at a handsome, intelligent, caring man with a gorgeous hairy chest and sexy eyes, and felt her heart leap within her. The desire in his eyes blazed out at her and she had fled, but now he pursued her, albeit slowly and clumsily, and excitement grew again. She waited, crouching beneath the cold water as he neared and stood upright, the water flowing off the matted hairs of his chest.

"Come on," James said, holding out a hand. "You don't want to stay in too long. We can walk back in the sunshine and get warmed up again."

Sam ignored his outstretched hand and turned away before standing, well aware that the water had rendered her underwear almost transparent. *No such luck with him*, she thought, glancing rapidly at James as he waded ashore. *Cotton briefs may cling but they don't show anything--except that the cold water isn't having any effect on him.*

There was no avoiding his gaze when they were both ashore and Sam stared down at the ground as they walked, her neck and face, she was sure, glowing like a beacon. The last of the sun felt warm on her skin and despite her unusual feeling of shyness, was glad that she had not gone in fully clothed. Already there was a slight nip in the air and there seemed little doubt that a cool night lay ahead. Dry, if somewhat dirty clothes were infinitely preferable to wet ones. *A pity my undies are still wet*, she thought. She became aware of James' eyes on her and her embarrassment and desire boiled over into anger as she whirled to face him.

Her anger wilted in his smiling eyes as they locked on hers. "Why don't you just take a picture?" she asked raggedly, unable to sustain her annoyance.

"What's wrong, Sam?" James asked quietly. "We're both adults, both unencumbered. I think you're attracted to me and I'm..." he blushed suddenly and looked down. "I'm certainly attracted to you."

"So you think because we're alone in the bush, you can behave..." Sam suddenly felt like she was playing a part, acting a role of which she wanted no part. *What can I say to show him I really do care?*

"If I have offended you in any way, I'm very sorry, Sam. The more I see of you, the more I want...oh, dear, that didn't come out too well. What I meant was I enjoy your company and I like having you all to myself." James grinned self-consciously and reached out, taking her cold hand in his. "I wish we could have gone to dinner that night in San Francisco. You might be surer of my intentions toward you."

If we'd gone out to dinner that night, you'd sure as hell have known my intentions, buster, Sam thought, very conscious of the pressure of his warm hand on hers. His touch and her memories were doing things to her anatomy she hadn't felt in a long time. Aloud, she said, "I wish we had, too." She stood and gazed into James' eyes for what seemed like hours, though the sun did not move appreciably in that time. "I...I suppose we'd better get dressed," she murmured.

James didn't answer, but moved closer, into her space and Sam experienced the novel sensation for her, of having to tilt her head back to look into his eyes. He leaned closer and his lips brushed hers, moved apart and touched again. Her breasts caressed his hairy chest, a merest whisper of contact, and she felt an electric current pass between them. Her muscles twitched with the desire to just grab him and press him to her nearly naked body. *God, slow down, gal or you'll make a fool of yourself...*She disengaged, reluctantly, and stepped back.

"I'm feeling cold," she whispered, refusing to look him in the eyes, hoping that the heat she felt must be radiating from her body would not reveal her lie.

Disappointment flickered momentarily across James' face but he forced it away with a chuckle. "Your dry clothes await, my dear. After that, I'll see what delectable sustenance I can find in my pack. I'm almost sure I have a packet of salted peanuts in there."

Sam laughed too, perhaps more heartily than the quip deserved. "A gourmet too," she murmured. She pulled on her clothes over still-damp underwear and at once felt more relaxed though also faintly sad. *Was I hoping he'd be more forthright?* she wondered. *Did I want him to do more?*

James quickly dressed but left his shoes and socks off, enjoying the cool grass on his feet. "Now for the feast," he said, moving toward his pack. He stopped suddenly and stared at the ground before looking all about him. "Someone's been here. Look."

Sam knelt and examined a square of white cloth set out on the short grass near James' pack. A small pile of fruit, a wooden bowl containing a gritty brown powder, two pieces of lean meat and a box of matches were neatly arranged on the cloth. She poked at the fruit with one finger. "Is it edible? I don't recognise any of these fruits--except these look a bit like tiny raspberries."

James sorted through the offerings. "Yes, they're wild raspberries. These are Davidson's plums, a few native pears, ah, and shelled Macadamias." He sniffed the powder in the wooden bowl before wetting a fingertip and tasting a tiny bit. "Kurrajong seeds, roasted and ground. That's very thoughtful; they're a bugger to prepare. And matches--we're going to eat well tonight."

"What about the meat?"

James nibbled on a morsel. "Wallaby, I'd say." He lifted a hand towards the mob on the edge of the clearing and called out, "Thanks, mates!"

James and Sam gathered a quantity of dry wood, logs and twigs mostly of *Acacia*, in the fading light, and with the aid of the matches soon had a roaring fire going. James kept an eye out for other 'bush tucker' and gathered some *Acacia* seeds, a few ginger fruits and a found a small cache of honey in an old log. The tiny blue-green stingless bees swarmed ineffectually as he relieved them of part of their store. While Sam managed the cooking of the wallaby steaks on green wood close to the flames, James added water to the Kurrajong flour, then a few wild ginger fruits, and *Acacia* nuts, a smear of honey and kneaded it into sticky dough. Then he scraped a hole in the ashes of the fire and placed the ball of dough into it, shoveling back the ashes and building up the fire again.

"Is that going to be edible?" Sam asked.

"Oh yes, a tried and true method, though I've usually just added Kurrajong flour to ordinary flour."

The wallaby steaks had been seared on each side to lock in the juices and Sam now moved them farther from the flames so they did not cook too fast. James had wandered off into the bush again, despite the darkness and had found a pepperbush, bringing back a few leaves. "Wallaby meat's great with the proper seasonings, but we'll have to make do. We can garnish it with salt from the peanuts, the pepper leaves, and some Davidson's plum."

"Those are plums?" Sam picked one of the large burgundy fruits with the blue sheen out of the small pile and bit into it before James could warn her. Her face screwed up in horror and she spat the piece out, jumping up and hurrying to the water's edge to rinse her mouth out. "My god," she spluttered. "That's tarter than a lemon. My jaws are still aching."

"Sorry," James said, stifling a smile. "I should have warned you. We can rub them over the meat for flavour, or if you want you can have a bit of honey with them." He picked up the plum she had dropped and picked bits of debris off it. "I've an acquired taste for them." James bit into the tart fruit and chewed appreciatively, though his mouth puckered slightly. "Hmm, a bit sourer than usual."

Sam chuckled at his expression. "Now who's got a sourpuss?"

"Not you, that's for sure," James murmured, delighted when she blushed. He used his pocketknife to cut the meat into chunks and put them in the bowl with a little of the plum juice, the crushed pepperbush leaves and a sprinkling of salt from his packet of peanuts. He then used a stick to sweep the ashes aside and rescued the unprepossessing lump of Kurrajong damper from the fire. Cutting it open, he gingerly tore off a hunk and sniffed it appreciatively. "It'll do." He passed it across to Sam, admonishing her not to bite into the crust.

Sam bit and chewed. "Hey, that's delicious--sort of nutty, peanut-buttery."

James grinned, inordinately pleased with himself. "Try some of the meat with it." He took a chunk of the juicy wallaby steak and wrapped the damper around it and bit into it. While Sam was chewing, he split open the native pears and hooked out the young seed clusters, emptying them into the communal bowl.

Sam picked one out and bit into it tentatively, her eyes opening wide in surprise. "They taste like peas."

"I'm no expert in bush tucker," James said modestly, "But with a bit of searching you can eat quite well in the bush. Of course, this lot was supplied, but we could probably have found most of it for ourselves if we had to."

"Who do you think gave it to us?" Sam asked around a mouthful of bread and meat.

"At a guess I'd say Ernie, but I didn't see anyone."

Sam shivered despite the heat of the fire. "I thought I liked him, but he scares me. Who...what is he, that he can disappear like that?"

"I'd say definitely a 'who', though he must be a very senior Karadji man. I've never seen a disappearing trick quite like that before." James grinned. "I don't think there's any need to be scared of him though. He's treated us to a good meal and got rid of that pest Guilford too."

They finished their meal with Macadamia nuts and wild raspberries. "A pity we don't have any wine, but at least the water's good."

"A perfect meal," Sam said. "You really know how to show a gal a good time."

"Ah, the night is yet young. We've had dinner, now we have the show." James led Sam out beyond the heat and light of the fire to a patch of grass in the open, away from overhanging trees. "Lie down," he instructed. When she hesitated, he added softly. "Don't worry, Sam, this is the 'show' part of our date."

They lay down side by side in the grass, feeling a gentle breeze cool their fire-heated faces. Staring up into the night sky, their eyes slowly adjusted to the darkness and the stars of the southern skies appeared in their glory. Sam gasped at the blaze of light strewn across the velvety blackness.

"We're lucky we are so far from city lights," James murmured. "And the moon won't be up for hours." He started by pointing out the Southern Cross and the Pointers that could be used to find south. "We don't have a Pole Star in this hemisphere, but if you watch long enough, you'll see all the stars turn around that area of sky there."

"Do you have the same constellations as we have in the north?"

"Some of them, because a lot can be seen from both hemispheres, like Capricornus there, my sign by the way..."

"Mine too," Sam murmured.

"... but some are just ours. Pavo, the chameleon, the swordfish," James moved his finger from star to star. "The Aborigines have their own names for them too." He pointed out different groups of stars, giving them Aboriginal names and their English translations. "Sometimes, it's not so much the stars that give shapes, but the absence." James traced out the 'Emu in the Sky', and then proceeded to tell her the legend behind it. "Aboriginal people use the night sky for many purposes. The rising and setting of some stars tells them when to move on to fresh hunting grounds, the images tell stories or offer valuable lessons by showing the mistakes of others. The Yolyngu tribe of Arnhem Land believe the constellation of Orion is two brothers in their canoe. They caught and ate a forbidden fish, so the sun punished them by sending a waterspout that lifted them up to the heavens. Now every time a Yolyngu child looks at the night sky, they are reminded of the need to obey the tribal laws."

James continued for nearly an hour and Sam hung on every word, but the chill of the night gradually bit into their bones. At last, she took advantage of a lull in the conversation to suggest they move back to the fire. They got up and moved back toward the glowing embers by the lake, becoming aware of the chorus of frog sounds from the water and the reed beds.

"I've never heard such a racket," Sam said.

"It's mating season. The males are all making a lot of noise to attract females and persuade them to mate."

"Is that what you've been doing?" Sam murmured. "Thank you for the dinner and show, James. I think now you invite me up for a cup of coffee."

"I don't have any coffee."

"That's all right, I don't want any."

They moved together, slipping into each other's arms, their lips hungrily searching, their bodies pressing close. After a few minutes, they separated and moved closer to the embers of the fire and in the warmth, removed their clothing and spread it on the springy turf. They lay down; their bodies and mouths eager again and after a while, produced their own rhythms and sounds to join those of the mating frogs.

*   *   *

Around them, unseen in the darkness, several large hairy beings watched Sam and James and waited for further instructions. The man with the rifle was far to the north and would not intrude on these humans. For reasons they did not fully understand, this mating was one of the most important events in recent history and they felt a measure of satisfaction that they had, in conjunction with the old one, brought the two humans together under such favourable circumstances. The keepers of the black stone would be pleased.

12

Guilford King had left Sam and James on the path after Ernie's magician's trick disappearance and had run northward after the crashing in the bushes that betrayed the escaping yowie. An initial worry that the unseen being might be something prosaic like a wallaby or a dingo was laid to rest by occasional glimpses through gaps in the dense foliage of an arm or a leg covered in dense golden-brown hair, and once, a great head turned to regard its pursuer, the sagittal crest on its head rising above large liquid brown eyes which held his for a moment before the beast turned and vanished into the undergrowth as he swept his rifle up.

Luckily, the path of the beast paralleled the track, and Guilford managed to keep up with his quarry for some distance. When he started to feel the pace, his breath coming in great gasps and the sweat pouring off him so much he knew he would have to give up the chase, the yowie stopped. Guilford stood on the track, gasping for air, his muscles trembling, and listened for any sound from the strangely still Australian bush. Nothing moved, no birds sang and even the insects were hushed in the hot afternoon sun. After a while, he breathed more easily and stepped off the track, cautiously moving toward where he had last heard the beast.

Guilford was two paces off the track when the animal seemingly lost its nerve and set off again, crashing through the bushes, on a course that once more paralleled the track up the valley. Cursing, Guilford cut back to the path, and resumed his pursuit.

The same thing happened twice more before sunset, by which time Guilford estimated he was over ten kilometres further up the valley. The path dwindled away to nothing and he resorted to dodging through gaps in the bushes, trying to force his way through thickets, knowing he could not hope to keep up with an animal several times his weight that could just walk through the tangled undergrowth. He cursed again and stopped and as he did so, the animal also stopped.

"What the fuck is going on?" Guilford muttered. *Why has it stopped too? Is it playing with me?*

The movement ahead of him started again, but irregular, a step and drag rhythm that had his forehead wrinkling in thought. *It's limping. It's hurt itself.* Guilford grinned and started forward again, cautiously edging around a tangle of vines. *There.* Twenty metres away, slightly obscured by intervening leaves, stood a tall broad-shouldered figure, thickly covered in coarse hair. It was leaning against a tree as if tired or hurt. *Got you, my beauty.* He raised his rifle and took aim at the broad sloping back, his hands shaking slightly with excitement. Guilford took a breath, steadying the sights and gently squeezed the trigger, his heart leaping in his chest as he saw blood and hair fly. The figure toppled and crashed to the forest floor.

He ran forward even as he levered another round into the chamber, his mind already fixed on the fame and fortune that awaited his triumphant return to civilisation. *Shit.* Guilford stared down at the fallen log with a great gouge of bark missing. He looked around wildly. *No way did I shoot at a tree. I must be disoriented. It's around here somewhere.* He started casting around, searching for the body of the beast he knew he had shot.

The bushes trembled and the beast crashed away from the hunter. With a frustrated cry, Guilford hurled himself after it, running again as the yowie, this time with no hint of a limp, kept some hundred metres ahead. The animal was close enough that Guilford had no difficulty following, yet far enough ahead that even in open patches he caught no more than a glimpse of his quarry as it disappeared into the vegetation on the far side.

The sun had disappeared behind the high walls of the valley's western ramparts an hour past and the light was becoming noticeably poorer. Guilford stopped and stared through the gathering gloom, the dregs of defeat bitter in his mouth. He checked his watch and looked back the way he had come. *Another hour of daylight*, he thought. *If I hurry, I could be back at the track by then. At least if I keep to that, I should find the others.*

A stone landed at his feet with a soft thump in the leaf-littered forest floor. Guilford swung his rifle up and stared into the forest. Another stone sailed through the air and clattered against a log, then another ripping through the foliage of a bush beside him. He caught sight of a fourth arcing through the evening air and started forward, watching the clump of trees whence it had come. A twig cracked to one side and he heard the thump of footsteps receding slowly, northward once more.

"You want me to follow?" Guilford muttered. "Okay, I'll follow, but sooner or later you're going to give me a clear shot, I promise."

The light continued to deteriorate and Guilford's pursuit slowed to a walk. He emerged from the forest into a broad, open meadow, dotted with large trees. At the far side, at least three hundred metres away, stood a tall hairy figure, just visible in the twilight. Guilford raised his rifle but he could not see the figure well enough to sight on it. *Do I chance a shot? If I miss it'll run and I'll lose it for certain. If I track it tomorrow I may be lucky.* The figure raised an arm as if acknowledging Guilford's decision, and merged with the tree line.

Guilford looked about him at the gathering darkness. The far line of trees was just an amorphous shadow now and the forest behind him lay black and uninviting. Using what little light remained he moved out into the meadow to one of the solitary trees, where he scraped together enough bark and fallen twigs to start a small fire with the aid of the lighter he always kept in his jacket pocket.

"Now if only that thieving Abo Ernie hadn't run off with my pack..." he muttered, before he remembered it was sitting on the track where he'd done his little party trick. There had been food in the pack, and water. Guilford shrugged. *I'll survive.* He heaped a few more branches on the crackling fire and sat back against the trunk, cradling his rifle across his lap and staring into the darkness. After a while, his head nodded forward only to jerk upright as a thrown stone scattered sparks from the fire.

Guilford leapt to his feet and strode out past the circle of light, waiting with rifle at the ready as his eyes became accustomed to the darkness. Nothing moved, though distantly, within the forest, he could hear the sounds of a dispute between at least two possums. He returned to the fire and sat down again, his back to the solid tree trunk.

It happened again. As his head drooped with tiredness he was disturbed, not by a stone this time but by a deep coughing roar from the darkness that made his hair stand on end. Guilford stood, but did not venture beyond the pool of light, staring into the featureless darkness. He heard nothing but seemed to sense something circling him, just out of sight. Raising his rifle, he considered the wisdom of firing at the unseen being, but decided against it. Once he started shooting, he might continue until he was out of ammunition. He tamped down his unreasoning fear and after a while the invisible presence receded.

An hour later, Guilford was dozing by the tree again when a wave of hostility washed over him. He looked up to see a pair of glowing yellow orbs in the darkness beyond the now smoldering fire. They switched off for an instant and he frowned before realising it was a pair of eyes and they had just blinked. He stared back, trying to work out whether the vaguely-discerned black form underneath the eyes was part of the creature or not. *Is it in a tree? Should I risk...?* The lights went out, only to reappear a minute later several metres to the left. *It's not in a tree then...but that would make it three metres tall...and what makes its eyes shine? There's not enough light from the embers and the moon's not up yet.* A faint fear that the creature may not be flesh and blood crept unwillingly into his mind. He recalled stories of Bigfoot where the creature seemed strangely incorporeal. *If it's not real I can't shoot it.* The fear grew and Guilford shrank back against the reassuring solidity of the tree trunk. *But if it's not real, its only weapon is fear. I refuse to be terrorised by something that's not real.* Guilford thrust his fear away from him, feeling anger build up in him instead. He sighted in on a spot between the glowing eyes and as his finger tightened on the trigger; they blinked out as a bullet slammed across the gap between them. Distant echoes of the shot rolled through the steep-sided valley, fading into silence. Nothing moved in the darkness, no sound spoke of a wounded beast. Guilford ejected the spent cartridge and levered another one into the chamber, fighting back his impulse to keep firing regardless.

The waning moon rose, and soon afterward, the eastern sky cracked open, spilling a rosy glow across the grey sky. Guilford yawned and stretched, exhausted after a sleepless night spent on guard against the unknown. He peed on the ashes of the fire, spreading the charred branches with his foot to ensure they were all out before picking up his rifle again.

Before setting off to pick up the trail, Guilford made a careful study of the skyline and what he could remember of the topography from the day before. *I think these are the Wild Dog Mountains. If I'm right, the Jenolan caves are to the west. That's where I'll head, then the main road to Katoomba and Sydney.* "But after I've settled your hash, my beauty."

There was no corpse on the grass in the direction he had fired a few hours before, so he shouldered his rifle and set off for the point on the forest edge where the creature had disappeared the previous day. He cast about until he found a few faint markings on the trees and on the ground that spoke to him of the passage of a large animal, and started off after it. *A pity that bastard Ernie's not here. He'd follow this trail without any trouble.*

The valley narrowed and became steeper as it climbed toward the ridge. A soak, hardly a stream, oozed from a rock face allowing a mass of mosses and ferns to gather in the crevices, the water gathering in a small pool at its base. In the mud on the edge of the pool, Guilford saw several footprints and bent to examine them. *Wallaby, possum, a bird or two...shit!* There in the wet mud at the water's edge were two large footprints, roughly man shaped and half as long again as Guilford's own booted foot. There was a strange double oval mark a little behind the footprints and Guilford stared at it for several minutes, trying to work out what it was. When it came to him, he laughed out loud. The creature had squatted at the water's edge, perhaps to drink, and had rested its bulk on the mud. The ovals were the imprints of its buttocks.

The image that settled in Guilford's mind became decidedly more human but he sat back on the grass for a few moments to check over his rifle. He found he had three rounds still in the rifle's magazine and another five in the pouch on his belt. Guilford took all the bullets out and examined them carefully, one by one, and then reloaded. *I'm only going to get one chance at this.* He ignored the thoughts at the back of his mind that spoke of the creature's similarity to man. *I'd be doing the species a favour by shooting one. Once the pollies know of its existence, they'll give it the protection of the law.*

Circling the pool, Guilford found more footprints on the far side and a few paces further on, a flattened area among the long grass where it had apparently lain down. As he examined the bed, one of the grass blades moved, flicking upward and Guilford froze, his senses alert. The creature must have been watching him by the pool and had only just moved on. He resisted the urge to hurry after it, determined he would not be led on like he had been the previous day. The wind blew gently up the valley and had no doubt been carrying his scent to the creature's nostrils all the time. Guilford judged the yowie had left the pool and turned back down the valley which was an excellent piece of luck. His scent and any small noise he made would be carried away from his quarry.

Unhurriedly, Guilford set off in pursuit, no longer charging after his prey, but instead employing all his hunting skills, attempting to put his mind inside that of the yowie. But in doing this, he made an assumption--that his quarry was an insensate beast--no doubt wily and cunning--but a creature with the mind of an animal rather than the mind of a man.

Guilford could see the direction the yowie was taking, and from his vantage point in the upper valley, could estimate it was heading toward a dense stand of bush perhaps half a kilometre further down the valley. He looked to his left and noticed a clear strip along the cliff edge. Estimating distances and times, he made his decision and ran, leaping over rocks and scrambling down slopes, hurrying to reach a position opposite the thicket before the yowie. He reached the area he had targeted and rested against a large boulder, sighting down to where the central part of the valley debouched into a small glade, no more than five or six paces across, just before the thicket. Thumbing the safety off, he scanned the vegetation for any sign of movement, knowing he would have time for one, maybe two shots before it reached safety. The bushes moved some twenty paces from the glade, then fifteen--ten. Guilford took a deep breath and braced himself against the rock, steadying his rifle.

Are you ready?

Don't worry, Guilford thought. *I know I've got one crack at this.*

Be careful.

Guilford frowned. *Why do I need to be careful? Five, four...*

Move fast.

Oh yes. Fast as lightning. Three, two...

Go, Rima.

Rima? The bushes moved and something brown hurtled out, long legs striding--three paces to the side of where he expected. Guilford squeezed off his first shot, knowing it would miss but unable to correct fast enough. Turf showered up from a point past the yowie's shoulder and he swung the rifle frantically, pulling the trigger again without aiming. Wood splinters flew from a tree. The golden-brown mass reached the far side of the glade apparently unscathed, the dense vegetation swallowing it even as Guilford's next bullets ripped through the foliage. Then the thicket erupted, shrubs and small trees whipping and bending as if in a cyclone. Growls and screams shook the air, slowly dying away to a deep silence as if the valley itself lay shocked.

Guilford leaned against the rock and took stock of the situation. He had hunted big game before, in all parts of the globe, and if he had had that result while hunting tiger, for instance, he would reasonably assume the beast had taken a mortal wound. *Give it a few minutes.* A wounded animal could be dangerous, and leaving it alone for the time it took to smoke a cigarette could give it time to bleed to death.

Ten minutes later, by Guilford's watch, he moved cautiously down to the glade and followed the trail of devastation into the forest. There was a stench pervading the still air of the thicket, a nauseating odour of cabbage and sewage and Guilford wrinkled his nose in disgust. Splashes of blood lay on several leaves and a clump of golden-brown fur clung to the rough bark of a tree, but no body was evident. Senses alert, Guilford moved deeper into the thicket, noting how the blood trail rapidly petered out. He grimaced, and followed, picking his steps carefully. At the far edge of the timbered area was an open expanse of bare earth and Guilford found several humanoid footprints, large and bare-footed, left by a yowie running rapidly. *An upper body wound then...*

Disappointed, Guilford followed for another few hundred metres until the tracks disappeared altogether. He shrugged and turned back to the site of the shooting, where he started to reconstruct the event. Blood spattered several leaves at about eye level and he moved through from the open area into the thicket following the same path. *The bullet struck it here, so...*he touched his left shoulder...*the beast lurched, struck the tree, recovered...*Guilford nodded, then dug into his inner jacket pocket, removing two creased and dirty ziplocked bags. He put the hair from the tree bark into one, and collected as many blood-spattered leaves as he could find, for the other. Carefully resealing them, Guilford retraced his steps to the pool to consider his next actions.

I'd like to follow the trail but there's not much point. If that black bastard was still with me I'd try it, but as it is...so what now? Guilford turned and looked up the steep valley to where it turned into a rock climb to the ridge. *I can make it up there, then across the tops and descend along one of the other ridges to the Katoomba Road. Then get a ride into Sydney.* He took his sample bags out again and turned them over and over, staring at the blood and hair. *Concrete samples,* he gloated. *That'll knock Professor bloody Hay into a cocked hat. I'll have them tested in three separate laboratories and have the results held and couriered to me at a press conference when I announce my findings, open the envelopes and be completely vindicated.* Guilford threw back his head and let loose a roar of triumph that echoed off the rock walls of the narrow valley.

13

S pence led his three companions back down to the camp at the foot of Tunbubudla, overriding objections that they should be on hand should the others need help. "Unless you know of a way to go through a non-existent portal, there's no way we can help them." That did not stop Spence from worrying however. He sat where he could see the mountain and stirred from his vantage point only to get food and coffee, or to use the bushes. Having known James for many years, he knew his capabilities and did not worry overly about his safety. His prime concern was he was missing out on an adventure, a possible answer to the riddles of the black stone and the yowies.

Nathan also worried, though in his case it was a concern for James' safety. He saw his own role very much as protector and had it not been for the presence of his fiancée Ratana Allira, he would not have budged from the place of the disappearance. Only a desire for Ratana's well-being persuaded him to follow Spence's advice and come down off the mountain.

Ratana fretted over the disappearances of James and Sam, and to a lesser extent of Cindy. She was certain that James could look after himself but she was less sure about Sam and Cindy. However, James would do his utmost there too. The other area of concern was over Guilford King. She had had dealings with the man in the past and knew all about his fanatical determination to achieve fame and fortune by exploiting the mysteries of Australia. There was no telling what the man would do when faced with the genuine paranormal. She could only hope that because Sam and James had been specially called to this quest, they would warrant special protection from whoever had called them.

Marc was the only one of the four to be more concerned with his own skin than with the fate of others. This was not because the young man was selfish or self-centred but because unlike the other three, he had had little experience of the paranormal before this expedition. A gifted photographer, his talents were sought after by a variety of Geographic magazines and in-between paid assignments he was more than happy to potter around on his own looking for the perfect photo. This search and a strong liking for Samantha Louis--or rather, for her younger sister Andi--had led him to join her in search of Aboriginal myths when his assignment in Tasmania finished.

The expedition had started in a very ordinary manner, but had quickly taken a turn onto a road that appeared to be at right angles to common sense and everyday reality. An attack by shadow creatures, a phantom Aboriginal elder, mythological monsters and teleportation had taken its toll of Marc's psyche. The first two, on the landslip near the town of Emerald had rocked his beliefs to the core and he was still amazed at how easily Sam had persuaded him to continue. From that point on though, it was almost as if he had been in a dream state, following along after the others but detached from their reality, observing but not really taking part. The existence of Yowies, the Australian equivalent of Bigfoot or Sasquatch, was exciting as he believed himself in no personal danger. The disappearance of five human beings from a path just in front of him was too much to cope with, coming as it did hard on the heels of the other incidents. If everyone else had been calm and contented he could have managed, but Marc picked up on the worry and his unease fed on it. Now he was debating whether a mental breakdown or precipitate flight might be the most appropriate action.

Nathan came over and sat down beside the young American photographer just as he made up his mind to pack up and chance a hike alone to the road and civilisation. He could read the state of Marc's mind from his body language and judged him very close to panic, so he offered him a muesli bar and started into a long and rather involved joke, the intention being less to get a laugh than to deflect his mind from his present worries. Nathan roared with laughter at his own punch line and ignored Marc's deadpan face, immediately launching into a series of short, snappy jokes that brought forth a smile, then a snort, and at last a grudging laugh.

"How the fuck can you joke with all this going on around you?" Marc asked.

"All what, mate? You mean this disappearance? Nothing to it, you can be sure Professor Hay has it well in hand."

"You're not worried?"

"Nah, there's no one I'd trust more than Prof Hay. Your mate Sam's in good hands."

Marc chewed his lip pensively. "What about that Guilford King?"

"He's more of a prick than a danger," Nathan laughed. "Besides, that old tracker's with them."

"You know him?"

Nathan shook his head. "Never met him before, but I know his type." He looked around carefully as if suddenly afraid of being overheard and leaned closer to Marc. "He has the look of an elder, maybe even a...a holy man, someone who has seen it all and is at peace with it."

"And you think because he's calm he's going to be able to protect the others?"

"Not just that, but if he's the sort of man I think he is, you don't have to worry. James, Sam and Cindy will be quite safe."

"Ah yes, the gorgeous Cindy," Marc said. "I wonder why she disappeared too. Spence said James and Sam were called to this venture but why the delectable Cindy?"

"Perhaps it was an accident. She was just behind Sam, and maybe she got too close when the portal opened."

"So just a blonde moment, you think?"

Nathan frowned. "You've used that phrase before, Marc--a blonde moment--to describe Cindy. What do you mean by it?"

"Uh, sorry if I've offended you, and I suppose you'll think I'm sexist, but I was just meaning it harmlessly to imply that as a blonde she's allowed to be an airhead sometimes."

"But she's not blonde."

"What d'ya mean? Of course she is. I don't know what's upstairs but I wouldn't mind getting to know her first floor better."

"What's your definition of blonde?" Nathan asked. "I'd have said she was brunette without even blonde highlights."

"You're shitting me? She's a beautiful pale gold blonde with a drop dead figure and come hither eyes."

Nathan's frown increased. "You are joking, aren't you? Surely America has good looking birds...you can't be starved of feminine beauty." He turned and beckoned to Ratana. When she walked over he said, "Marc here thinks Cindy is blonde with a good figure. What do you think? Is he barmy or what?"

Ratana considered carefully. "Well, I'm not seeing things through a male's hormone-tinged eyes, so I'd say she was pretty, but her short hair doesn't suit her. She should wear it shoulder length at least. And Marc, you need your eyes tested. That colour is not blonde; it's more of a mousey brown."

"Is this some form of Aussie joke you're playing, like with those drop bears?"

"No joke, Marc, but this is really curious." Nathan called Spence over to them. He came reluctantly, still upset over his exclusion, but he listened to Nathan's outline of what he called the 'Cindy enigma'.

"You've noticed it too, huh?" Spence asked. "It was something that niggled at my mind from time to time while she was with us, but I could never get myself to concentrate on it. Now she has gone, our minds can consider the different things we saw."

"You really saw something different?" Marc asked incredulously. "No shapely blonde?"

"Not even close," Spence said with a smile. "Tell me though, all of you; did Cindy remind you of anyone you know? Think carefully."

"She looked a bit like a girl I knew at uni," Ratana said. "In fact, now I think about it, a lot like her."

"She's the spitting image of Cathy Edwards, one of the nurses in the base hospital in Cairns," Nathan reflected. "Nothing untoward, Ratana," he added hurriedly. "Just a friend."

"One of the Miss California contestants I went out with a couple of years ago," Marc said. "When she first tottered out of the trees I thought it was her."

"And I thought she was a certain young lady I...er, had a drink with a couple of weeks ago." Spence frowned and looked round at the others. "You see what this means?" he asked.

Nathan nodded, but the others looked puzzled. "What?" Marc asked.

"We saw Cindy not as she was, but as our minds believed she looked, based on someone we each knew. That means that someone or something was manipulating our minds, tapping into individual memories, to hide who she really was...or what she was."

Marc shivered. "Please don't let's consider a 'what'; I'm much more comfortable with 'who'."

"Why would the identity of Cindy need to be disguised?" Nathan asked. "And who was putting that idea into our minds?"

"It might have been Cindy herself," Ratana replied.

"If it was, then Cindy is not human," Spence said. "I've never come across a person who can do that in uncontrolled conditions."

"Uncontrolled?"

"Outside of a laboratory, in the open where all the environmental conditions are variable," Nathan clarified.

"If it wasn't Cindy, who else could it have been?" Ratana asked. "We hadn't met up with Ernie and Guilford yet, so unless you suspect one of us..."

"Persons seen or unseen, powers visible or invisible," Spence said with a grin.

"Gee, thanks for that," Marc grimaced. "That makes me feel a whole lot better."

"I can't think of any way to determine who was manipulating our minds," Spence went on, "So maybe we could concentrate on the 'why'."

"Is that going to be any easier?" Marc asked.

Spence shrugged. "Let's try it and see. Have you got anything better to do?"

"Just getting the hell out of Dodge!"

"I wouldn't advise that in the circumstances," Spence said seriously. "I think you'd be safer here with us. Out there..." he gestured at the grassy woodland, "... You'd be anybody's."

"Okay, thinking about why Cindy was disguised," Ratana said slowly, "Why does anyone disguise themselves? To deceive others," she answered herself.

"And if you are going to deceive someone, it is because they would object if they saw you for what you really are," Nathan added. "So who was the object of Cindy's deception?"

"She's no longer with us," Spence continued, "And because of that we've all cottoned on to her actions, so it's unlikely to be one of us. I'd guess James or Sam...or both."

"Unless she saw Ernie and Guilford coming and was getting in early."

"Possible," Spence agreed, "But I think James and Sam are likelier targets. Did you notice James seemed confused?"

"He had a lot of headaches," Ratana commented.

"Yes, but only after Cindy arrived. Then we had Sam's missing time episode and James' strange behavior like inviting Guilford along. Some of his other decisions were odd too, like dividing us into two groups on the trail."

"Which leads us to ask what her intentions are toward them."

"Not good if you can't be open and honest about it," Ratana said firmly.

"So James and Sam have gone through that portal to god-knows-where with a being that may be hostile," Nathan said gloomily.

"Or two such beings," Marc commented thoughtfully. "Do you remember when Ernie and Cindy met? They didn't say anything, just stood and stared at each other."

"Hey, that's right," Nathan agreed. "I wondered for a few moments if they knew each other, and then I forgot all about it."

"Forgetfulness seems to be common around Cindy," Spence said. "If you thought that and forgot it, it might be important. Cindy didn't want you to know she knew Ernie."

"Which means they're in cahoots," Marc summed up firmly.

"And they both went with James and Sam."

Ratana shook her head. "I don't believe Ernie's evil. I got a very strong feeling when I met him that he was...well, holy or something. Someone in touch with the spirits."

"Um...there are two types of spirits. Remember the Quinkan?"

Marc shuddered. "I'd rather not, and I must admit, up till now I'd managed to...well, if not forget them, at least put them at the back of my mind."

"Interesting," Spence said. "How do you actually feel about the shadows, Marc? I assume you hadn't come across any before."

"They scared the crap outa me." Marc stared around at the brightly lit eucalyptus scrub and shivered. "I can think about them in the daytime, but unless I can shut them outa my mind, I'll be shitting myself come sundown."

"They are creatures of the night," Spence agreed, "Though I have heard occasional reports of daytime sightings."

"Great."

Spence laughed. "I doubt you have much to worry about. I've only ever heard of them in very specific places and never around Tunbubudla."

"They weren't supposed to be around Emerald either," Nathan said quietly.

"This isn't getting us very far," Ratana said. "We believe the being called Cindy has deceived us all for unknown purposes, has captured James and Sam for an equally unknown purpose--so what do we do? Can we rescue our friends or do we just sit here chatting?"

"What can we do?" Spence asked. "If we knew where they had gone, maybe we could find another way there, but we don't. They could be a kilometre away or ten thousand. We have no way of telling."

"So we're going to do nothing?" Marc asked.

"No, we're going to brew a cuppa, have a bite to eat, then as the day is still young, we're going to do a bit of exploring back up the mountain. Maybe there is something we missed."

Two hours later found them back up at the site of the disappearance. Despite the earlier traffic, when they had sought the missing five persons, there were still signs on the ground if you knew what to look for. Nathan knew a bit about tracking, though he had never become proficient at it, and Ratana had been actively discouraged from the practice as it was not judged to be an activity suitable for a woman. Spence was the most adept at noticing the tiny blemishes left on ground and vegetation and interpreting them, yet it was Marc who noticed the first of these clues to the disappearance.

"That's Sam's shoeprint. I'm certain of it. Those are Propet Walkers' soles. She's worn them before."

"Are you sure? They don't look very different."

"I'm sure," Marc said. "You don't get that brand over here and I've seen hers before."

"Okay." Spence squatted just off the track and peered at the faint marks in the dirt. "This is as far as she came. See, there are other marks here, almost as if they were crowding up--then nothing. She didn't go forward, or back-- just poof." He made a gesture with his hand as if a puff of smoke was dissipating in the still air.

"Can you identify any other footprints?"

"Well, I'd say that was Ernie." Spence pointed at the scuff marks of bare feet. "There are several boot marks..."

"James and Guilford," Ratana chipped in.

"...But I can't see any prints from Cindy."

"There's something back here," Nathan said, a few paces behind the others, "But it must be Ernie as it's barefoot...that can't be right, it overlays a boot mark and Ernie was leading. It's pretty big though--how tall was Ernie?"

Spence came back to examine the faint marks on the ground. "You're right, someone in bare feet followed James or Guilford but hell's bells, he must have massive feet unless I'm reading this completely wrong." He spread his fingers on his left hand wide and held them over the footprint. "My hand spread is about twenty-two centimetres, not much short of my own foot size, but if that is the toe and that the heel..." he pointed, "... then his foot is over...bloody hell, this isn't Ernie, it's a yowie."

"No kidding?" Marc snapped off a few pictures with his digital camera. "You mean they were followed by a yowie?"

"Looks that way, but when?"

"Could be any time since we left here this morning," Marc observed. "Is it important?"

They cast about for other prints and markings, and knowing what they were looking for, soon discovered others. Spence bent over the new ones, frowning as he interpreted the spoor. "Has anyone stepped onto the path since we got back?" Everyone denied they had, so Spence pointed out what was puzzling him. "Here's Marc's print--quite distinctive tread pattern--from early this morning, but it partially overlies one of the yowie footprints. He must have been close behind a yowie."

"But that would mean it was here between the first group passing and Marc following up," Ratana objected. "There wouldn't have been time and we'd have seen a three metre creature anyway. It would have towered above the bushes."

Marc nodded. "That's true. I have been careful not to tread on the path since coming back and I was only a couple of minutes behind Cindy this morning. But I'm sure I would have seen a great hulking brute ahead of me. You must be mistaken."

"No mistake," Spence said. "A yowie passed by just ahead of you, Marc, and just behind James and Guilford."

"But that's where Sam and Cindy were," Marc objected. "They would have raised holy hell if they'd seen a Bigfoot treading close behind."

Nathan's gaze met Spence's. "And there are no footprints left by Cindy," he said softly to the older man. "I don't see there is any other reasonable conclusion we can reach."

"What are you talking about?" Marc asked.

"It looks like a yowie followed Sam and preceded you."

Marc frowned. "But that's where Cindy was...Cindy? A yowie?" He laughed uneasily. "Is this another of your jokes?"

"Think about it, Marc. We can see from the footprints there was a yowie following the first group. There are no footprints we can identify as coming from Cindy. As far as the four of us can judge, Cindy had no objective reality--she looked like whatever we imagined. Now an ordinary person has no need for that sort of disguise, we'd pretty well accept anyone that turned up at face value. What we wouldn't accept--couldn't accept--is a cryptozoological mystery in the flesh."

"But...but she was so normal, so...she was a young woman, not a monster."

"I never said she was a monster," Spence reproved. "In fact, I'd say there is at least human intelligence shown here."

"I'm not saying it's impossible," Ratana said, "But is there actually any proof that yowies or Bigfoot can do this sort of thing? Mentally disguise themselves?"

"Proof? No, but there's plenty of anecdotal evidence. There's a guy called Lapseritis in the States who has written a book about what he calls the psychic sasquatch. He says they can escape notice whenever they want, sometimes through a form of hypnosis. I'd say that's pretty much what Cindy has done to us."

"But we don't know why?"

"To isolate James and Sam, I'd guess. Though why they want them, I don't know." Spence grimaced. "I just wished they had taken me. I've spent even longer than James looking for these creatures, and Sam is a tyro. It's just bloody not fair."

Return to your camp.

"What did you say?" Spence asked.

"I didn't say anything," Marc replied, looking around nervously at the thick undergrowth.

Nathan shrugged and Ratana shook her head. "Not me, but I heard something."

Return to your camp.

"Shit, there it is again. Who is that?"

"Perhaps we'd better do as he...it says," Nathan suggested.

"Trusting soul, aren't you," Marc grumbled. "We don't even know who or what it is."

"He does have a point," Ratana said. "How can we be sure it means us no harm?"

The bushes further up Tunbubudla shook and a series of growls riveted their attention. The disturbance drew closer and involuntarily they withdrew, keeping their eyes firmly on the unseen threat.

"Now I really do think it's time for us to leave," Spence said.

They withdrew hurriedly, Marc leading the retreat down the mountain and Spence wistfully bringing up the rear, scouring the vegetation for a glimpse of a yowie. The growls and bush shaking continued, following them and herding them down onto the flat land around the base of 'The Twins' whence their camp lay. As they entered it, the sounds died away, leaving them in relative silence, with only the normal sounds of the Australian bush surrounding them.

Welcome, said a strange voice.

They turned and looked wide-eyed at a tall young man standing in the middle of their camp.

Spence stared, fighting at the wool that seemed to invade his mind. "Let me guess. You're Cindy's boyfriend and you're not human either."

14

James and Sam woke within minutes of each other as the first rays of the
sun stabbed over the eastern cliffs. They shivered and automatically
turned to one another for warmth, but while this action made some parts
warm, it also exposed others to the chill breeze that blew up the valley ahead
of the sun's warming rays. James kissed Sam tenderly and, getting to his feet,
set about trying to coax some life back into the almost-extinct ashes of the
fire. Sam decided clothes were a first priority, followed by a quick visit to the
bushes and a wash in the lake. She started toward the shrubbery then
hesitated, thinking back to the previous morning and the alarming thing that
had happened.

Sam opened her mouth to call back to James and ask whether it was safe,
but she caught sight of him squatting by the fire, dangling, and she laughed
instead. *Damned if I'm going to play the weak woman more than I have to,* she
thought. She looked at James fondly and smiled at the thought of the
previous night. *Mind you, girl, it ain't so bad when your man is strong and enthusiastic.*
With another chuckle, Sam pivoted on her heel and strode into the
shrubbery.

By the time Sam got back from the lake, her face and hair still wet, and
shivering slightly, James had coaxed new life into the fire and had rescued the
scraps of the previous night's repast.

"Not much of a breakfast," he said with a grimace. "Some slightly stale
bread and a few berries, plus my packet of peanuts."

Sam made a face. "I'm famished. Do you think our benefactors might see
their way clear to providing a bit more food?" She looked around at the open
spaces, where a few wallabies were feeding on the grass, and at the flocks of
lorikeets squawking noisily as they squabbled over the nectar in eucalyptus
tree blossoms. "What about it?" she called. "I'd like bacon and eggs over
easy, hash browns with syrup, orange juice, toast and a large pot of strong
coffee, with cream and sugar." She listened for a few moments before
turning away with a shrug and a grin. "Worth a try, I guess."

"They may not provide breakfast, but you can be sure they won't leave us," James said. "They brought us here for a purpose and I'm sure it wasn't what...er, we got up to last night."

"Got up to last night? James, you say the most romantic things." Sam smiled sweetly, and then fixed James with a steely gaze. "There is a time and place for naked men. I suggest you get some pants on before company arrives."

James grinned and turned, sprinting over the turf to fling himself headlong into the still, chill waters of the lake. He splashed around and swam across the lake and back before hauling himself out, drying himself off with his bush shirt and donning underpants and shorts.

Sam handed him a chunk of the kurrajong damper bread, toasted and crisped around the edges.

James leaned over and kissed her lightly before taking a big bite. "Mmm, it's good. Thank you, Sam."

Sam chewed her own piece, still thinking wistfully of crispy bacon and soft-centred eggs. "So what do we do today?" she asked. "Wait here for instructions or go off looking for answers?"

"I don't know. The path we came down ends at the lake, so unless we just retrace our steps..." A distant, echo-muffled 'crack' interrupted him, followed within moments by two or three more reports wrapped up in a rolling reverberation.

"Those are rifle shots," Sam said flatly.

"Guilford doing his own brand of scientific sampling, I'd guess," James replied. "Damn the man. Why did we have to be lumbered with him?"

"You invited him along."

"Yes, I did, didn't I? And I can't figure out why. I loathe and detest the creep."

Sam grimaced. "You too? Do you have the feeling we've been manipulated?" she asked.

James made a non-committal noise. "I think those shots settle what we should do. I don't think we should head up the valley again."

"I'd be just as happy to stay here, but I sure wish we had some food. Do you think you could find some more in the forest?"

"Possibly, but only fruit. Still, I'll have a...Jesus! Where did you come from?" James jumped at the sight of Ernie, the old Aboriginal man, sitting by the crackling fire.

Sam did a double-take too and stared suspiciously at the old man. "How did you get there? I didn't see you sneak up."

"Gidday Ms Louis, Aparrerinja. I thought you might like a little brekkie." Ernie grinned and held up a plastic bag of groceries and a frying pan.

Sam took the bag and looked inside it while Ernie busied himself setting the pan on a ring of stones over the embers. "You have got to be kidding," she said, pulling out a carton of eggs, several rashers of bacon, a bottle of orange juice and a thermos of coffee, as well as bread, butter, paper plates and utensils. "Where did you find all this?"

"In a supermarket and a cafe, Ms Louis. I am sorry to say I could not find any hash browns and to tell the truth, I'm not even sure what they are. I hope this will be sufficient."

"You gorgeous man. Are you taken, by any chance?"

Ernie grinned widely. "I'm afraid so, Ms Louis."

"Call me Sam, please. Well, I suppose I'll just have to make do with the man I have then." She smiled at James and started setting out the food. Suddenly she stopped and frowned before looking quizzically at Ernie. "How did you know? I only asked for these things a few minutes ago. Have you been here all along?" She flushed slightly. "Even last night?"

"No Sam, I was elsewhere. My friends heard you and told me."

"Your friends?"

"Over there." Ernie pointed toward the forest. A huge, shaggy-haired creature stood in the shadows beneath a tall tree. As James and Sam stared, it raised a hand briefly above its head before slipping back into invisibility.

"Th...that was a...a yowie?" Sam stammered, her face pale.

James was staring hard at the shadows as if he could soak the image of the creature up into his brain. "They can talk?" he asked. "They're intelligent?"

"They're smart, Aparrerinja, but they don't exactly talk, not like this anyway. They did tell me what Sam wanted for brekkie, so I went out and got it."

"From a supermarket?" Sam shook her head. "Even if you did that sudden appearance and disappearance thing, you still wouldn't have time."

Ernie smiled, the corners of his eyes crinkling in amusement. "I'd hate to have only twenty-four hours in a day. I'd never get anything done."

"Oh, hell, I'm not even going to ask you to explain that one," James groaned. He tipped some butter into the frypan and cracked a couple of eggs into it, jiggling the pan to distribute the crackling butter. After a few moments he flipped the eggs expertly, and then slid them out onto a plate. He passed it to Sam and started another couple.

"My god, you know how to do eggs over easy!" Sam exclaimed. "You are a keeper if you can make a gal breakfast the next morning as well as..." She blushed and choked on a mouthful of egg.

"You slept well?" Ernie asked innocently.

"Some of the time," James replied with a grin. "All I wanted anyway."

"That is good. There is a lot for you to do today."

"Oh? What?"

"Wait and see. Finish your brekkie first, mate."

"Yes, Ernie." James grinned and tucked into his own eggs.

After clearing away the breakfast things and making sure the fire was out, Ernie led Sam and James back to the path and up the valley a little way, the plastic bag of supplies and rubbish swinging incongruously from one hand. Sam stared with delight at the fresh vistas of vegetation in varying shades of green, the blossoms on shrubs and vines, the multi-hued butterflies and darting dragonflies that haunted the edges of sunny glades. Flocks of birds passed overhead and wallabies bounded off the path in front of them. James was less interested in their surroundings and stumbled often as he was continually looking around to try and catch sight of a yowie in the surrounding forest.

"Pay attention, Aparrerinja," Ernie said. "You will see a yowie if it is necessary, but for now there are more important things to consider."

The old Aboriginal tracker led them off the trail onto a path that looked as if it had once been in use but not for some time. The weeds and undergrowth almost choked the gap between the shrubs and once they entered the forest proper, they lost all sight of a path, moved across undisturbed leaf litter.

Sam gasped as they plunged into the cool dimness of the forest. "It's like a cathedral--the trunks of the trees are like pillars..." She chuckled as she looked around. "I keep expecting to see rows of worshipers."

"They are here, Sam," Ernie said quietly. "Every right-minded being holds the wild places of this world in reverence."

"There are a lot of people who don't," James murmured.

Ernie nodded. "It was not always so, but it has been for thousands of years. Humans have spread like a plague over the land, always taking, seldom giving back until..." He was silent for a minute, his dark eyes hooded and unfocused. "It is not for me to speak of these things. Others will do this; ones who have seen the events unfold."

"Who are these ones you speak of, Ernie?" James asked.

Ernie shook his head. "You wouldn't want me to spoil the surprise now, would you, hey?" He grinned. "Come on, we're nearly there." He set off across the open forest floor, the plastic bag swinging.

The land sloped gently upward, though the great buttressed roots of the huge forest trees masked the lie of the land until abruptly, they passed from the gloom of the forest to a thin strip of brightly sunlit bushes and a sheer wall of rock.

James craned his neck, looking up the cliff, past fragments of vegetation caught in cracks and irregularities of the stone to the distant rim of the cliff set against an azure sky. "You're not expecting us to climb that, are you?"

"Just a little way," Ernie said.

"I...I don't have a head for heights."

"You will be all right, Ms Louis. They are only about twenty feet up."

"What is?" James asked.

"The answers."

Ernie reached up and moved quickly and lightly along a series of tiny toeholds, his bare feet almost seeming to kick depressions in the rock face, for when Sam started up she found the ledges and cracks amply wide enough and secure enough to hold her in safety. James followed and in only a few minutes they found themselves on a ledge that had been invisible from below. The rock face receded to form a shallow shaft, a hollow a little under two metres in height that plunged into the rock for about ten paces before ending in a smooth wall of seamless rock. The morning sun angled into the shaft, lighting up the bare walls, revealing its emptiness.

Ernie put down his shopping bag and pulled out two torches which he handed to Sam and James. "You'll need these. Follow me." He stepped into the shaft.

James flicked his torch on and off. "Where the hell are we going to need these?" He shrugged and followed Ernie, looking to make sure Sam was close behind him.

Five paces into the shaft, James suddenly slowed, startled, and stared at Ernie and the smooth wall in front of them. The old Aboriginal turned and beckoned him onward, striding toward the end wall...which seemed as far as ever. James frowned and took another five paces, and then another five, yet the back wall seemed no closer. He glanced behind him at Sam and beyond her to the sun-soaked ledge seemingly only a pace or two behind.

Abruptly the sun went out, as if someone had flipped a light switch. James gasped involuntarily and Sam gripped his arm tightly.

"What happened?" she said tightly. "Where are we?"

"We have passed through a portal, Ms Louis." Ernie's voice, echoing slightly, came out of the absolute darkness. "There is nothing to be frightened of."

"I'm not frightened," she declared, her voice shaking slightly.

"Well, I bloody am," James muttered. "Can't you give us a bit of warning when you do that sort of thing?"

"Why don't you put your torches on?" Ernie asked. "You need to see where you are."

They obeyed without further comment and two tiny pools of light lit the stygian darkness. James and Sam could see each other and small portions of the floor and walls of what looked like a long stone passageway. Ernie hovered at the edge of the light and pointed to a lightly phosphorescent strip on the floor.

"Follow it," Ernie instructed. "Do not deviate. These caverns are vast and while you would come to no harm if you stepped off the path, it would be tedious looking for you."

"You're not coming with us?"

"I have not been summoned." He stepped back into the darkness and as the torch beams followed him, he appeared to step through a doorway and vanish. James moved after him before thinking better of his action and turning back toward Sam.

"I'm not sure I want to contemplate beings that can summon or dismiss someone as powerful as Ernie," James said.

"He would not willingly send us into danger," Sam murmured. "I trust him."

"Yeah, I guess I do too." James shone his torch down the rock passage, along the faint gleam in the rock floor. "Well, shall we follow our instructions?"

The passage stretched out well beyond the range of their torches, so they concentrated on keeping them on the floor near their feet. It soon became apparent that the torches were more for their own peace of mind than of any real use. The floor of the passage was smooth and free of debris, the ceiling high and without any projections that might cause injury. On an impulse, James had both torches switched off and instead of near darkness resulting, the faint gleam of phosphorescence in the floor strip suddenly glowed brightly, illuminating their faces in a greenish pallor.

"That's handy," James said. "If our batteries go flat, we'll still be able to see."

Switching their torches back on, Sam and James continued deeper into the mountain. The floor sloped downward gradually and after a while Sam thought she could detect another sound over the almost continuous echoing slap of their feet. She thought there was something familiar about it and tried to identify it before saying anything, but the faint sound eluded definition.

"Someone's left a tap on," James said, holding up his hand and coming to a halt.

"That's it. Dang, I thought I recognised it--dripping water."

"I'm not surprised. There are whole lakes under parts of Australia and while I don't know of any under the Blue Mountains, there's bound to be springs and seepages."

"And of course, there is no guarantee we're still in the Blue Mountains," Sam added. "Ernie's portal could have taken us anywhere."

"That's true. I hadn't considered that."

They continued on down the passage, the sound of dripping water getting louder by the minute. An irregularity in the ceiling rock, the first they had seen, exuded a trickle of water that dripped steadily into a water-worn basin on the floor. The pool overflowed into a tiny rivulet that meandered down the passage ahead of them. Gradually the sound of dripping water fell away behind them to be replaced by a gurgling and rippling sound from the stream that raced along beside them. After several crossings of the water course as it swung from one side of the passage to the other, Sam stepped into it accidentally and exclaimed in surprise.

"It's bigger than it was. How can it get bigger if it's all from that same drip?"

James squatted beside the stream and played his slightly yellowed beam of light over it. The ripples and vortices threw back the light, illuminating the walls and ceiling in shifting patterns. "You're right, it is bigger." He stood up and moved from wall to wall, examining the surface. "The walls are wet. There must be considerable seepage adding to the flow."

The stream continued to grow in size and the floor of the tunnel, instead of remaining smooth and flat, developed a broad groove along the left-hand side that channeled the water into it. Soon, another sound impinged on their senses--the sound of water falling. Sam and James slowed their pace, cautious about what they might find. Abruptly, the gleam of phosphorescence at their feet flared into a strip across the passage and the stream hurled itself across it and out into blackness, falling like thunder into the void.

"Shit," James said. "End of the line. Where the hell do we go from here?" He shone his torch beam out into the darkness and could follow the stream water down to sparkling spray some twenty metres or so below them. "I'll tell you one thing," he muttered. "I'm not jumping into that."

"There are stairs over here," Sam called. The beam of her torch revealed broad steps cut into the rock.

"Let me go first," James said promptly.

"When you know me a little better, James, you'll realise I don't let a man lead me, particularly when I've found it." She started down them, with James following. A couple of minutes later, they stood on a broad stone shelf about half a metre above the black waters of what appeared to be a large underground lake. The rock shelf stretched about ten metres in length and five metres wide and was bare and featureless. The rock wall behind them was smooth, the only feature being the broad stairs that rose towards the black on black mouth of the tunnel and the cascading stream.

"Now what?" Sam asked. "There's no way forward unless we swim, and I ain't swimming. There's no telling what might be lurking in there."

James examined the edge of the platform and leaned out over the edge, shining his torch down into the water. "The rock is thin," he reported, "And there's a space underneath. I wonder if we are supposed to go under there." He looked round at Sam and noted the yellowing beam of her torch. "I'll go in and have a look if you think you can haul me back up."

"Don't you dare," Sam exclaimed. "I'm not going to risk losing you so soon after I've found you. No, if we can't find a logical way off this platform we go back. Ernie should have given us full instructions."

"I don't like just giving up."

"We're not, but if these guys really have summoned us, they need to provide us with the means to answer their call. If they don't have the courtesy to do that, they can go whistle for somebody else."

James had been staring out over the lake, into the stygian darkness. "Switch off your torch a moment, Sam." He clicked his off and when, a moment later, she followed suit, a luminous circle shone out over the water from some distant point. "I think that's where we are supposed to go."

"James, at your feet. Look."

He looked down, stepping back in alarm as a faint glow from under the rock ledge grew steadily brighter. After a few moments, the tip of a small aluminium rowing boat nosed out from under the platform and sat rocking slightly in the wavelets churned up by the falling stream.

"Is that our ride?" Sam asked.

"Ride, be damned," James muttered. "There are oars in it and guess who'll be rowing?"

James clambered into the boat and helped Sam down into it, sitting her in the rear while he took up his position amidships, facing her. He fitted the oars in the rowlocks before saying with a grin, "It's been a while since I did this. No criticism now." He dug in the oar blades and pulled. One blade dug deep and spun the boat while the other scooped water up and showered Sam.

"Damn it, James," Sam spluttered, wiping water from her face. "Let's have less energy and more finesse." She smiled and leaned forward to pat his knee. "I've always said it's not the size of a man's stroke that counts; it's what he does with it."

"Hmm, I need a bit of practice."

"Not much," smiled Sam, "But I'll give you all the time you need. In the meantime," she pointed off to their right, "I think we need to be heading for that luminous patch."

James soon remembered how to row and their progress, while a bit unsteady and involving a certain amount of spray, drew them out into the vast underground lake. The only sound was the splash and gurgle of the oar blades and the ripple of the passage of the boat through the water. James concentrated on rowing, while Sam offered up course corrections as the little boat yawed and rocked under his enthusiastic efforts. As he improved, Sam found herself with little to do and snapped on her torch, playing it over the oily black waters.

A large ripple appeared off to their right, its foamy wake almost a jet stream of froth. Sam sat up straight and focused all her attention on the fast moving motion of the disturbance. When it continued to parallel the boat for some distance, Sam tapped James on the knee. "Take a look at that. Something big is moving under there and it's following us."

James stopped rowing and switched his torch on, scanning the disturbed water in its weakening beam. After watching it for a few minutes, he switched his torch off and took up the oars again. "There's something there all right. It looks like it might be a big fish or something."

"Nothing's been normal on this trip. Why expect it now?" Sam continued to illuminate the water, hoping for a glimpse of the creature.

Without any warning, the wake created by the creature abruptly ceased. Sam looked all about, hoping to regain sight of it. Then the water five metres from the boat rippled and broke as a rounded, greyish domed head, like an upside down metal bowl the size of a beach ball, rose steadily and sedately out of the water, a snort of exhaled air showering them both with a fine spray of water. The long snout of the creature, complete with whiskers and large eyes, gave the impression of an oversized seal bobbing effortlessly alongside the boat. Sam and James sat mesmerised by the unfolding spectacle of another unknown creature.

"My God! What is that thing?" Sam whispered.

A four-foot long, elegantly curved neck dispelled the image of a seal. The torch's beam danced in the rippling water and reflected off the sleek hide of the creature. It swam closer and lifted its head higher into the air. Peering down into the boat, its large, liquid brown eyes, rimmed by coal black eyelashes, blinked at them with curiosity. It shook its head, revealing a long, dark mane of hair running down the back of its neck and sank, slipping back under the water.

James cautiously peered over the side and announced, "It has flippers. It's swimming; keeping pace with the boat. Well, I'll be. I should have known."

"What is it? Should have known what? James, what is that thing?" Anxiety crept into Sam's voice. "Is it dangerous?"

"It's a bunyip, a fabled water monster from these parts." James turned to look at her, his face reflecting the wonder in his voice. "It's the Australian version of the Loch Ness Monster. They even have a Maori version in New Zealand called a Taniwha."

"You're kidding me?" Sam jumped as the creature rose again, a little further from the boat, but it came no closer, remaining stationary in the water. "It looks like a baby seal with a giraffe's neck and a dolphin's body. More like a badly put together kid's puzzle. *This* is what Nessie looks like?"

"Heuvelmans was right after all," James murmured.

"Who's Heuvelmans?" Sam asked, her eyes fixed on the creature.

James continued to stare at the bunyip while he talked. "Bernard Heuvelmans, the father of Cryptozoology, always claimed that one group of water monsters, including the Loch Ness one, was some sort of long-necked seal. This little fellow certainly seems to vindicate him, doesn't he?" James decided not to say anything about the reputation some bunyips had for attacking livestock and sometimes people.

The bunyip started swimming again, executed a neat roll with its entire body then rose high out of the water and came down with a splash of its two large front flippers. The cool spray that hit the boat soaked both of them to the skin. By the time they had wiped their faces free of water, the creature had disappeared beneath the water, leaving the surface roiling in its wake.

James sorted the oars out and started rowing toward the luminous target once more. Sam kept twisting around in her seat, playing the beam of her torch over the water, seeking out any hint of the bunyip's presence. "What would it eat down here?" she asked, adding quickly, "Don't tell me if your answer is 'people'."

"Fish, I would imagine, and the fish would eat insects washed down by streams. However, I think there must be a connection with the outside world as that animal had well-developed eyes."

"And why is that significant?"

"Creatures that live in perpetual darkness have no need of vision and often lose that sense entirely. Our bunyip is either a recent arrival or there's a passage to the outside somewhere."

"Perhaps where we're going," Sam said. "That light is a lot bigger and it's starting to look as if there is a tunnel there."

James stopped rowing and looked over his shoulder. "You're right." The glow from the light they were approaching showed up his pensive features. "You know, I don't want to seem alarmist, but the whole scale of this operation is a bit daunting. What sort of an organisation commands the loyalty of Karadji men like Ernie and Mick, has a technology that encompasses UFOs and teleportation and is associated with yowies and bunyips? I mean, what's left? Time travel?"

Sam nodded. "I know what you mean. And what does an organisation like that want with us?"

"Well, we're not going to find out floating on this lake. Are you ready to brave the unknown, dear Sam?"

"Brave a bit more of it, you mean. Press on, fearless leader."

James steered the rowing boat into the tunnel and up to a low stone platform similar to the one on the other side of the lake. He tied up the boat using a piece of rope in the bilges and a metal ring set in the stone, after which he helped Sam from the boat. They stood and looked around, the platform being bathed in greenish-yellow phosphorescence that seemed to emanate from the ceiling rather than any definite light fixtures.

"There are stairs over there," Sam said, pointing.

They climbed the wide stone stairs cautiously and at the top, found themselves in a short passageway leading to a spacious, well-lit cavern. James led the way into the huge chamber, his mind being aware of the many objects in the cavern, but his attention focused on the figure in front of him.

A woman dressed in a long white robe, her blonde hair cascading about her shoulders, stood some twenty paces away, regarding Sam and James gravely as they emerged from the passage. She held out her hands and and a calm voice sounded within their heads. *Welcome Professor James Hay and Ms Samantha Louis. We have been expecting you.*

15

ery good, Spencer Tuhua, the young man said. *These others must be Ratana Allira, Nathan Wambiri, and Marc Lachlan. You are all welcome.*

"Why isn't he moving his mouth when he speaks?" Marc whispered to Nathan.

The young man smiled. *That is because I do not have complex vocal cords, tongue and palate, like humans. I cannot actually talk as you can.*

"Then how..." Spence started to say, when Marc interrupted.

"Fuck that, he said he's not human."

Be at ease, Marc. I mean you no harm.

"The fuck you don't," Marc muttered, but he lapsed into a sullen silence.

*In answer to your question, Spence, I can talk to you through the speech and auditory centres in your brain, in the same way as we can influence the visual centres to create an illusion, like this body you see...*The young man gestured down the length of his body with both hands...*I think my thoughts and transmit them to your brain which then translates my thoughts into sounds for you.*

"Telepathy's impossible," Spence said.

The young man smiled. *Evidently not.*

"You're a yowie?" Nathan asked abruptly.

The young man smiled warmly. *My name is Wulgu and unlike you I only have one name. We are few in number and can identify each other easily by the...shall we say flavour...of each other's minds. Humans need a name tag, so I am known as Wulgu, a name of significance among our kind for legend has it that the first male of our species was also called Wulgu. And yes, I am what humans call a yah-wee, or yowie.*

"Is your form so fearsome that you have to wear a disguise?" Spence asked. "Men have seen yowies before."

Not fearsome necessarily, Wulgu replied, *But intimidating to some. I do not want to engender fear, so I adopt an illusory body.*

"You have an enviable vocabulary too," Spence said with a smile. "Better than many humans. And your accent appears to display a touch of Kiwi for some reason."

A wave of amusement swept over the four humans. *The vocabulary is yours, Spence. Did I not adequately explain how I am talking to you? Every word and its pronunciation come through the stimulation of your cortical neurons. While you hear a New Zealand accent, Marc hears an American one, Nathan an Aboriginal, and Ratana the lilt of her Torres Strait homeland.*

"Shit, I thought you were just a Bigfoot on a working visa from the States."

You have an interesting thought pattern, Marc. Hang onto it, because humour will help in the difficult times.

"You understand humour?" Ratana asked. "I thought that was a human characteristic."

Wulgu sighed and a mild melancholy washed over them. *Humans do not always understand their place in the tapestry of life. They seek a preeminent position for themselves and seek exclusivity for feelings and beliefs that are common among what you call the lower animals.*

"Are you going to show yourself as you really are?" Spence asked.

Is this body not easy to look at?

"Maybe, but it's not real. I've wanted to see a yowie all my life. I want to see the truth of it, as you really appear."

You want the truth? You can't handle the truth. Wulgu broke into peals of rather forced laughter. *That was a joke? Whose mind did it come from? Ah...Marc's. It is a 'movie'? Ah...yes...I see. Thank you, Marc.*

"No trouble, I'm sure." Marc frowned and tried, unsuccessfully, to conceal his consternation.

"So? As you really are?"

If you wish it, Wulgu said, *But I shall monitor your vital functions and if I detect fear, I will resume this form.*

Wulgu's body increased in size, the proportions changing as it grew. Arms became longer, legs shorter, the chest swelled and the stomach distended. The shoes disappeared and the feet pushed outward, increasing in length and breadth. The head changed shape, the top rising up in a great sagittal crest, from which huge muscles attached that operated the mighty jaws, even as heavy brow ridges developed and the chin receded. Wulgu's neck shortened until it seemed as if his head sat atop broad shoulders. His eyes swelled and deepened in colour and his lips thinned beneath a large flattened nose. Covering him from the crest on his head to the tops of his huge feet was a pelt of shiny dark brown hair.

Satisfied, Spence? Wulgu asked.

Spence nodded, swallowing hard and resisting the urge to step back out of range of those long arms. Ratana and Nathan also stood their ground, their minds reflecting the belief they had in the spirit nature, mostly beneficent, of the yowie.

Marc retreated several paces and he could not look directly at the huge creature towering above them to a height of three metres. His eyes slid off to the side and his thoughts were fixated on safe ideas. *Special effects. Absolutely fucking great special effects.*

"Thank you," Spence whispered. "And...and this is what Cindy looks like too?"

The being you call Cindy is a female yowie by the name of Rima. She is smaller than I and far more beautiful. Wulgu's mind reflected something akin to love as he thought of her.

"What was Cindy's...Rima's purpose?" Nathan enquired. "Why was it necessary to have her with us at all?"

Control, Wulgu said simply. *It was necessary to manipulate events and people so that your James and Sam could be isolated and moved without undue stress.*

"And Guilford King?" Spence asked.

He is a bad man. Rima volunteered to remove him.

"Remove him? You...you had him killed?" Spence's eyes opened wide.

Wulgu stared back at Spence and his lips curled, revealing large canines. *We kill only in defence of our own, and then only when there is no other option. We are not wanton killers like humans.* The yowie's features softened slightly and the teeth disappeared behind thin lips again. *The bad man has not been killed, though he would try to kill us without compunction. We have removed him to a place where he cannot harm the members of this experiment.*

"Experiment? What experiment?"

That is not for me to say, Spence.

"You can't just leave it at that. Are we being experimented on? For what purpose? Why? On whose authority?"

I cannot tell you, and would not even if I knew, without permission.

"Who gives orders to a yowie?" Nathan wondered.

Marc giggled. "Where does a thousand pound yowie sleep? Anywhere he damn well pleases."

I am glad to see that Marc seeks refuge in humour, Wulgu observed. *I feared this experience might be traumatic for him.*

Spence looked around at the heat-shimmered air of the Tunbubudla bush with its scents of dust, eucalyptus and pine. He looked up at the peak and the strip of vegetation from whence they had so recently been herded. "What is your purpose in contacting us, Wulgu?"

I am instructed to keep you safe.

Ratana had been edging closer as Spence and the yowie conversed. Now only a pace or two away, she tentatively reached out her hand. "M...may I touch you, Wulgu?"

Wulgu looked down on the tall Torres Strait Islander woman. *You believe I am a spirit*, he said gently. *Can you touch a spirit?* When she did not answer, the yowie stretched out one long arm and touched a huge forefinger to the palm of her hand. *I am real, Ratana.*

Spence frowned. "Hang on, safe from what? You...or rather, Rima...has already removed Guilford. What other danger is there?"

The world is a dangerous place, Wulgu replied.

Nathan moved up alongside his fiancée and stroked the yowie's hand, grasping the thick and powerful fingers gingerly. He ran his gaze over the mountain of bone and muscle and whistled softly. "Incredible," he murmured. "Wulgu, I have to ask. As you are not spirit, where did you come from? Are you *Gigantopithecus?*"

I could as well ask you if you are chimpanzee because you share many characteristics with the ape, Wulgu replied cryptically.

Nathan's eyebrows lifted. "You know about chimpanzees? Ah, of course, you found it in my mind."

I did, but I knew of them already. We have...access to much knowledge.

"God, there are so many questions I want to ask," Nathan said.

"He's not God," Marc giggled. "Just very powerful."

I think we should get you all to a place of safety. We can have someone care for Marc too, as I think this is all too much for his mind. Wulgu lifted his great head and snuffed the air. *Come, we must be going.*

"Where?" Spence asked, "And why? This camp is as safe as anywhere and James and Sam know where it is if they return."

They will not be coming back here, but something else may, so I will take you elsewhere. Wulgu started off with a rolling gait that quickly became a fluid stride, looking back over his shoulder to see if the others were following.

"Bloody hell," Spence muttered. "If I didn't believe in the Patterson movie before, I do now." He trotted after the yowie, shaking his head.

Nathan grasped Marc's arm and led the unresisting photographer while Ratana brought up the rear, carrying her own pack and Marc's camera.

Wulgu led them off through the eucalyptus woodland, veering away from the left-hand peak of Tunbubudla. The going was a lot easier than when they had arrived, as they did not have to push their way through thorn thickets, tangled grass or patches of dense shrubs. Wulgu strode nonchalantly through everything and the four humans trotted along in his wake, the flattened vegetation proving no obstacle.

"Hey, Wulgu...slow down a bit, will you?" Spence panted after about twenty minutes. "I'm an old man and you're setting a cracking pace."

The yowie stopped and let the humans catch up. He looked down at Spence with a slight smile. *As you wish, old man, but I think you want me to slow because of Marc, not because you are unfit.*

Spence grunted. "Are we going far?"

That depends. It is my intention to take you to the other peak of Tunbubudla, but we shall see when we get there.

"But why are we going? You implied there was some danger and that something else may come to our campsite. What are you afraid of?"

Wulgu looked at him in silence and for a moment, Spence feared he had offended the giant yowie. *Say nothing to Marc, but I think the Quinkan, the Shadow People are near.*

Spence glanced at Marc, but the young photographer was chatting quietly with Nathan and seemed unconcerned about the imminent threat of something he admitted terrified him.

"He didn't hear you?"

Only you can hear me at the moment. I have switched to a personal mode of contact. You can do the same with me. Just think what you wish to say, but preface it with my name. When you have done it once, it will become easier.

Wulgucanyouhearme? Damnhecan'tIfeelsostupidhellohelloanyonehome? Myleg'sitchywhat'sthatsound? CanyouhearmeWulgu? OhdamnwhatamIdoingwrong?

Slow down old man, I can hear you perfectly well, but you must learn to discipline your thoughts. At the moment you are babbling. Think my name and use your lips and tongue to form the words silently.

Wulgu, Spence mouthed, *Can you hear me?*

Yes, clearly now. Do not worry, old man, it will become easier with practice.

"What's happening?" Ratana whispered. "Can you hear something?" She cocked her head on one side and a look of pure delight crossed her face. *Oh Wulgu, that is so wonderful.* She listened again, then, *Spence, can you hear me?*

"Bugger me!" Spence exclaimed. *Ratana? How is this possible? Telepathy has never been convincingly demonstrated.*

Trust your senses, Uncle. Wulgu has explained it to me. He says it is like a stream blocked with debris. Once the floodwaters have removed it, the stream will continue to flow as long as water runs in it. He says we must practice.

Well, damn me! Nathan, Marc, can you hear me? Nathan. Marc. Hello? "They can't hear me." Spence looked crestfallen.

Your thoughts have the force of a urinating wombat, Wulgu said, his own thoughts reflecting great mirth. *Humans are generally weak-willed when it comes to mind communication. Let me open the way for you.*

Spence watched Nathan's face and saw the look of incredulity that flooded it as the yowie spoke to him mentally. A moment later, Nathan spoke to him and for a minute or so; silent speech flew back and forth between the three humans and the yowie.

What about Marc?

I shall not open Marc's mind, Wulgu explained. *At the moment he denies even my existence, refusing to even see me though I am standing in front of him. He explains my general thoughts as audible speech by you three, but if he were to be invaded by silent speech, I fear his mind could withdraw in upon itself completely.*

Nathan nodded and tapped Marc on the shoulder. "We're stopping for a few minutes to listen to the noises of the bush, mate. Nothing to worry about, but can you keep quiet for a bit?"

"Yeah, sure, okay." Marc sat down on a fallen log and sat looking off into the distance, chewing on a piece of plucked grass and ignoring the three humans. *And the...the...*his mind slid away from the other thing, refusing to recognise its presence.

Okay, what now? You said something about the Quinkan, Wulgu?

They are near.

Nathan shivered. *I can't stand the thought of them after Emerald, but they weren't really a threat, were they? I mean, that spirit saw them off pretty quickly.*

Wulgu delved into Nathan's memories. *You saw him?* His mind radiated surprise and wonder. *But remember, he is not with us, so we are not protected.*

You know him? Who is he?

Wulgu did not answer, nor was there any hint on the edges of his thoughts.

Nathan shrugged mentally and tried a different tack. *The Quinkan are spirit creatures. There are many ways in legends of dealing with them.*

Wulgu looked troubled. *They are something else.*

What do you mean? Ratana asked. *Quinkan can be countered if one is prepared.*

They are not truly Quinkan, Wulgu admitted. *We call them that for they resemble the legend but the Shadow People come from elsewhere, slipping through the cracks in the fabric of reality.*

So the legends may be based on real experiences of these beings in the past?

Perhaps.

"Shit," Spence muttered. *So you can't fight them?*

Not with much success, old man. The best defense is avoidance, so we'll head quietly for the other peak, away from the site of disturbance.

They roused Marc and pressed on again, deeper into the thickets around The Twins. The air became still and humid in the dense vegetation and soon everyone was plagued by swarms of small flies attracted to their sweat. Insects thrummed in the undergrowth and in the shaded area under the trees, swarms of medium-sized black and white, and black and blue butterflies danced or clung to dead twigs.

Nathan got Marc's attention and pointed them out. "Crows and blue tigers," he said. "They use these gullies and dense thickets as a refuge during the dry season. They're mostly males," he added.

Marc emerged from his bemused state long enough to take a few photos, including one of the yowie, though he did not seem to realise it. "Where's Sam?" he asked. "She'd like to see this."

"She's not here just now, Marc," Ratana said gently. "We are going to see her later, but if you take some nice photos she can see those."

Marc nodded. "Good idea, I'll..." A fearsome roar blotted out the rest of his sentence, a roar dripping with rage and grief. Marc collapsed to his knees and rolled over into a fetal position, his eyes tight shut and his hands over his ears.

Wulgu stood with his head raised high, his great mouth with its long canine teeth open and a hideous howl of incoherent sound bursting out into the suddenly silent landscape. Spence, Nathan and Ratana stood dumbfounded, staring as the unholy cry faltered into whimpers and sobs. Abruptly, Wulgu leapt forward and took hold of a sapling with a trunk as thick as Spence's upper arm and, seemingly without effort, ripped it from the ground. In a shower of earth, Wulgu swung the small tree around his head and slammed it to the ground with an inchoate cry of rage. He swung again, battering the foliage of surrounding bushes, stripping the branches of their leaves before snapping the trunk in two and hurling the pieces aside. A stench of garlic and sewage pervaded the area.

"Wulgu!" Nathan yelled aloud. "What the hell is the matter?"

The yowie swung round at the sound of a human voice and his great arms reached out toward Nathan, his hands grasping at the air. Wulgu roared again and then turned and charged a much larger tree. He gripped it and ripped at it so that the trunk bent and shook, but it resisted his efforts to destroy it. In a final burst of rage he ripped a huge slab of bark off and hurled it to the ground, standing over it with shaking shoulders and gusting breath.

After several minutes he looked up and met the gaze of the three shaken humans. *Guilford King has shot Rima.*

Ratana uttered a small cry of grief and Spence swore bitterly. "Is she seriously hurt?" Nathan asked quietly.

I do not know. She was with another of our kind, leading him away from the others when it happened...

Is his name Oonoo? Ratana asked.

Wulgu's head came up and he stared at the Torres Strait woman. *How did you know?*

I can hear him, she replied wonderingly. *He says she is alive. It was only a flesh wound to her arm.*

Wulgu turned away and Ratana whispered that she could hear him talking over a great distance. "I think he's talking to Cindy...to Rima. She's somewhere in the Blue Mountains, I think, and she's all right."

"How can you hear them at that distance?" Spence asked. "I can't hear a thing."

"I don't know."

Something moaned at their feet and they stared in horror at Marc's tightly curled body, his eyes screwed shut and the hands over his ears. His weak cries tore at their hearts like that of a hurt puppy.

"Shit, what can we do?" Spence muttered. He dropped to his knees and shook Marc's shoulder. The young photographer responded by whimpering and curling tighter. "We've got to do something; otherwise this could completely unhinge him." Spence shook him again. "It's okay, Marc. Wulgu got some bad news but..."

Nathan stopped him. *He's denied Wulgu's existence. That argument won't work. Let me try.* He squatted beside the trembling young man and spoke conversationally. "That was one hell of a storm, mate, and it came out of nowhere. Did you see that whirlwind? It was a small tornado, shrieking like a demon and flattening everything in sight." Marc stopped his moaning. "Damn near made me shit my pants, mate, when it uprooted and snapped that tree in half. I hope you got some pictures, I was too busy hiding to see it all."

Marc opened his eyes, a hunted expression lurking deep within them. "Tornado?" he whispered.

Spence nodded. "Damnedest thing, but we're all unhurt, so we need to press on. Do you think you're up to it?"

Marc uncurled and looked around, flinching as his gaze moved across the bulk of the yowie, but taking in the destruction of the vegetation. "Fuck," he muttered. "I gotta get some pics." He got to his feet shakily and pointed his camera, seemingly oblivious of the trembling of his hands. "Whew, what's that stink?"

He needs help, Wulgu. I'm sorry to ask when you have your own troubles, but can we get him somewhere secure?

When we get to our destination, I will ask.

Ask who?

"And just what is that smell?" Nathan said, fanning the air in front of his face.

My kind has many defenses, Wulgu stated, his thoughts reflecting no emotion. *Odour is one of them. In times of stress or when we wish to discourage humans, we emit a scent that persuades them to go elsewhere.*

"Skunk ape," Spence said. "That's a name for a Bigfoot-like creature in the American South." *I'm sorry, Wulgu. I don't mean to cause offence.*

I am not offended, old man, though humans smell very odd themselves. Wulgu snuffed the air again. *We should go. I fear my rage and grief have attracted attention.* He turned away and set off at a steady lope, the others following as quickly as they could.

It was not far to the eastern peak of Tunbubudla, and they reached it hot and thirsty in the early afternoon. Collapsing in the shade of a pile of boulders, they drank greedily from their water bottles and despite there being no ready source of replenishment, nearly drained them.

Finish it and give the bottles to me, Wulgu said. *I will fill them for you.*

Nathan looked around at the arid landscape in surprise. *Where from? There are no streams near here.*

I know a place.

Let me come and help you. Nathan struggled to his feet.

No. Wulgu took the bottles and strode off up the slope, disappearing among the boulders almost immediately.

"Where are you going?" Marc stared up at Nathan anxiously. "Don't leave me here. There are...things." He looked over his shoulder and raised a finger to his lips. "They'll hear," he added in a whisper.

"It's okay, mate. I'm not going anywhere." Nathan sat down by Marc and started telling him stories of his childhood in a low voice.

Spence leaned close to Ratana and murmured, "Nathan is in the news a bit these days with his Aboriginal activism, but I'd forgotten what a kind soul he really is."

"He's a good man," Ratana agreed. "I'm lucky to have him."

"How are you holding up under this onslaught of new things?"

Ratana rocked her hand back and forth. "So-so, and you?"

Spence snorted. "I've been interested in the paranormal and cryptozoology all my life and as a Maori tohunga I've come across my share of odd things, but these last few days have my senses reeling. I'm exhausted, but my mind is working overtime trying to assimilate everything. First we have that 'saucer' sighting, and then people disappearing, yowies, and now telepathy." He chuckled and flicked an ant off the leg of his shorts. "I'm starting to think I'm in an issue of the Fortean Times."

"And don't forget the rest of us had that run-in with the Shadow People," Ratana added.

"Yeah, that must have been terrifying. I've seen shadows before--you know, the corner of the eye things--and once or twice something man-shaped but featureless, but never a whole swarm of them. Lucky for you the Aboriginal spirit came along."

"I'm not so sure it was 'luck'," Ratana said slowly. "We were sent down here by this Tjakkan spirit of Grandfather Mick, so surely he would not just cast us adrift. It would be logical to think he was keeping an eye on us."

"You think the Aboriginal spirit is this Tjakkan?"

"I don't know. I have absolutely no information about Tjakkan except that it was him that Mick got his power from. If I was to guess, I'd say yes, but it could as easily be another servant of Tjakkan. Maybe we should ask Wulgu. He may know."

Spence laughed wryly. "You don't have the impression we've been sidelined? James and Sam were called to this and now they've been removed, so the rest of us are surplus to requirements. I think Wulgu is a somewhat exotic babysitter sent to look after us until James and Sam have completed their assignment."

"I think you're right, but that's okay. Just to meet a yowie in the flesh is amazing, and to be able to communicate...is that a snake?" Ratana leapt up and faced the jumble of rocks from which a dry rustling sound grew louder.

Something dark darted out of the rocks, the sunlight itself dimming around it as if the light was being sucked up. Another followed, and then with an avalanche of scaly slithering, shadows poured from the cracks and crevices between the boulders. Streams swept toward Spence and Ratana while others leapt toward Nathan and Marc. Within seconds, all four were on their feet, frantically batting at the insubstantial shadows, ducking and weaving to avoid them. The tenebrous touch of the dark shadows drew personal fears and buried memories from them of snakes, rats, spiders or the horror of things moving in a dusty sepulchre.

"Keep your mouths closed," Nathan yelled. "They're trying to...get inside us..." He dissolved into a paroxysm of coughing.

Marc fell to the ground, his eyes wide, skin pale, and his mouth open in a rictus of terror, a thin wail of horror issuing from his tortured throat as the beings fluttered and beat at his face.

We can't stop them, Spence yelled inside his head. *We have no defence.*

Nathan! Nathan! Ratana called, but her fiancé just rolled on the ground near Marc, clawing at his throat and uttering choking sounds. She tried to reach Nathan but fell to her knees, her vision misting over as the shadows enveloped her head.

A roaring sound swept over her and she felt herself pulled to her feet and pushed up the slope. The shadows swirled away from her eyes and she saw Wulgu leaping and roaring with rage among the rocks, a broken-off shrub in each hand as he swung and battered at the swarming shadows.

Run! Wulgu mind-bellowed. *Up the slope.*

Nathan can't run, he's choking, Ratana screamed back.

Old man, take the female, I will bring her mate and the weak one. Hurry!

Where the hell can we go? Spence howled. *You said there was no defence.*

Just follow. Wulgu grabbed Nathan under one arm and scooped up Marc, who had thankfully lost consciousness, before bounding past Spence and Ratana as they staggered upward, surrounded by a cloud of the Shadow Beings. He burst up through the last of the vegetation into the zone of crumbled igneous rock that made up the solidified throat of the extinct volcano. Ahead lay a perpendicular face of smooth rock but the yowie did not hesitate, running up to the broken rubble at the base of it before turning to face the two humans stumbling after him.

Spence saw the rock wall barring their way and faltered. *We've had it*, he thought.

Wulgu dropped his burdens unceremoniously and ran his hands over the cliff face in a weaving pattern. *Strength, old man*, he said and picking Nathan up, threw him at the rock face.

Ratana gasped in horror, then again as Nathan sank into the rock as if into a pool of water. The cliff closed behind him, as bare and featureless as it had been a moment before.

It's a portal, Spence said. *Come on!* He led the charge up the last bit of slope and hesitated at the brink. *What about the shadows...*Wulgu grabbed his arm and hurled him at the rock, bundling Ratana into it a moment later and stepping through with an insensible Marc under his arm as the balked shadows crashed impotently against the rock.

16

IIt seems you have the advantage, ma'am," James said politely. "You seem to know us."

Indeed I do, said the woman in white. *Please forgive me. I meet so few humans I forget the niceties of social intercourse. My name is Amaru and I will be acting as your host. Be welcome and at peace.*

"Thank you," James said, but Sam frowned.

You are troubled, Samantha Louis? Amaru asked.

"Your lips are not moving in sync with your words."

That is because I am not really talking as you talk. I am talking to you with my mind.

"You're kidding?"

No, Samantha Louis.

"Just Sam. You are the one who brought us here, sent for us?"

Amaru nodded. *I and others.*

"You couldn't have just asked?"

Amaru smiled. *And would you have come to a complete stranger, in a cavern beneath the Glass House Mountains?*

"I might," Sam said, "If I thought there was a story in it."

There is no story, Sam, for you can tell no one of what you see and hear.

"Then why are we here?" James asked. "Who are you and what is your relationship to Mick Wambiri?"

Your honorary grandfather? I have never met him, nor even spoken to him. He does not know of my existence.

"Why then should he send me here?"

What reason did he give you, that you would obey him?

"He said his spirit guide told him."

Then I suspect that his spirit guide and the ones we call the 'Others' are one and the same, for they warned me of your arrival and instructed me on our course of action.

"Who are these 'Others', and what is this course of action? Why are we here?"

I will tell you soon, but first I must make sure your minds are adjusted. You will have a lot to assimilate.

"And how do you propose to do that?" James asked.

First, let me remind you of the one you call Ernie. He appears and disappears in front of you in ways you do not comprehend, does he not? This is because he is not what he seems. The being you call Cindy is also not what she seems. I believe you each saw something different about her, and whenever you started to think about what she said or did, you got a headache.

"That is true." James nodded, feeling his heart beat faster at the hint of secrets to be revealed.

"You call her a being," Sam said, frowning. "Not a young girl. Why?"

She is a yowie, but to prevent alarm disguised herself by interfering with your visual and auditory centres.

James' eyebrows shot up. "Why was that necessary?"

She was there as a guide, Amaru said. *She was able to perform this more easily when your minds were distracted. Now, the point I wish to make is that what you see is not necessarily what is really there. When you look at me, you see a tall, blonde-haired woman of your own racial type, garbed in a white gown; but that is not who I am. I would like to appear as I really am, but I do not want to alarm you.*

Sam stepped closer to James without conscious thought. "You...you're not a...a monster, are you?"

Amaru smiled. *No, my shape is similar to yours, but I am not quite of your species.*

"Now you intrigue me," James said softly.

That was my intention, Amaru said. *You now desire to see my true shape. Sam, please be assured I mean you no harm.*

Sam nodded. "Go ahead then," she said, her voice exhibiting a tremor of nervousness.

Amaru's image rippled, shrinking in height, changing in proportions. The white gown remained, but the body underneath became browner, hairier, more muscular, and her face changed drastically. Her nose swelled and a shelf of bone protruded above her eyes which became hooded, deepening in their sockets. Amaru's chin receded and her delicate mouth enlarged, pushing forward, the lips parting to reveal buck teeth.

"Damn," James muttered. "*Homo sapiens neanderthalensis.*"

Sam gripped James' arm but stared in fascination at the change enveloping Amaru. "What did you call her?"

"Neanderthal man...or should I say, Neanderthal woman?" James replied with a smile. "But you are wrong, Amaru. You are of our species. Only a variant."

Maybe we were once, thirty or forty thousand years ago, but evolution has drawn us apart. We are now genetically distinct.

"Why have you remained hidden? How many of you are there?"

We are only a few hundred strong, worldwide. As for the other question, I think you know the answer already.

"I thought Neanderthals were cavemen from Europe," Sam said. "What are you doing in Australia?"

We are doing what we were called to do, Amaru replied. *But come, everything will be made clear soon enough, for you have been called for a purpose. We have need of you.* The Neanderthal woman turned and started walking deeper into the illuminated cavern, the structure of her legs and body imparting a peculiarly rolling nautical gait to her motion.

They passed through the cavern into another that was packed with what at first looked like empty cases and stands. Amaru led them down an aisle and as they drew level with a large box-like structure, a light flicked on inside it and both James and Sam gasped at what was revealed. Inside the box and apparently stretching away over kilometres of open grassland to snow-capped mountains was a diorama of a group of primitive humanoids trudging through the waist-high grass. A scattering of plant-eating beasts dotted the landscape and to one side, several hundred metres away it seemed, a pack of carnivores squabbled over the bloodied remains of a kill.

"Australopithecines," James said.

After a few minutes of gazing at the scene, they moved along to the next box that revealed another diorama, this time of a wooded scene and a forest pool. Larger, more human looking, creatures sat around the pool, while the trees and undergrowth partially revealed many smaller animals.

"*Homo erectus*?" James guessed. "These scenes are very well presented, and as far as I can tell, completely authentic, but you didn't prepare these for us, did you?"

No, Amaru said. *Our young use this room, and others, for their education.*

The next diorama held a snowy scene with glaciers and mammoths in the background. The forefront displayed a battle between two groups of humans, one squat and muscular, the other tall and straight-limbed. A member of the former group lay dead on the blood-spattered snow while the others of his tribe withdrew under the threat of his killers.

One of many conflicts between your species and mine, Amaru said softly. *Neanderthals were not war-like, preferring to live in peace with their neighbours, but humans would not let them.*

"Why do you refer to your people as Neanderthals, Amaru?" James asked. "That is the name given to you by humans. What do you call yourselves?"

Amaru smiled sadly. *We call ourselves 'The People' or 'The People of the Stone'.* She delved into her robe and brought out a chunk of shiny black quartz, threaded on a leather thong. She held it out but twitched it away when James tried to grasp it. *This is our totem, the centre of our beliefs. We have always followed the call of the Black Stone.*

"What do you mean by the call?" Sam asked. "Is that like James' quest?"

We will get to that soon. Amaru beckoned them onward, past other dioramas and a series of artefacts set on stands near the scenic exhibits. *Now that civilisation is starting,* she said, *it is instructive to display the objects that fascinate humans. As you see, there are a number of legitimate tools and objects of beauty, but also many weapons.*

They wandered down the aisles looking at and handling stone axes, wooden spears, primitive pots, necklaces, clothing made from skins, copper, bronze and iron implements, swords and maces, together with wheels, jewellery, woven garments, coins and wooden carvings.

"These are all in incredibly good condition," James said, feeling the weave of a snow-white linen kilt from pharaonic Egypt. "Or are they replicas?"

They are the genuine article, Amaru assured him. *My people collected them down the ages as they were produced.*

"But Neanderthals died out," Sam objected. "Or at least...I mean...obviously not, but we thought they did. Why is there no mention of you in history if you were out and about collecting things?"

We did not do it openly. We took articles and left in return something of equal value. Sometimes, I think we engendered tales of fairy folk.

"Why, though? Just to make a museum?" James shook his head. "Don't get me wrong, any museum on earth would kill to get this collection, but if, as you say, you are a different species, where are your own artefacts? Why collect just those of my species?"

Your kind has a saying --'know thy enemy'.

James frowned. "We are enemies?"

Not willingly, but humans have a history of violence, as this record shows. Even you said that museums would kill to get this collection.

"For God's sake! That was a metaphor. It wasn't meant literally."

Perhaps not, but the fact it is a metaphor at all is illuminating. Have a look here. Amaru pointed to what looked like a television screen set on a pedestal. She tapped out a code on a key pad and pictures flashed up in full colour.

For a moment, Sam stared at scenes of marching men, pageantry and banners. She listened to the shouting masses a few seconds longer before she recognised it. "Nazi Germany," she said.

"The Nuremburg Rallies," James agreed, "And Hitler. But these are in full colour. I've only ever seen black and white footage."

These are not ones you have seen, Amaru said. *We took these ourselves.* She pointed at the screen again. *Look.*

The scene changed to methodical activity as units of the German army, SS and quasi-military units plundered the art wealth of Europe, locking up priceless paintings and sculptures in salt mines and bank vaults.

They literally killed to get that collection.

Sam shook her head, tears in her eyes. "You can't use the Nazis as the standard for human behaviour."

No? Amaru's fingers danced over the key pad and the scene changed to a bitter struggle between red-coated soldiers and native tribesmen. *Rorke's Drift, South Africa.* Another code and a tidal wave of mounted armoured men died in the mud, mown down by a small contingent of longbow men. *Agincourt, France.* Amaru's fingers tapped out further codes and they watched, their spirits sinking, as a great procession of armed men, from the distant past to modern day, hacked and stabbed and shot their way through the ranks of their fellow men.

The scenario changed and individuals hunted down victims, men, women and children, murdering them in cold blood and in the heat of passion. Lynchings took place, executions, stonings, crucifixions, and beheadings. The screen altered once more, displaying the carnage that took place on modern roads, the misery that arose from greed, rape, cruelty, abuse, and the rampant destruction of the environment, ending in a blinding flash of light and the horrific tall hats of atomic explosions marching across continents.

James was weeping openly and Sam sobbed on his shoulder as Amaru brought the show to an end.

That last has not happened...yet.

"Why are you showing us all this?" James whispered.

Because I need your thoughts on the matter, Amaru replied. *Why is mankind so violent?*

James shook his head, wiping the tears from his eyes with the back of his hand. He took a clean handkerchief out of his back trouser pocket and passed it to Sam. She wiped her eyes and blew her nose, tucking the fabric into her own pocket.

"You should be asking a psychologist or an anthropologist," he said. "I'm just an ecologist, but I'd say it was something innate."

Amaru frowned, her misshapen face screwing up further. *Innate? You think murdering others of your own species is natural?*

"No, but competition is. As long as there were relatively few people on the planet, the wandering hunters could avoid each other and conflict. As numbers increased, competition for resources became keener."

That is, if you don't mind my saying so, rather simplistic, Professor Hay.

"I never claimed to be an expert, but it seems to me that wars generally take place either because somebody else has what you want, or because somebody else believes something you don't."

Enough to kill for it?

"Evidently."

And what is the solution?

James shrugged. "People have been looking for solutions for ever. Tolerance for differing viewpoints certainly comes into it, and the ability to see that other people are much the same as you. I've always thought that the two most divisive forces on earth are religion and nationalism. How you would get people to change is another matter."

"What are you doing about it?" Sam challenged. "You are quick to blame us, but you're human too. Why haven't you Neanderthals stepped in if you are so against all this violence?"

Amaru stared at Sam for a few moments before nodding. *A fair question. Come with me and I shall give you the answer.* The Neanderthal woman turned and pattered off down the aisle, leaving Sam and James to follow.

"Is all this for real?" Sam whispered as they walked. "Cavemen and high technology seem a bit incongruous."

"There's certainly a high level of strangeness here," James agreed. "On top of which she speaks fluent English, though with a bit of an Australian accent. I suppose that's not too strange, given she's living in Oz."

Sam raised her eyebrows. "I wouldn't have said it was an Oz accent, rather straight Californian."

"Really?"

They stepped through an archway into a much smaller cavern, almost a room, with several large, fabric-covered armchairs arranged around a low coffee table. On one wall was a large television screen and Sam groaned inwardly at the thought of another lecture on man's inhumanity to man.

Nothing like that, Sam, Amaru said gently. *Please, sit.* She indicated two armchairs opposite hers. Amaru stood and waited until the two humans were seated before sitting down. *May I offer you refreshment? Anything at all.*

James stifled the urge to ask for a gin and tonic, just to see what Amaru would say, and asked instead for a coffee. "Jamaican Blue Mountain, if you have it." Sam asked for a Pepsi and Amaru nodded, but made no move to get the drinks or order them. Instead, she say demurely with her hairy hands folded in her lap and looked at Sam curiously.

Forgive me staring, Amaru said quietly. *I have often wondered what you would look like.*

"What do you mean? You know me?"

I knew that you must exist, somewhere, sometime, but until a week ago I did not think it would be anytime soon. Two nights ago I was sure.

"You are talking in riddles," Sam said. "Please explain yourself."

In a moment. Here is your refreshment.

A young Neanderthal swayed through the archway, holding a wooden tray. Smaller than Amaru, the male Neanderthal was otherwise almost identical to her except he wore only a pair of khaki shorts. Bowing to Amaru, he offered the tray to Sam and waited while she removed a tall glass of Pepsi, condensation beading on the cold glass.

James took a steaming cup of coffee from the tray when it was offered. He sniffed, and then sipped. "It is Blue Mountain. That's incredible, or do you normally drink this?"

We do not drink stimulants in any form, Amaru replied, taking a glass of fruit juice from the tray and thanked the young Neanderthal, dismissing him with a nod. *I sent for them when you requested them.*

"You don't drink them yet you had them in your stores?"

Amaru smiled and sipped at her fruit juice. *Sam, you wanted to know why we have not intervened in human history? If you think about it for a moment, you will see why. We number only a few hundred yet, given enough power, we could enforce peace on the world. Why would this not work?*

"You would have constant rebellion," James said slowly, "And you would, over time, have to become just as violent in order to keep the population subjugated."

"So there is no hope?" Sam asked sadly. "No way to rid the world of violence and cruelty?"

I did not say that, but before I talk on this matter, I must lay a little background. Amaru grinned, the effect on her strange-shaped face startling James. *You are wondering how cavemen can be technological. Well, thirty thousand years or so ago, we were not. My people were a variant of yours, living in Europe and adapted to cold climate. We existed by hunting, we used fire, buried our dead, conducted magic rituals, wore clothes and were in balance with nature--as were our cousins* Homo sapiens, *your ancestors. One of the ways in which speciation occurs is by separating out the gene pools...*

"Allopatric speciation," James murmured.

Exactly. The Ice Ages divided the human populations. Neanderthals could thrive amidst the ice, whereas sapiens *preferred the warmer climates. By the time we were contacted, the differences were almost too great. Although we shared a common ancestor, our two lines could no longer interbreed. We had become separate species.*

"Hang on, you said 'contacted'. Contacted by whom?"

The gods. A feeling of amusement swept over Sam and James and they both grinned. *That is what we called them at first, but now we just call them 'The Others'.*

"But who are they?" Sam asked.

I do not know, but I suspect they are non-human and possibly extra-terrestrial.

"Aliens?" James nodded. "We saw a UFO over Tunbubudla."

That was one of ours. Amaru held up a hand. *I will show you later. For now, I must continue with my narrative.* Amaru sipped from her juice again, gathering the thread of her thoughts. *There was one other important difference between my people and* sapiens. *We have no functional larynx and articulated speech was denied us, so we developed other means of communication.*

"But you are talking..."

Not by using a larynx. Neanderthals talk with the mind, as once all humans did. Sapiens *learned to vocalize and lost the use of mind-talk and with it came violence.*

"I don't see how that follows."

Minds in complete communication allow for no misunderstanding, for complete empathy. Violence toward another thinking being is almost impossible. Neanderthals kill only in self-defence and only as a last resort.

"Incredible." James shook his head. "But hang on, how is it that we can hear you? If you are telepathic but we aren't, you wouldn't be able to contact us."

I did say that all humans were once this way. Your ancestors effectively lost the ability because you did not use it, but the 'muscle' has not completely atrophied. I can open up the link with you and you hear my thoughts. Amaru paused, and then added, *And I can hear yours.*

James and Sam gaped in astonishment, and Sam suddenly blushed. "You heard me thinking about another lecture."

162

I don't believe this, James thought. *Science has never found a telepathic capability or even any organ that could conceivably perform it. Come on then, Miss Smartypants--blue, circle, and seven. Let's see you hear...*

Blue, circle, seven, Amaru said quietly. *But I do not have pants, smart or otherwise. It is true, James. Accept it and I will show you later how it is done.*

"Bugger me," James breathed. "Uh, sorry, Amaru. It takes some getting used to."

"Can you hear everything we are thinking?" Sam blushed deeper, cringing in her chair.

The old Neanderthal woman smiled again. *Yes, within limits, but etiquette requires me to ignore most of what you think. Now, to continue--we found that we were too few to influence* sapiens *and persuade them to our peaceful ways, so we sought another, more lasting, solution. The 'Others' pointed it out but we could not start to implement it for thousands of years.* Amaru laughed. *They suggested the science of genetics to cavemen to whom procreation was still a mystery. It was meaningless at first, but by degrees they educated us, protected us, guided our faltering footsteps, and after a few millennia we became proficient at mapping out the human and Neanderthal genome. This was a little before the last Ice Age ended.*

"You're kidding?" Sam said. "You were mapping genes while the rest of us were banging rocks together?"

Technically, no. Your sapiens *predecessors had quite a high level of civilisation before they fell back into savagery about twelve thousand years ago. But in effect yes, we developed a technological society and have maintained it for the last fifteen thousand years. I should stress that this is not because we are inherently more intelligent but rather because we were given a leg-up by the 'Others'.*

"This civilisation you say mankind had," James said, leaning forward intently. "How did it manifest itself? Cyclopean cities and sea-faring nations? Are you talking about an Antarctic society and a crust slippage? The legend of...of Atlantis?"

We can talk about this another time, James. We have full records of the period. But for now I must continue my story. We had a detailed knowledge of Neanderthal and human genomics and guided by our mentors we discovered that the factors that made humans aggressive and ourselves passive, were inbuilt. We actually identified the genes responsible. Along with this came a realisation that the aggression genes were coupled with fertility and a drive to achieve greatness. Our own lack of aggression doomed us to passivity, a declining population, and introspection. We developed telepathy but knowing each other's minds led to stagnation even as it eliminated violence. Each species needed something the other lacked.

"Your knowledge of genetics enabled you to see the problem, but not how to correct it?"

Our two lines diverged some two hundred thousand years ago. We separated, mutated, underwent natural selection and gradually became distinct species, though the process was not irrevocable until a little less than thirty thousand years ago. The problem was, our two lines needed to interbreed, to mingle our genes and to temper your natural aggression and creativity with our telepathic empathy and love of peace.

"I thought we had interbred," James said. "They've identified Neanderthal genes in the human genome."

Yes, there are some, but not enough. Interbreeding took place early on, within the first hundred thousand years, but after aggression gripped the human species, they had less interest in interbreeding.

"Make war, not love," James said with a sad smile.

Something like that.

"And now it's too late," Sam said. "So why do you keep watching, torturing yourselves with what might have been?"

It may not be too late. In the last few hundred years, our own scientists, acting on remarks made by the 'Others', have discovered a way of hybridising species to form viable, intelligent offspring. You have experienced one of these already--the yowie.

"The yowie is artificial?" James gaped. "But it has a long history, in many countries. Sasquatch, Orang Pendek, *Gigantopithecus*..."

We borrowed aspects of legendary creatures so our creations would blend in with folklore. The yowie has genes from many sources but they are predominantly Neanderthal and gorilla. We like to think they show the best aspects of both species.

"Intelligent?"

Very much so. Also gentle, telepathic and...well, they have a few other talents as well. Maybe you can meet one later.

"I'd like that," James said sincerely.

Now, to continue, Amaru said, *Our hybridisation work led us to believe we could change the human gene content by introducing Neanderthal genes, more or less hybridising the two species long after the separation point. After all, it had worked with Neanderthal and gorilla, as well as with other, more distantly related species.* Amaru held up a hand to forestall James' questions. *It did not work. None of the offspring of Neanderthal and* sapiens *were viable. We despaired, and the 'Others' stepped in again, revealing an important combination of genes present in* sapiens *and, to a lesser extent, in us.*

"You rely on these 'Others' a lot, don't you?" James asked. "Do you do everything they say?"

Amaru sat silently for a few minutes. *I can see in your mind you have a picture of aliens dictating to us, telling us what to do--a sort of master and slave relationship. That is not true, though they are vastly superior to us in every way.*

"Yeah, right," Sam muttered. "They've certainly got you believing it."

Maybe in time you will come to see the truth of it, Amaru said mildly.

"So what were these genes you found?" James asked.

Seventeen genes scattered among the races of humans, five of which derive ultimately from Neanderthals. We seek to find an individual with all seventeen, for such an individual may heal the division between our species. About fifty years ago, we developed the technology to test for these genes and we have been sampling humankind ever since.

"How could you sample people?" Sam asked. "Wouldn't people object?"

"I have a feeling they weren't consulted," James growled.

We sought to make the experience non-traumatic but when we found people had memories of the procedures, we had to hide it behind a façade that would not be believed...

"Alien abductions," James said. "You're behind them, not little grey aliens...or is that what the 'Others' look like?"

I do not know what the 'Others' look like, but the ones who did the sampling are in fact, small and grey-skinned. We created them too.

Sam gasped. "I...I had missing time two nights ago. Was I abducted and tested by your greys?"

Amaru nodded. *And once before, just before you came to Australia, as you sat in your apartment in Collinsville. We found then that you have eight of the necessary genes. Naturally you were brought to my notice as another human you knew had the other nine genes.*

Sam frowned. "Marc? Or my sister Andi?"

"I think she means me," James said quietly. "I have had missing time and a scar to prove it." He rubbed his shoulder as he spoke. "You have tested me too."

Yes, James, you have the complementary nine genes. A union between you and Sam would produce the one we seek, the healer of our species.

James stared at the old Neanderthal woman and then burst out laughing. "I'm sorry to have to disappoint you, but gene transfer isn't quite that easy. I may have nine genes and Sam the other eight, but chromatids cross over as sex cells form. Those nine and eight genes are going to get mixed up thoroughly. You'll be lucky to get a sperm or egg with more than three or four of them."

Normally, you would be right, James, so we took some precautions--made some subtle manipulations. All your sperm cells now carry the full complement of the nine targeted genes. Amaru smiled gently at Sam. *And all your eggs have been cultivated to carry the eight you have. Any child born to the two of you is tremendously important.*

"I don't know how you do things in your species," James said with a frown, "But in humans there's a little more to it than just mating. Any woman who has my child is going to be my wife, married because I love her and she loves me; not because of some alien genetics program."

"You tell 'em, buster," Sam growled. "I resent the shit out of you even testing me, let alone fiddling with my private bits. I'll see you in hell before I consent to any of your manipulations."

You are already pregnant, Sam, and the foetus has all seventeen marked genes, Amaru said with a satisfied look. *We have named her Gaia, after your mythological mother of the Earth.*

17

S pence felt himself sink into the rock and for what seemed like several seconds the crystalline nature of its substrate swam in front of his eyes. He wondered how he could possibly breathe as he filtered his way through solid stone and then found he wasn't. The discovery shocked him and he attempted to gasp but could not move a muscle. The greyness around him thinned to murky white and suddenly flashed into brilliance as he tumbled, throwing out his arms to break his fall. He found himself sprawled beside Nathan and sat up just as Ratana fell out of the wall toward him. A moment later, Wulgu stepped through and lowered an unconscious Marc to the floor.

"Where the hell are we?" he croaked, his hammering heartbeat almost drowning out his voice. "Have those things come with us?"

They lack physicality, Wulgu assured him. *The portal will exclude them. Now stay and see to your friends, I will be back shortly.*

"Where are you..." Spence cursed as the yowie strode away. He got shakily to his feet and looked around at a small, featureless cavern with rough white-painted walls and a brilliant light source set into the ceiling about five metres above his head. The space was devoid of furniture or any sort of apparatus and Spence wondered what powered the portal set into the wall they'd just come through.

A groan distracted him from his contemplation of the empty cavern and he looked down at Nathan as he lay on the stone floor with Ratana kneeling beside him. He squatted and put a hand on the young Aboriginal man's shoulder. "You okay, mate? You took a bit of a beating out there."

Nathan nodded. "I think so." He smiled at Ratana. "Good to see ya, darlin'. How's Marc?" He rolled his head to look at the young photographer's supine body.

"He's out to it," Spence said. "I reckon it just got too much for him and he fainted. Can't say I blame him."

Nathan grinned weakly. "Me neither. There were moments there I wished I could have passed out."

"You are all right now though?" Ratana asked anxiously, holding Nathan's hand.

"Yeah, I reckon. I mean, I keep having nightmares but that'll pass." He looked around at the blank cavern walls. "Where are we, and where's Wulgu?"

"Nicely alliterative, mate," Spence grinned. "The yowie went to do something, he didn't say what. As to where this is..." he shrugged, "Inside Tunbubudla or anywhere for that matter. I don't know anything about the capabilities of portals."

"Should we wait here for him or go and look?" Nathan got to his feet and dusted off the seat of his pants.

"We should wait," Ratana said. "Besides, Marc can't go anywhere right now. We should stay with him."

Nathan glanced down at the still body. "Nah, he'll be okay. I just want to see what's through that door there. You with me, Uncle?"

"Sure, why not." Spence followed the young Aborigine over to the arched entrance to the small cavern. They walked through a short passage and looked into a larger cavern. This one was not empty. Ringing the walls were banks of machines, many of them with banks of lights or screens and at them stood people...*no, not people*...tapping at keyboards. Spence stared, his hand on Nathan's shoulder. "Bugger me," he breathed. "When did we come aboard the spaceship?"

"What are they?" Nathan whispered.

"Greys," Spence replied softly. "Traditionally, these are the inhabitants of flying saucers. Didn't you see the Roswell Tapes?"

"Those were fakes."

"Well, of course they were, any fool could see that, but the person who made it knew something about saucer folklore. But this," Spence gestured around the room, "This is the real thing."

"Are they friendly?"

"Sure, they're just likely to operate on you to remove organs and implant transmitters if you can believe the UFO nutters."

"In that case," Nathan whispered. "I think we'll just go back and wait for Wulgu."

As Spence and Nathan started to withdraw, one of the Greys turned its head and saw them. It uttered a twittering cry and every large head on the small bodies turned to stare with huge black eyes at the interlopers. Five of them raced over the stone floor, their feet twinkling and surrounded the two men before they could withdraw. Twittering and uttering fluted cries that incongruously made Spence think of dolphins, they pushed and tugged at the men with surprising strength, leading them into the middle of the cavern.

The Greys were no taller than waist high on Spence, and their grey domed heads tilted back to fix the men's faces with unblinking stares from large black-in-black eyes that resembled wrap-around sunglasses. They had no ears, only tiny holes in the sides of their heads, nostrils without an external nose and a thin lipless slash of a mouth. Squeaking and trilling, the little creatures tugged at the men's clothing, ran cool long-fingered hands over their bodies and separated them from their watches, passing the time-pieces back and forth with little cries of excitement.

"Hey, that's my watch," Spence cried out, making a half-hearted attempt to grab it back. At the sound of his voice, all the Greys stepped back and their almost continuous burbling cries shut off as if a switch had been flicked.

"That got a reaction," Nathan muttered. He bent down at stared into the face of one of the Greys. "Boo!" he said suddenly.

The Grey jumped back, expressionless. A whisper entered Nathan's mind, not unlike Wulgu's mind speech but sibilant and drawn out. *Whoss isssss youss?*

"You heard that?" Nathan asked.

"I did indeed," Spence confirmed. He faced one of the Greys and spoke slowly and clearly. "I am Spence. This is Nathan." He pointed toward the passage and the smaller chamber. "We came through there, with Wulgu."

Wulgusss, repeated the Grey. At once, two detached themselves from the group around the men and raced away, disappearing through an archway at the far end of the cavern.

A few minutes later they returned, scurrying at the feet of the hairy giant. Wulgu frowned and the Greys immediately hurried back to their consoles, though they still glanced round at the men as they worked.

I thought I told you to wait in the portal room.

"Yeah, you did, but you didn't say when you were coming back and we got curious," Spence said.

Please do not talk out loud. It upsets them.

The Greys? Why?

You call them Greys? Ah, I see. Yes, you are correct. Now will you please come back to the portal room? The yowie started to usher them back the way they had come.

"Hang on." Nathan ducked under Wulgu's arm. "Just who are these guys anyway? Are they aliens like Spence says? What are they doing?"

169

Wulgu reached out and grabbed Nathan's collar, hauling him away. *Their real names would be meaningless to you; no, they are not aliens; and they are doing their work despite your interference.* The yowie pushed Spence and dragged Nathan back into the portal room.

"I do have some questions, Wulgu," Spence said.

I will not answer them. It is not my place to.

"Who will then?"

Wulgu was silent for a while, then, *Garagh says he will talk to you.*

"Who's Garagh?"

Be quiet and come with me and you will find out. Exasperation flavoured Wulgu's mind speech, so Spence just shrugged. *Now, stand close to Marc.*

"Why?" Ratana asked.

Are all humans so annoying?

"Not all of us," Nathan replied. His grin slipped as the chamber rippled with static and changed. He looked around at a comfortably furnished chamber and jumped when he saw the two beings standing to one side.

One looked rather like the tiny Greys, though if you were describing this being based on skin colour, Blue-grey would be closer to the mark. He had the same domed head and wrap-around black eyes, but he stood as tall as a man and had extremely long, almost prehensile fingers. The only familiar thing about him was the neatly pressed white laboratory smock he wore, but this piece of clothing served only to make him look more alien.

The other creature was man-like, but a warped parody of a man--thickset, bandy-legged and with a skull that looked as if a plastic doll's head had been put into a heated oven. Intelligence shone out of dark brown eyes set under prominent eye ridges and a nonexistent chin had the effect of pushing an already prominent nose into a snout-like protuberance. He was covered in reddish hair and wore a pair of baggy blue shorts.

Thank you, Wulgu, said the man-like creature, broadcasting mentally. *You are all welcome. Please be seated and take refreshment.* He waved at the chairs and flasks of fruit juices and water set on a low table. When nobody moved he spoke again. *No harm will come to you. My name is Garagh, and I am what I believe you call a Neanderthal. My colleague here...*The Blue-grey inclined its swollen head...*is Doctor Ponatuo. I have asked him here to tend to your distressed friend.*

"I iss pleasssed to meet you," Dr Ponatuo hissed. "I belief you prefer vocalissed ssspeech?"

"Er, we are used to it," Spence replied, *But we can manage either, I think,* he finished mentally.

"Ah, yesss, you iss very good, but I likesss to practiss my Englisssh." He walked over to where Marc lay on the floor, and bent over him. "What iss the matter wit' him?"

"I think it was the shock of too many new things," Ratana explained. "Er, all this..." she waved her hand around vaguely, "...and the shadow creatures. He just fainted and hasn't come round."

"Come round? Ah, you mean he hasss not woken up." He examined Marc and lifted his eyelids. "He iss not unconsssciousss, he jussst doesss not want to fassse up to reality. I t'ink he iss in catatonic ssstupor."

"Can you cure him, doc?" Nathan asked.

"Oh yesss. But it may help to keep him asssleep for a while. I will hypnotisse him and give him sssome delayed sssuggesstionss. It will help him cope better." *Wulgu, would you help me please?*

The yowie lifted Marc gently and carried him from the chamber, Dr Ponatuo loping behind. Garagh, the Neanderthal, gestured toward the chairs and drinks.

Spence seated himself and looked suspiciously at Garagh. "Where are James and Sam, our companions?"

Wulgu has explained mental speech? Garagh asked. *I wish you to feel at ease.*

"I guess," Spence replied, shrugging his shoulders.

"You can't speak vocally?" Nathan asked. "If it's all the same to you I'd rather you weren't poking around in my head."

"I agree," Ratana said, "But not for that reason. I just think that we are most comfortable talking naturally and I've experienced enough new things today. I think I'd like to give that one a rest for now."

Neanderthals lack the vocal apparatus enabling true speech, Garagh said. *But I can induce the appearance of it by subtly manipulating the appropriate parts of your brains. I will still be talking mentally, but you will imagine my lips are moving.*

"I'm not sure that makes me feel better," Nathan replied. "You're still poking around in our minds."

"The appearance of speech will be fine," Ratana said. "Listening to you now, I can't tell the difference."

Very well, then in answer to your question, James and Sam are well and are being entertained by one of my companions in another part of this complex beneath the Glass House Mountains.

"They are in good health?"

Indeed. Their health and well-being are of great importance to us.

"When can we join them?"

Soon. They are learning why they are here. When they have grasped and accepted their parts in unfolding events, we shall reunite you.

"And what is this part they play? What events are you talking about?"

You may ask them when you see them next. It is not my place to talk about private matters.

"What about the events?" Ratana asked. "All right, you have brought Sam and James here for a purpose and I accept it is personal and you can't talk about it, but what about the events taking place that led you to bring them here? Can you talk about them?"

Garagh nodded. *Yes, for though your companions are central to our purpose, your help will also be needed.* The Neanderthal man poured himself a glass of water and sipped at it pensively. *Thirty thousand years ago, I brought my tribe out of Europe and across the Asian land bridge to Australia...*

Nathan giggled, thinking that Garagh's continued speech while he drank the water was like a ventriloquist's show.

"What?" Spence said. "Sorry, I think I misheard you. How long ago?"

Thirty thousand years.

"That's nuts," Nathan said. "Nothing lives that long."

"I have to agree," Spence added. "Even bristlecone pines only live three or four thousand, and tortoises are the oldest animals at a couple of hundred. This has some mythological meaning for you, obviously. By you, you mean your people, perhaps."

No, Garagh said gently. *I mean myself. I have lived for over thirty thousand years.*

"And you don't look a day over twenty thousand," Nathan said with a laugh.

"Do you have any proof of this claim?" Spence asked.

You can ask Wandjina, Garagh replied. *He was there too.*

"Wandjina?" Ratana asked. "Why would you call someone after the Aboriginal creator spirit?"

You will have to ask him that. It is the name by which I have always known him.

"So let me see if I have got this right." Spence said. "You say you are thirty thousand years old and offer by way of proof a man who calls himself a god and was with you back then? You will understand why I'm not convinced."

Garagh smiled. *Yes, I'm sorry, I forgot. You are a scientist and do not believe anything you cannot measure. Well, in this case I do not have the proof you need. You can either accept my word or dismiss it. It does not matter to me.*

Spence coloured slightly and looked away. "You were saying...you, or your people, came out of Europe?"

Yes. Your species was pressuring mine. We only wished to hunt and observe the seasons and our customs, live peaceably with our neighbours, but we were pushed gradually out of the best caves, away from the best hunting sites, and sometimes even killed. One day I found a black rock where none had been before. I picked it up, marvelling at the colours that playing over its shiny black surface--and the sky spirits spoke to me. They told me that I had been chosen to lead my people away from their ancestral hunting grounds, far to the south-east, where my people would achieve a destiny far more worthy than any that could be had there. Naturally, I did not immediately believe them, for how could I know they were indeed sky spirits and not evil ones from the dark places? I asked for a sign from the sky and they gave me one. That night, a great star fell from the sky, but it did not fall to earth. It hovered above our cave, turning the night into day, and the sky spirits spoke to us all, asking of us obedience and promising great rewards. Garagh smiled and shrugged. *How could we refuse?*

"Who were these sky spirits, these saucer people?" Spence asked. "Did you find out?"

I have never seen them, Garagh admitted. *We call them the 'Others'.*

"And they speak through a black rock? Is this the same black rock that sent us here?"

Garagh nodded. *The 'Others' communicate through them. I carry one always.* The old Neanderthal man lifted a small black quartz crystal on a leather thong from amongst the long reddish hairs covering his chest and leaned forward. *Through this I can hear the 'Others'.*

Spence and Nathan leaned forward to examine it, and when Nathan sat back, Ratana took his place. "Are you listening to them now? she asked. "Are they telling you to say this?"

No. They allow us autonomy of action for the most part, being content to advise and guide us, but sometimes they will issue a direct command.

"What is it they wanted you to do?" Spence asked. "Are you allowed to tell us?"

Our task was to monitor the growth of human civilisation and its impact on the environment. When it became obvious that your species was overrunning the planet and heading for catastrophic environmental breakdown, they asked us to attempt an intervention.

"Bloody hell! They don't ask much, do they? Do you have the resources for an intervention? A global network? The technology?"

We have the means to end the human race but we will not use it. Your species is no more at fault than a child born with a cleft palate is at fault for its condition. The fault stems from millennia ago when our two species diverged. You carry a mutation that stimulates extreme aggression. It was our initial task to ameliorate this condition by breeding in the passive allele from Neanderthal stocks. We failed in this and now our species are too far apart for interbreeding to occur. Even were it not so, our genetic base is now too small. With extended life comes decreased fertility and we now number less than five hundred individuals, of whom only ten are children. We have a doubtful future.

"I'm sorry," Spence muttered awkwardly. "What can you do then? I agree with you that mankind is ruining the earth, though I'm not at all sure what can reasonably be done about it."

The 'Others' have told us that a child will be born who can save both species.

Nathan grinned. "A Messiah?"

If you like. She has been conceived already.

"No kidding? Where?"

In the Blue Mountains a week ago. To your friends James and Sam.

The three humans gaped, speechless. "Th...that's imp...impossible," Spence stuttered. "James was up north a week ago and Sam was still in the States. Besides, they're not an item."

More time has passed than you are aware of.

Spence stared at Garagh. "Lost time again?" he whispered. "Why?"

To make sure the embryo survives. It is essential to our purposes.

Ratana frowned. "They agreed to this plan of yours?"

No, but they mated without our help. We merely ensured the right gametes came together to produce an embryo with the required genetic makeup.

"Oh, they will be pleased," Ratana murmured. "Where do you get off doing this to people?"

You disapprove? Garagh looked mildly surprised. *It was necessary. The alternative would have been far worse.*

"I thought you said you would not end the human race."

Not end it, but induce sterility until the numbers dropped to the carrying capacity of the planet.

"Jesus, even that's bloody draconian," Spence said. "How would this messiah of yours save things?"

We don't know. The 'Others' tell us that a child bearing particular genetic markers, which it does, could save both our species. They have not told us how.

"But you trust them?"

They have shown themselves to be trustworthy over the last thirty thousand years. Can you point to a human government that has fulfilled its promises for that long?

Nathan snorted. "You'd be lucky if you could trust one for thirty months."

"Well, I suppose it's not down to us anyway," Spence said. "This is a child of James and Sam. It will be their decision to keep it or not. We're just on the sidelines."

Not entirely, Garagh said. *Why do you think I am telling you all this? I want you to join your friends, Spencer Tuhua, and persuade them to co-operate.*

Spence laughed ruefully. "You've obviously never tried to get James to do anything against his will. And from what I've seen of Sam's character, she'll be immovable too."

Do your best, I beg you. This child is of vital importance.

Spence nodded and Ratana joined in. "We can give it a go, but if James and Sam are adamant, I will support their decision, whatever it may be."

Thank you, Ratana, but I have another task for you and Nathan.

On cue, an Aboriginal man walked into the room and greeted the three humans. Ratana leapt to her feet, while Nathan grinned and Spence nodded. "Ernie," she cried. "What are you doing here?"

"I have come to speak to you and Nathan, but first, Spencer Tuhua, you have a duty elsewhere. Wulgu will take you, he is waiting just outside."

Spence made his farewells to his friends but hesitated in front of Garagh. "Will I see you again? I have a feeling you could answer many of my questions."

We will see each other again, I am sure. Garagh stood and waited while Spence left the chamber.

You will not wipe his memory of these events afterward? Ernie asked on an intimate mode. *It might be safer.*

No, Wandjina. The child will have need of human protectors as well as parents. These three humans will serve well.

But not the other young man?

I could not ask it of him, he has been through enough. His memory of the last few days will be erased and some false memories implanted.

Very well, Garagh. It is your decision.

Ernie sat down cross-legged in an armchair and smiled at the young Aboriginal man and the Torres Strait Islander woman. "You know that the one called Cindy is a yowie? She has been wounded by Guilford King and the situation is quite serious."

Ratana's eyes opened wide and glistened suddenly. "I thought it was just a flesh wound. Oonoo said..."

"No, no, you misunderstand. She is hurt but recovering quickly. The situation that has arisen from the shooting is serious however. Guilford King collected her blood and hair at the site of the shooting and has submitted it to three independent laboratories for analysis. This could potentially be disastrous if the attention of the world is drawn to us at this time. We do not want firm evidence for the existence of the yowie to emerge."

"What will the results of the analysis show?" Nathan asked.

"That an unknown primate is wandering around the Blue Mountains outside of Australia's largest city."

Nathan grinned. "That'll put the proverbial cat among the pigeons."

"We must stop it."

"How do you propose to do that? I can't see King doing it willingly."

"We could destroy the samples," Ernie said.

"How?"

Ernie hesitated. "Suffice it to say it could be done. What I want to ask you is what effect this would have on proceedings. Would it solve the problem?"

"It could," Nathan replied cautiously. "The lack of any concrete evidence would reduce the whole thing down to the declaration of one man."

"The problem is," Ratana added, "King has a reputation as a scientist-- rapacious, single-minded and bullying, but also multi-published. If the samples mysteriously disappeared, from three separate laboratories, he could make a lot of mileage off a conspiracy of silence or something. And if he has kept back any samples, he might just resubmit them with tighter security."

"That's true," Nathan agreed. "If you've got the capability to make them disappear, maybe you could just switch the samples."

"That would be harder," Ernie admitted. "What would you switch them with?"

Nathan shrugged. "Anything. It scarcely matters what."

"Blood and hair of something ordinary, a wallaby maybe," Ratana added. "But what if they have been tested already? If the results are sitting in an envelope somewhere, or in an email, or on a computer, then switching the samples is not going to help.

"Another problem might be that when he gets the negative results back from the labs, he just goes ahead and has a press conference anyway. He won't have the solid evidence but his name still carries some weight, so you need to discredit him somehow, make him look ridiculous."

"I doubt the samples have been tested yet," Ernie said. "He arrived in Sydney two days ago and held a small press conference yesterday where he showed the samples, and announced which labs had agreed to test them. He also plans to open the results at the next press conference in a week's time. He said the world will see them at the same time he does."

"That's just stupid," Nathan said. "What if he got a negative result? It would blow his case out of the water."

"He obviously feels confident enough in the results," Ratana said. "After all, he knows he was there and knows what he shot. For him, the lab results will be a foregone conclusion. And think how spectacular it'll be, opening up the old 'Oscar' envelope to announce the winner. If nothing else, King is a showman."

"So we need to switch the samples immediately," Ernie concluded.

"You can do that?" Nathan asked.

"I think it could be done. King announced the names of the laboratories doing the testing and I have technicians tracking down the spatial coordinates at the moment."

"And when you find them?"

"Then you go in and get them."

"Us?"

"Why not? You said you wanted to help."

"Yeah, but...er, you guys must do this all the time. Wouldn't it be better to send a professional?"

If we had time, we could send a Grey, Garagh said quietly. *But we cannot wait until the night and I cannot send him in the daytime. Neither can I send one of my own people. Imagine the uproar if either an alien or a caveman were seen in a city laboratory.* The old Neanderthal smiled broadly, his old, misshapen face crinkling with good humour.

"They won't be too happy to see one of us either," Nathan grumbled. "How do I explain my presence if...when...I'm caught?"

"You won't have to do any explaining," Ernie reassured him. "We'll put you into the lab when it's empty, wearing a white coat or whatever uniform they wear there. You go straight to the refrigerator, remove the samples, label the fake bags appropriately with a marker pen, and step back through the portal. If anyone stops you, bluff your way out if you can. If you can't, we'll be keeping an eye out and will bring you back."

"Why can't you do it?"

Ernie smiled sadly. "If you and Ratana refuse, I will do it myself."

"And what happens to us?"

"Nothing. We will remove your memories of this place and the things you have experienced. It will be as if it never happened."

"I'm doing it," Ratana said firmly.

Nathan frowned and massaged his temples lightly. "Yeah, I guess I'll do it too."

Ernie and Garagh led the two young people through a series of caverns to where a small group of little Greys were clustered around a machine that seemed to rely more on beauty and graceful lines than on strict utilitarian functionality. Instead of the usual straight lines and box-like body, the inner workings of the machine were contained within curving lines of glass, metal and wood. A glowing screen, across which ran multi-coloured figures, was under the control of one Grey, whose long fingers danced over a curved keyboard. Another turned a series of knobs, his attention focused on the screen, while two others manipulated jointed-arm extensions of the machine that swept to one side and ended in crescent-shaped sections. Between the two crescents rippled a disturbance in the air, but despite the wavering scene between the arms, the image seen through the disturbance was not of the cavern. The Greys made some last adjustments to the dials and the rippled air snapped clean and clear, as if a rumpled sheet of plastic had suddenly been drawn tight.

Nathan and Ratana stared into the circle between the crescents, holding onto each other as vertigo swept over them. The scene a metre from their noses was an aerial shot of a building, apparently from a hundred metres or so in the air.

"Redfern Laboratories," Ernie said.

The scene lurched and Nathan closed his eyes and stumbled, while Ratana gasped. They plummeted through the roof of the building, down through ceiling, pipes and insulation and into a laboratory, where they seemed to hover a metre over the heads of three people sitting at benches.

"What if they look up?" Ratana whispered.

Ernie laughed. "They can't hear you, nor can they see you. If they were very keen sighted, they might see dust motes tumbling in a small vortex, but nothing more."

"Now what?"

"Now we wait for lunchtime," Ernie said. A Grey brought a white lab coat and a box to Ernie. "Who's going to do the first one?" he asked.

Nathan gulped and glanced at Ratana. "I will."

"Good man." Ernie handed him the lab coat, a marker pen and two plastic bags, one containing some stained, wilted leaves, and the other a small tuft of hair.

Minutes passed, and the three people stretched, chatted a bit and wandered out of the lab. The Greys altered the orientation of the portal, bringing it to floor level and verticality. Another fiddle with the dials and the portal expanded until it was almost two metres across.

"There we go," Ernie said. "The fridge is straight ahead. You have the replacement samples? Good, off you go."

Nathan took a deep breath and, after a glance at Ratana, advanced shakily on the portal. Gingerly, he stepped over the threshold and found himself in the laboratory. Heart beating faster, he looked back but the cavern and Ratana had disappeared. The only thing that betrayed the position of the portal was a slight sparkle to the air as if tiny flecks of mica danced in a beam of sunlight.

Voices broke in on Nathan's thoughts and he turned and hurried toward the fridge. Opening it, he started rummaging through bags and bottles inside, looking for leaves and hair. There weren't many samples and he found the ones he wanted almost immediately. With shaking hands, he took them out and carefully copied the notations onto the bags he had brought with him. Placing these into the fridge, he pocketed the ones from Guilford King and turned to leave, just as the door of the lab opened.

A young woman walked in and was several paces into the room before she saw Nathan. "Oh, I didn't see you...who are you? What are you doing here?"

"Gidday," Nathan said with a smile. "I'm looking for...Johnny. This is where he works, isn't it?"

The woman hesitated. "There's no Johnny here. What's your name?"

"Look, there's no need to be afraid. Come in and shut the door."

The woman's eyes opened wide and she backed out of the room rapidly, shouting for help. As soon as she was out of sight, Nathan stepped back through the portal and the Greys closed it.

"Piece of cake," Nathan said with a grin. He handed the samples to Ernie and the lab coat to Ratana. "Your turn."

It took half an hour before the portal machine zeroed in on the second laboratory--Highfield Analysis--but the room was deserted when the portal opened. Ratana went through and was back within five minutes, breathless but with a broad smile on her face. "That was fun," she said. "I want to do the third one too."

"What's in the new samples?" Nathan asked Ernie as Ratana rummaged through the last fridge.

Ernie just smiled. "Wait and see. Guilford King is going to wish he hadn't done any of this."

18

S am stared at the old Neanderthal woman, the blood draining from her face. "You arrogant bitch," she whispered.

James got up and moved across to Sam and stood beside her, one hand on her shoulder. "What the hell were you thinking?" he snarled. "That we would thank you for using us for your damned breeding program as if we were cattle or something? You had no right."

Amaru frowned and looked from one to the other. *What is the problem? This child is vitally important to both our species. Surely you can see that?*

"Well, let me tell you your species can go hang itself if you are typical of it," James said. "If you've studied our species as thoroughly as you say you have, you'll know that whenever any tyrant has introduced a breeding program, all right-minded people have fought against him."

"It's immoral," Sam added. "And deeply repugnant. I feel as if...as if I've been raped."

Amaru started to laugh and then stopped suddenly as she caught the look of fury on Sam's face. *I see no humour in the situation but I thought you were using hyperbole to make your argument*, Amaru explained. *Surely you realise that the impregnation was by natural means? You only became pregnant when you and James coupled beside the lake a week ago.*

"Two nights ago," James corrected.

A week, Amaru reiterated. *You lost some time in the tunnel. We had to be sure implantation of the embryo took place.*

"Implantation is not that rapid," James said, staggered at the revelation. "You'd need at least two weeks for that."

Normally, yes. However, we have refined our techniques of embryo development and we have accelerated growth to about the third month.

"What?"

"What's she talking about, James?"

"If I understand her correctly, she is saying we lost time again--about a week--and while we were gone they accelerated the development of the embryo so it is now about three months old."

Sam's hands dropped to her belly and she looked down at them. "Three months?"

"How can you accelerate something like that?" James asked. "You'd risk..." his voice tailed off as he thought better about declaring his misgivings.

There is no risk, Amaru assured him. *Given how important this child is to us, do you think we would do anything to jeopardise the health of either mother or child?* The old Neanderthal shrugged. *As for exactly how it is done, you would have to ask our scientists. Remember, we have been studying such things for thousands of years.*

"I'm not ready for this," Sam said. "When I decide to have a baby it is going to be my choice. I can't just rearrange my whole life because it suits somebody else. Take it back, rear it outside my body if you must, but take it away, please."

Does a baby arrive only by choice? Amaru asked. *Can you truly plan such an event?*

Sam bit her lip and shook her head. "Obviously not. Besides, that is not the point. You took away any choice I had in the matter by...hang on, I'm on the pill. I can't be pregnant."

We negated the effects of the contraceptive chemicals when we gave you a physical checkup, flushing them from your body. Rima switched the pills in your pack with a placebo.

Sam swore, colourfully. "That makes it worse. You have used me at every stage, right from when you made me come over here to Australia."

Not used, Sam, only guided. You already had feelings for James and our sampling had indicated you may have been the one to carry the genetic markers. Your sister Andi was another possibility, though she lacks two of the desired markers. We influenced your mind, I admit, but only to do something you had contemplated already. After all, did you not mean to couple with him in San Francisco when you first met him? Your memories and desires were easy to read.

Sam flushed deep red. "Those are private thoughts," she forced out. "Again, you have no right."

James hid a grin. "You wanted me then?" he whispered. "I sure as hell wanted you, and not because of any damn breeding program. I was falling in love even then."

Sam twisted in her seat and stared up at James, tears in her eyes. "You were? And now...?"

"Now I'm in love, Sam. I've known since you first walked into my office in Townsville."

"Me too." Sam's hand grasped James' and he bent over and kissed her lingeringly on the lips. She squeezed his hand and turned back to Amaru. "This doesn't let you off the hook. You're still a bitch in my book."

Ah! Amaru turned toward the cavern entrance with some relief. She stood a few seconds before Spence entered, with Wulgu just behind him. *You are welcome, Spencer Tuhua. My name is Amaru, daughter many times removed of the one you know as Garagh.*

James goggled at the huge yowie, whose head towered above them all. "Is...is that...my God. Spence, is that a...a yowie?"

"Hey Jimmy, hi Sam. Yeah, that's Wulgu. Ain't he something, though? You can say hello to him, if you like." Spence turned toward the mountainous creature. "Wulgu, this is Professor James Hay and Samantha Louis. James, Sam, this is Wulgu."

I am pleased to meet you at last, James and Sam. Your coming has been anticipated.

James sat down on the edge of an armchair and stared at Wulgu. "Did I just hear him...?" *No, I must be imagining things.*

I am not a creature of imagination, James and Sam. You really did hear my inner voice. If you think back at me, I can hear you.

Jesus!

A feeling of mirth washed over Sam and James. *Your friend Marc said something similar.*

"Marc?" Sam said quickly. "How is he? And the others?"

He is being looked after, while Nathan and Ratana help Garagh and Wandjina with a problem.

"Wandjina?"

You know him as Ernie.

"And you're a yowie?"

My kind is called that sometimes.

James looked away suddenly. "I'm sorry, I'm staring."

Perhaps we can talk later. I have much to discuss with you.

"I...I'd like that." James stood again as Wulgu left the cavern the way he'd come. "Bloody hell," he breathed. "That was something."

Spence grinned. "Told you so." *You can hear his thoughts too?*

James jumped and Sam stared.

"God, the expression on your faces," Spence crowed. *Wulgu explained it to me as a dammed up stream. Once the dam is broken you can communicate mentally. He says it is something we all have.*

Spencer Tuhua, Amaru interposed quietly. *I appreciate that you have many new things to discuss with your friends, but I would be grateful if you could turn your mind to our current disagreement and convince James and Sam that we have their best interests at heart.*

"Eh? Oh, sure. Congratulations, by the way, Sam. You too, James. Garagh told us the good news."

"I don't think congratulations are in order," Sam grated.

"Who's Garagh?" James asked.

"A Neanderthal man. I gather he's the leader of the tribe. He claims to be thirty thousand years old."

"Surely not? Cellular degeneration..."

"Can you please forget about these details, James? We have more important things on our minds now."

James nodded. "You're right, of course, Sam. It's just that there is so much happening."

Spence grinned. "I told Garagh he'd have a fight on his hands with you two."

"It's not funny, Spence, so wipe that smirk off your face."

"Yeah, sorry, Sam. I was just envisioning anyone trying to make you do something you didn't want to do." Spence managed to look serious. "You'd better tell me all about it."

James nodded. "If I may...The Neanderthals have appointed themselves, or been appointed by aliens, as the guardians or guards--I'm not quite sure on that point--of humans. They say they've been doing this for thousands of years. Now, they claim our species is violent by nature whereas theirs is peaceable. They would like to weld the two species together but our genetic makeup is now incompatible..."

"Genetic drift?" Spence asked.

"Exactly. They claim to have identified genetic markers in humans that would, if gathered together in one individual, produce someone who could 'heal' the two species in some undefined way. A sort of messiah, if you like. In the course of routine abductions and testing of the human race, they came across Sam with eight of the seventeen necessary genes, and me, with the other nine. They engineered things so that we mated...made love, and produced a child that will have all seventeen genes."

"Yeah, that's a good story but it can't happen," Spence said. "No, strike that, not impossible--but it would have a vanishingly small chance of happening. Crossing over would scatter the genes. Unless they're linked of course." He looked at Amaru. "Are they?"

The old Neanderthal woman shook her head. *Two lots of three on chromosomes seven and eleven, but the others are all independently assorted.*

"There you go then," Spence concluded. "One in a billion, or less."

"Except she claims that when Sam and I were abducted, they fixed our gametes so that those genes would have to be passed on."

"Ah, that's a neat trick."

"Then after we conceived..."

"We, indeed," Sam sniffed.

"... We lost time again and they accelerated the growth of the embryo to about the three month stage. They've even had the cheek to name it--Gaia."

"Gaia? That's Greek for 'good mother' isn't it? There was a dinosaur..."

"You're thinking of Maiasaurus," James interrupted. "This is Gaia, also Greek, basically meaning 'Mother Earth'."

"Ah, yes, that's right. Then there was the Gaia hypothesis by Lovelock..."

"Damn it, will you guys stop flapping your jaws about inconsequential details and sort this pile of shit out?"

"Sorry, Sam," James soothed. "Well, Spence, what do you think? Are we justified in being angry with these damn interfering Neanderthals?"

"Definitely, but may I ask Amaru some questions? Just to satisfy my curiosity--and maybe clarify a few points."

Sam shrugged and James said, "Go ahead, though I doubt she'll tell you anything useful."

If I can answer, I will, Amaru said.

"Okay. First of all, how important is this child Gaia to you?"

There has not been a more important individual conceived in the last thirty thousand years.

"Why is she so important?"

I'm not sure I can answer that, Amaru said hesitantly. *In theory, it is because our two species were supposed to be one, or at least closely related, but we have grown apart. Your species is active and ruining the planet and ours is passive and dying out instead of both being vigorous and environmentally friendly. The 'Others' say this Gaia child can achieve this, which is why we have been guided to bring her into being, but how she will do it, I do not know.*

"You haven't been told?"

No.

"Have you any thoughts on why a totally human child is so important? Why should these seventeen genes all be human ones?"

I have pondered that question often, Amaru admitted. *After all, we have the capability to engineer Neanderthal genes with those of several animals, but we have been expressly forbidden to experiment with humans. All I can think is that humans either have some hidden capability that will help the 'Others' achieve their goal, or else some of those genes came from a distant Neanderthal ancestor.*

"Just while we are on the subject...sorry, Sam, but I must ask...what Neanderthal-animal hybrids have you created?"

Gorilla, Amaru replied. *Yowies were the result. Also dolphin, orca, otter and seal.*

"Good God," James exclaimed. "That water creature we saw in the underground lake--was that one of your hybrids?"

No, that was a natural creature, related to a seal. They are on the brink of extinction though, surviving only where we can protect them. You have seen Greys though. They have cetacean ancestry.

"Okay," Spence said. "Getting back to the main subject--did you not think that such interference in human morality could be counterproductive? Humans are fiercely independent and bitterly resent being manipulated, particularly in the field of reproduction."

I can see that now, Amaru admitted. *But can you appreciate my dilemma? We have waited fifteen thousand years for these two individuals, containing between them all seventeen genes. Then we have to make sure they mate. Luckily, they are inclined to do so without our help, but the problem of crossing over is insurmountable unless we manipulate their gametes. Should we interfere or leave it to chance?*

Spence considered a few moments. "You said Sam and James were already inclined to do the naughty." He grinned broadly. "Why couldn't you just let nature take its course? I mean, you have a long history of abductions and you'd already tested and manipulated Sam's and James' gametes. Couldn't you just have been sneaky and not told them? Then in nine months, Gaia would be born and nobody would be any the wiser."

A large number of embryos spontaneously abort in the first few weeks of pregnancy, Amaru said calmly. *What if Gaia was one of them? What if, before they had an opportunity to try again, something happened to one or both of them? They are each one in ten billion. Together, they may never arise again. I could not take the chance. Then there is the raising of Gaia. That cannot be left to chance. We could not risk the parents might separate or that we would not have an input into her education. We had to make Sam and James aware of the great responsibility we had laid upon them.* Amaru looked at Sam with a gentle expression. *Forgive me, Sam. It was my decision and not one I took lightly. Believe me, I can feel your hurt and pain, but I did what I thought to be right. I had hoped you might see this from my viewpoint, from a wider perspective.*

"Oh, I can," Sam sighed. "It still doesn't give you the right though. I'm the one that has to go through this pregnancy. I'm the one that has to rear the kid for the next twenty years or so..."

"Not alone," James murmured. "Whatever you decide is okay by me, even if it's not wanting me around. I hope you'll let me be with you though."

Sam smiled and squeezed his hand. "You'll be the first to know."

You will have us too, Sam, Amaru said. *If you want us.*

Sam nodded. "I need to think about that."

I love you Sam.

??

It's me. Trying out that opened up stream. It seems to be working.

James? Holy shit. I can hear you.

And I can hear you, loud and clear.

Did you mean it?

What? Oh, yes, that. Yes, I love you and want to be part of your life. Read my mind, Sam. Go deep. I won't hide anything.

!!

Yes.

I love you too, James. See?

(Both) Yes!

Spence laughed out loud. "What sappy expressions you're both wearing."
I'm guessing you're talking mentally?

Sam blushed. James grinned but asked, *You can't hear us?*

Nope, rest easy. I gather as long as you direct your thoughts at a particular person; you sort of lock onto that person's mental signature and can't be overheard.

Do not tell them otherwise, Amaru. Garagh's mental voice spoke to the old Neanderthal woman alone.

That's right, isn't it, Amaru? Spence asked.

Is what right? Spence explained what he had been talking to Sam and James about, and Amaru nodded. *You can be as private as being alone.* She hesitated before continuing. *Sam, I must ask. Have you reached a decision concerning Gaia?*

"I won't terminate it...her, if that's what you mean."

I am glad, Sam, but that was not exactly what I meant. Her genetic makeup is only part of the solution. I would like to be sure she is emotionally stable and is educated in a loving household. I do not know what the 'Others' intend for her, but I'd like to make sure she has a good start.

Sam squirmed. "I...I've never had a child before, but I'm sure I will grow to love her. I can provide for her at least."

"We can provide," James said firmly. "Don't shut me out, Sam. I beg you."

Sam turned and looked at James and for many seconds, neither spoke. Amaru kept her eyes averted but monitored the silent conversation, forcing her face to hide her growing elation. *They have accepted Gaia and will raise her,* she called to Garagh. *Should we tell them of...?*

No! You will not let even a hint of that escape your mind.

"Okay, here's the deal," Sam said to Amaru. "I want to be sure you accept this right from the git-go, no misunderstandings. James and I will raise Gaia, educating her properly and if you want to lend a hand that's okay too, but you run it past us first. When she reaches the age of eighteen, you can ask her...ask, mind...if she wants to participate in this solution of the 'Others'. If she decides against it, there is to be no argument, you back off and leave her alone. Is that understood?"

I understand, Sam.

"Do you accept it as well as understand?" James asked sharply.

Amaru gazed at him enigmatically. *I accept your conditions.*

"Do you swear you will? Do you have a deity or holy name you bind yourself to for cementing promises?"

Amaru smiled. *The closest thing we have to a god are the 'Others', though in truth I do not know if they are one or many. They are beings, I am sure, but so powerful, so knowledgeable, that they might as well be a god. I can take an oath on them if it will reassure you.*

"I cannot see how that would bind you. I think we will just have to accept your word on this."

Amaru inclined her head. *I thank you for your trust.*

An awkward silence fell over the four people, though Sam and James shared intimate thoughts, tentatively planned the future.

Spence cleared his throat. "Er, so...is that it? Are we here for anything else, or can we go home now?"

You may go if that is your wish, though you are welcome here whenever you want. We will show you how you can contact us. You, Spence, said you wanted to get to know Wulgu better. Ratana and Nathan are to be trained by Wandjina, and we have work for you, Sam and James, if you agree.

"I'd like to stay," Spence said, "But I think we'd better take Marc out to civilisation first. If we can come back, I'd like to."

Amaru nodded. *That is a good decision. Sam, James, while you are gone, you can start Gaia's education.*

Sam's eyebrows rose. "Start how? You mean by playing music to her, or singing?"

"She's a bit young for that," James agreed. "Even for an accelerated three month old fetus."

I meant by talking to her, showing her things, answering her questions. Things like that.

"I'm sorry, you've lost me. You mean when she's a toddler? We'd do that anyway."

I mean now, Amaru said. *Use your mind to talk to her.*

James laughed uncertainly. "But she's only a week...or an accelerated three months old. Her brain is only just forming. It's not functional, even for motor skills, let alone learning."

Do not confuse 'brain' with 'mind'. The mind has pre-existence and is only awaiting the formation of a suitable vehicle to work with. Communication is possible.

"How can it be?" Sam asked. "Nobody's memories go back to the womb."

Seldom, it is true, Amaru admitted. *But sometimes, memories go back even further than the womb. I am told that putting on a body is like waking from a vivid dream. You forget quickly. But as for communication with the unformed brain; do not take my word for it. Try it.*

"Try what?" James gave Amaru an incredulous look. "Even if it was possible to communicate, there's no knowledge, no vocabulary. There is no way brain cells without language pathways can verbalise."

She will tap into your own brain for what she needs. Try it.

James grimaced and shook his head. "This is idiotic but I'll give it a go." He concentrated and then sat down abruptly, looking baffled. "How?"

Ah, Amaru murmured. *Let me go first, the way is narrow and delicate. Unless you know...there...yes, try now.*

Gaia?

?

"I felt something," James yelled, leaping to his feet. "Try it, Sam."

"I'm way ahead of you, buddy." *Gaia, I'm your mother, Sam.*

?

I love you Gaia. This other mind is your father, James. He loves you too.

!

Can you talk to us baby? Look into our minds. See?

MotherSam.

That's right baby. Can you see the others? James? Amaru? Spence?

FatherJames. Amaru. Spence.

Oh, yes, baby. Search my mind, take what you need.

"Bugger me," Spence breathed. "Was that Gaia?" *Hi, kid.*

Tallbabygoat?

Spence and James burst into fits of laughter, leaving Sam to explain to Gaia. For the next hour, all three humans poured out their minds to the tiny foetal brain, feeling as if their thoughts, their beliefs and their knowledge were being sucked up like water in an arid land. Finally, it became too much.

Tired. My body and brain now sleep.

Okay, baby. We'll talk again. We love you, Gaia.

Amaru looked around the three tired but contented humans. *Do you accept the responsibility of Gaia?*

"Oh, yes. Very definitely," James murmured.

"My oath," Spence grinned.

Sam stared grimly back at the old Neanderthal woman. "Just try and stop me."

I would not dream of it, Amaru said. *Rest now, while I organise your return to your vehicles. I will ask Wandjina, the one you call Ernie, to return with you. He will explain further what comes next.* She rose and left the cavern, her mind already busy issuing commands and conversing with Garagh.

How long do we have, Garagh?

Gaia will be born in six months. We can give her another six months after that.

Pain flowed through Amaru. *Only that? I like Sam; I do not want to deprive her of her baby so soon.*

Do you question the commands of the 'Others'?

No, but...

Delay could be deadly. Besides, it may not be forever.

There was a long silence and eventually, Garagh felt a mental acquiescence.

Amaru, you will accelerate the development of Shinara. We must be ready.

19

The tires of the Toyota Landcruiser hummed monotonously on the well-surfaced expanse of the Bruce Highway as James drove northward from the Glass House Mountains toward Townsville. The drone of rubber on road only altered as freshly sealed potholes interrupted the smooth passage of the vehicle on its way back to normality. Almost complete silence reigned within the cab, Sam sitting next to James in the front, while Nathan, Marc and Ratana sat in the back. Ernie had accompanied them as far as Rockhampton, before asking to be dropped off at the bus depot to catch a ride westward toward the Simpson Desert. He would not say why he wanted to go there and they did not ask, though Nathan tried to slip his mind into Ernie's without permission. His probe met an adamantine shell and bounced back, the old Aboriginal man turning to Nathan with an enigmatic look but saying nothing. This silent response rebuked Nathan and he withdrew into himself.

Marc had ridden with Spence in his old Jeep as far as Rockhampton before the young American photographer transferred to the Landcruiser. Spence declined to come further north just then, saying he had business in the south that would occupy his attentions for the next month or so.

"I'll come to your wedding though, you randy old bugger," he told James, embracing him outside the bus depot. "You look after your lady and the wunderkind."

"Don't you worry about us, Spence," Sam said, giving him an enthusiastic hug. "And you'd better not be a stranger either. Keep in contact and come and see us whenever you can."

Yes, please talk to me, Uncle Spence. You tell such interesting stories.

Okay kid, whenever I can. Look after yourself and your parents.

I will.

The trip northward took place in almost complete silence for many miles, though conversation raged unheard around Marc, who spent most of his time staring out the window at the landscape. Sam and James continued an almost uninterrupted three-way discussion with Gaia, whose thirst for knowledge was insatiable. In the day or so since her awakening, she had grasped the meanings of most of the words in her parents' vocabularies and many others besides. It was a source of some embarrassment to Spence when the fetal girl started using the swear words gleaned from his interestingly convoluted mind. The fact that she used them in the correct context was the only saving grace, and the incidents led to long discussions on such diverse topics as the origin of words, usage in polite society, censorship and cultural differences. Gaia agreed to limit her use of such words on the proviso that they would fully explain the origins of them and not try to hide any from her.

Nathan and Ratana also talked at length about their own plans for marriage and the tasks they had been set by Ernie, who called himself Wandjina.

I'm uncomfortable calling him Wandjina, Ratana said. *Wandjina is a great creator spirit and it borders on blasphemy for any man to call himself that.*

Nathan yawned. *It's only a name. We all use nicknames from time to time.* He snickered. *Perhaps it pulls the birds.*

Ratana stared at her fiancé and tried to probe his mind delicately.

Nathan grinned and deflected her easily. *Bad manners, Ratana. Didn't Wandjina teach you differently?*

I'm just worried about you, Ratana replied. *You seem a lot more sarcastic and belligerent these last couple of days.*

Perhaps I just see things a bit more clearly. Those Neanderthals are great at using people and, well, perhaps I just don't want to be used.

You don't think what they're doing is worthwhile?

Nathan shrugged. *How the hell do I know? What didn't they tell us? And as for the old fella Wandjina, perhaps he's not quite right in the head. I mean you'd have to be schizo to think you were a god.*

Ratana stayed silent, withdrawing into the turmoil of her mind. Everything her fiancé said was reasonable enough on the face of it, but when she was talking to Amaru or Garagh or Ernie--she could not think of him as Wandjina--what they said gleamed with truth and honesty.

Marc yawned and turned away from the window, looking around at the silent people in the vehicle. "You're all very quiet," he said. "What's the matter? Disappointed none of it worked out?" He shook his head. "You shouldn't be," he went on. "I've been on a lot of expeditions where the goals looked easy on paper but evaporated in the field. So what if the black rock thing didn't pan out? We had a good time, didn't we? Saw some bush, did a bit of trekking, took some photos, sank a few beers."

Sam turned round in her seat to look at Marc. "What do you remember of the last week?"

"Not much. The days just sort of merged into one another. In fact, for me, the trip was just one big chill out. After all, we didn't find anything, just wandered around for a while and relaxed."

"It was rather pleasant, wasn't it?" James commented.

"Yeah, but where did you and Sam disappear to? I don't remember seeing you for a while."

"Oh, we were there. We just wandered off to get to know each other better."

Marc grinned. "You sure did that. Sam, you're a dark horse. You never told me you had the hots for James."

"Well, I don't tell you everything I do, any more than you told me the sordid details of how you pried those photos away from the Townsville Bulletin reporter." She held up a hand in mock terror. "Don't tell me. That comes under the heading of too much information."

Marc laughed and rummaged in his camera bag, pulling out a sheaf of glossy photos. "They're not going to be of much use now that the story fizzled. Besides which, they're not my photos so I can't use them. Do you want them, Sam?"

"Sure. They'll be a memento of a great holiday if nothing else."

"So did you take many photos in the end?" Nathan asked. "You were clicking around at various times."

"Yeah, I got some but nothing really interesting--some of the bush, you guys, and a few of the aftermath of that mini-tornado." Marc took his digital camera out and switched it to 'Play'.

"What tornado was that?" Sam asked.

Careful, Sam, Ratana thought. *That was when Wulgu went berserk after he found out Rima had been shot.*

Ah, sorry. "Let's see what pictures you took of me, Marc. I take a lousy picture."

"Hang on; I want to see the ones of the tornado first. Ah, here we are...not much really, a bit of flattened bush, broken trees, one uprooted, but it must have been damned sudden because the light is good, no trace of overcast...hello, what's this?" He stared at the screen on the back of his camera.

"What have you got?" James asked carefully, his voice casual.

Marc frowned, peering at the screen. "It's a bit out of focus for some reason, as the others are clear and crisp. It looks like a guy in a gorilla suit."

Ratana leaned over to look. *Oh shit, it's Wulgu. He's taken a bloody picture of Wulgu.*

Marc grinned suddenly. "It's you isn't it, Nathan? Playing one of your fuckin' tricks on me again. What was the name of that thing you said...a wool-goo? No, that's not right...a drop bear." He scowled as abruptly as he had grinned. "Well this is one American tourist you didn't fool." Marc tapped the delete button and the scene shifted. "I'm not taking that home as proof of a hoax you played on me, thank you very much."

"You seem very sure of yourself," Nathan commented. "Are you sure you haven't just deleted the definitive Bigfoot picture?"

What the hell are you doing? Do you want him to remember?

"Oh, I'm sure," Marc laughed. "You carefully set me up for all this, all of you, with your talk of mysterious animals and weird shadow creatures. You had me half believing you for a while, but I saw through you."

"Yup, you worked that out very quickly," James said. "I didn't really think we could fool an experienced photographer, but it was fun trying."

"Beats me where you got the gorilla suit from though, and where it went," Marc continued. "I helped pack up the baggage in Townsville and when we came out, but I didn't see a suit. It would be too bulky to put in a pack."

"It was Spence's," James said. "He does a lot of lecturing on the subject and he carries one of them as a prop in his Jeep. That's why you didn't see it."

Marc nodded. He returned to his perusal of the pictures on his camera, deleting several others before packing it away again. He yawned and asked how far it was to Townsville.

"About another five hours. We'll stop for a break soon." James turned on the car radio and asked Sam to find some decent music. She surfed the AM and FM bands looking for something within range and pleasant to listen to, catching the end of a local news broadcast.

"... in an uproar yesterday morning. Self-proclaimed Bigfoot hunter, Guilford King, presented eviden..." The rest dissolved into a crackle of static. Sam twiddled the knob but the sound faded away.

James slowed and pulled over slightly as a large truck, with horn blaring, swerved out and past them. "Find that station again--quickly."

Sam searched and was at last rewarded with a few low quality phrases. "... King is helping New South Wales police in their inquiries...missing for over two weeks...news bulletin brought to you by Cheesy Snacks, the taste on..."

"Damn. What's happening?" James asked, staring at the radio. He switched off the static-polluted music and thought for a moment, frowning. "Do any of you know what that was about?"

Sure, Nathan replied. *King shot Rima and submitted blood and hair samples for analysis.*

Ernie had Nathan and I substitute other samples for the real ones, Ratana added.

"Nope, don't know a thing," Marc said.

"We need a paper." James pulled back onto the highway and accelerated to the speed limit and beyond. Ten minutes later, he pulled up by a faded, rundown weatherboard shop and dashed inside, emerging a few minutes later with a local paper and a national one. He tossed one into the back seat and started turning the pages of the other.

"What are we looking for?" Marc asked.

"Guilford King. Anything on him."

"Who is Guilford King?"

Sam raised her eyebrows. "You don't remember him?" *Whoops.* "Er, he was a hunter we saw briefly. James and I saw him when we were, er, off walking."

"Damn, nothing in here," James said. "I'm into 'Sports' and 'Classifieds' already."

"There's something here, Uncle," Ratana said quietly. *Do you want me to read it out? If I don't, Marc is going to wonder why not, but if I do...*

Go ahead; we'll worry about what to say afterward.

"Okay, here goes." Ratana read, "Sydney, Wednesday; Bigfoot Hunter Shoots Himself in Foot. Guilford King, a cryptozoologist of note on the Australian scene revealed at a press conference last week that he had shot and wounded a large primate in the Blue Mountains, west of Sydney. The large primate in question is said to be the legendary "Yowie" or "Yowee", subject of many alleged sightings along the east coast.

"Samples of blood and hair collected at the scene of the shooting were submitted to three independent laboratories for testing. Mr King took the unusual step of asking for the results of the tests to be delivered in sealed envelopes to Mr Joshua Keenan of the law firm of Jones, Keenan and Armbruster, to hold until yesterday's press conference. 'I am confident of the results,' Mr King is quoted as saying.

"Mr King opened the press conference with a long statement (see page 57 for details) about his cryptozoological studies--Cryptozoology is defined as the study of hidden animals--culminating in a description of a hunt for the Yowie--Australia's equivalent of the Bigfoot--in the Blue Mountains.

"'I tracked the beast and shot it, wounding it,' Mr King said. 'Although it escaped into thick forest, I was able to collect blood and hair samples which will show the nature of the beast I shot. I have here...' Mr King held up three buff envelopes at this stage '...the results of the tests from three independent laboratories which will prove, once and for all, the existence of a large non-human primate in Australia's forests and hills.'

"In a performance more suited to the circus ring than to a scientific inquiry, Mr King then asked Mr Keenan to open the envelopes and read out the findings. Mr Keenan's disclosure stunned the audience of reporters, scientists, police and, it would seem, Mr King, who left the conference without further comment. The findings from all three laboratories were 'Human blood' and 'wallaby hair'.

"The Assistant Commissioner of New South Wales' police force, Winston Andrews, made a statement immediately after Mr King's precipitate departure in which he said, in part, 'We will be asking Mr King for his assistance in finding the site of the alleged shooting so that our forensic pathologists can examine the site thoroughly.' In answer to a question about the identity of the human blood, Commissioner Andrews replied 'No comment.' On being asked whether the blood was that of German tourist Hans Stedler, missing in the Blue Mountains for two weeks, Commissioner Andrews again refused to comment.'"

James laughed delightedly. "That'll shut him up," he crowed.

"Who is this Guilford King, that you all hate him so much?" Marc asked, looking around the cabin of the Landcruiser. "It just doesn't seem the sort of thing you'd do."

"Hate is a bit strong, Marc," James answered. "I'd say we dislike him intensely. He's one of those extremely opinionated people who don't mind who they hurt or trample to get what they want. King has, at one time or another, ridiculed every other cryptozoologist in Australia and many overseas ones too. His favourite ploy is personal vilification so...well, I feel immensely cheered he's got his come-uppance for once."

"It won't hold him back, Uncle," Ratana commented.

"Yeah, he'll be right back into it in days, once he thinks of a plausible reason for the blood samples becoming mixed," Nathan added.

"What about the police?" Sam asked. "Will that have any effect? Could he really have shot a person?"

No, it was Cindy--Rima, but we switched the samples, Ratana replied. *We don't know whose blood Ernie used in the replacements.*

"I doubt it," James said, "I think the samples probably got switched or else it's a hoax of his that backfired." *That's for Marc's benefit*, he silently explained.

Conversation died away as the journey resumed and it was late evening by the time they arrived in Townsville. James drove through the light traffic to the Strand and Sam's and Marc's hotel where Sam packed up the rest of her belongings and paid the now quite sizeable bill for the rooms. Marc opted to stay one more night and fly out for Sydney and beyond the next day, having booked a flight as soon as he arrived at the hotel.

"It's been interesting," Marc said, shaking hands all round. He hugged Sam, whispering to her, "Next time you think of me for a project, make sure there actually is one."

"What time's your flight tomorrow?" James asked. "We'll come and pick you up."

"Nah, it's at six in the morning, so I appreciate the thought but I'll grab a taxi."

"You're sure? It's no trouble."

"I'm sure. Y'all take care now, y'hear?"

Sam laughed. "That's the most American you've sounded the whole trip." She hesitated and then handed Marc a sealed envelope. "Would you post this to my sister Andi when you get Stateside?"

Marc turned it over in his hands. "It's not going to get me in trouble with Customs, is it? Why don't you just post it from here?"

"It's just a letter, nothing more, and...well, I have my reasons."

Marc shrugged and slipped it into his back pocket. "Okay."

They left Marc in the foyer of the hotel and got back into the university Landcruiser. James drove Ratana and Nathan up to the university where they had rooms in the Halls of Residence. "You'll be okay?" he asked as he dropped them off.

"Sure, Uncle," Ratana replied. "All I want is a takeaway pizza and a good night's sleep. See you at the lab tomorrow?"

James nodded. "I'll be in around mid-morning for a couple of hours. I have to put in a report and do a bit of admin stuff. You've got enough of your own work to keep you going?"

Sam looked at James as he drove back out onto University Drive and toward his Mundingburra house. "What's going on in that mind of yours?" she asked. "You're hiding something. Your mind becomes quite slippery when you're doing that."

James grinned. "Just thinking about getting you home. I hope you're not too tired."

"I'm tired, but not that tired." She smiled, and then abruptly blushed. "Oh, what will Gaia think? We can't."

"Explain it to her--not the reproductive aspects but the pair-bonding. She's an intelligent kid, she'll understand."

"You think?" Sam looked dubious but fell silent. A few minutes later she said, "She does understand. She says she has enough to think about for now so she'll switch off her sensory input tonight."

"There you go then," James leered. "No excuses, woman."

"What the hell makes you think I want one? I'll bet you call it quits before I do."

"You're on." James grinned and glanced sideways at Sam. "What was that about the letter you gave Marc? You were hiding something then."

"I got a message from Amaru. We have to go away for a time, and I didn't want Andi to worry."

"Go away where? When? And for that matter, why?"

"I don't know, soon, and I don't know. You know Amaru, she can play things close to her ample chest."

James grunted. "As long as we get the opportunity to get married first. We have to sort out Immigration and Residency too."

"Don't worry, we will." Sam slid across the seat and nibbled James' ear, as she slipped a thought past his mental defences.

James jumped, the vehicle swerving slightly on the almost deserted roads as he turned off Ross River Road onto Mango Avenue. *Bloody hell, Sam, that's not like you.*

You don't know the half of it, buster. I think making love while we are telepathically connected is going to be an awesome experience.

James pulled into the driveway of his house and parked the vehicle. Gone were his thoughts of the past few weeks and the staggering vistas that had opened up from their Glass House Mountains experiences. All that filled his mind were the more personal possibilities of life with the woman he loved. The future would look after itself; for now there was the present to enjoy. He slipped his arm around Sam's waist and walked her up the path toward their house, his mind already entwined with Sam's.

Interlude 1

*T*ownsville Bulletin
November 24
Local university professor, James Hay, and award-winning journalist Samantha Louis of Illinois, USA, were married today in a quiet civil ceremony held at the Palmetum. Best man was the New Zealand researcher and adventurer Spencer Tuhua, and the bridesmaid was a friend of the family, Cindy Rima. The happy couple will enjoy a short honeymoon on Magnetic Island.

The Australian
November 30
Guilford King, hunter and researcher into the mysteries of Australia, was released from police custody today after the German tourist, whom King was suspected of killing in September, walked out of the Blue Mountains yesterday. Hans Stedler, 27, of Dusseldorf in Germany, was in good health despite his nine weeks in the Mountains. He was unable to explain his whereabouts for the time and can remember very little after the first few days. Among his last memories is that of a bright light and doctors at Sydney's South Side Hospital are of the opinion that Mr Stedler fell and struck his head, accounting for the light and his subsequent loss of memory. He is believed to have been living in some small town in western New South Wales these last two months as his condition is not that of a man lost in the bush. Police are asking anyone who might have knowledge of the whereabouts of Hans Stedler over the last few weeks to contact their local police station.

Police are questioning Guilford King over his access to Mr Stedler's blood and are examining the premise that there was collusion between the two men to perpetrate a hoax. Neither Mr King nor Mr Stedler was available for comment.

Townsville Bulletin
     December 4
     Police were called yesterday to the hilltop villa on Magnetic Island where Professor James Hay of James Cook University and his new bride Samantha were honeymooning. Neighbours reported a bright light in the sky a few moments before a power outage blacked out the Island at a few minutes after eleven in the evening. A security guard at nearby Ocean View Resort reported what he called a 'searchlight' bathing the grounds of the villa shortly after the blackout and the presence of several large figures moving into the house. A spokesman for the Magnetic Island police, Sergeant Kevin Spiller, told reporters that although Professor and Mrs Hay were missing from the house, there was no evidence of foul play. Investigations are continuing.

Townsville Bulletin
     December 8
     The hunt for Professor James Hay and his wife Samantha was widened to the mainland today. The couple went missing from their honeymoon villa four days ago after neighbours reported seeing lights in the sky and several large men entering the house during a blackout that cut all power to the island for the space of an hour. The power company has been unable to trace the fault responsible for the outage and believe power may have been cut deliberately. Police are also investigating this premise.

Townsville Bulletin
     December 23
     The search for Professor James and Samantha Hay, missing from their honeymoon cottage since December 4, was called off today. Police said the case will remain open and information from the public is always welcome.

The story continues in *A Glass Darkly*
Book 2 of the *Glass* trilogy

About the Author

Max Overton has travelled extensively and lived in many places around the world-- including Malaysia, India, Germany, England, Jamaica, New Zealand, USA and Australia. Trained in the biological sciences in New Zealand and Australia, he has worked within the scientific field for many years, but now concentrates on writing. While predominantly a writer of historical fiction (Scarab: Books 1 - 6 of the Amarnan Kings; the Scythian Trilogy; the Demon Series; Ascension), he also writes in other genres (A Cry of Shadows, the Glass Trilogy, Haunted Trail, Sequestered) and draws on true life (Adventures of a Small Game Hunter in Jamaica, We Came From Königsberg). Max also maintains an interest in butterflies, photography, the paranormal and other aspects of Fortean Studies.

Most of his other published books are available at Writers Exchange Ebooks, http://www.writers-exchange.com/Max-Overton.html and all his books may be viewed on his website: http://www.maxovertonauthor.com/

Max's book covers are all designed and created by Julie Napier, and other examples of her art and photography may be viewed at www.julienapier.com

If you want to read more about other books by this author, they are listed on the following pages...

A Cry of Shadows
{Paranormal Murder Mystery}

Australian Professor Ian Delaney is single-minded in his determination to prove his theory that one can discover the moment that the life force leaves the body. After succumbing to the temptation to kill a girl under scientifically controlled conditions, he takes an offer of work in St Louis, hoping to leave the undiscovered crime behind him.

In America, Wayne Richardson seeks revenge by killing his ex-girlfriend, believing it will give him the upper hand, a means to seize control following their breakup. Wayne quickly discovers that he enjoys killing and begins to seek out young women who resemble his dead ex-girlfriend.

Ian and Wayne meet and, when Ian recognizes the symptoms of violent delusion, he employs Wayne to help him further his research. Despite the police closing in, the two killers manage to evade identification time and time again as the death toll rises in their wake.

The detective in charge of the case, John Barnes, is frantic, willing to try anything to catch his killer. With time running out, he searches desperately for answers before another body is found...or the culprit slips into the woodwork for good.
Publisher: http://www.writers-exchange.com/A-Cry-of-Shadows/

Adventures of a Small Game Hunter in Jamaica
{Biography}

An eleven-year-old boy is plucked from boarding school in England and transported to the tropical paradise of Jamaica where he's free to study his one great love--butterflies. He discovers that Jamaica has a wealth of these wonderful insects and sets about making a collection of as many as he can find. Along the way, he has adventures with other creatures, from hummingbirds to vultures, from iguanas to black widow spiders. Through it all runs the promise of the legendary Homerus swallowtail, Jamaica's national butterfly.

Other activities intrude, like school, boxing and swimming lessons, but he manages to inveigle his parents into taking him to strange and sometimes dangerous places, all in the name of butterfly collecting. He meets scientists and Rastafarians, teachers, small boys and the ordinary people living on the tropical isle, and even discovers butterflies that shouldn't exist in Jamaica.

Author Max Overton was that young boy. He counted himself fortunate to have lived in Jamaica in an age very different from the present one. Max still has some of the butterflies he collected half a century or more ago, and each one releases a flood of memories whenever he opens the box and gazes at their tattered and fading wings. These memories have become stories--stories of the Adventures of a Small Game Hunter in Jamaica.
Publisher: http://www.writers-exchange.com/Adventures-of-a-Small-Game-Hunter/

Ascension Series, A Novel of Nazi Germany
{Historical: Holocaust}

Before he fully realized the diabolical cruelties of the National Socialist German Worker's Party, Konrad Wengler had committed atrocities against his own people, the Jews, out of fear of both his faith and his heritage. But after he witnesses firsthand the concentration camps, the corruption, the inhuman malevolence of the Nazi war machine and the propaganda aimed at annihilating an entire race, he knows he must find a way to turn the tide and become the savior his people desperately need.

Book 1: Ascension
Being a Jew in Germany can be a dangerous thing...

Fear prompts Konrad Wengler to put his faith aside and try desperately to forget his heritage. After fighting in the Great War, he's wounded and turns instead to law enforcement in his tiny Bavarian hometown. There, he falls under the spell of the fledgling Nazi Party. He joins the Party in patriotic fervour and becomes a Lieutenant of Police and Schutzstaffel (SS).

In the course of his duties as policeman, Konrad offends a powerful Nazi official who starts an SS investigation. War breaks out. When he joins the Police Battalions, he's sent to Poland and witnesses there firsthand the atrocities being committed upon his fellow Jews.

Unknown to Konrad, the SS investigators have discovered his origins and follow him into Poland. Arrested and sent to Mauthausen Concentration Camp, Konrad is forced to face what it means to be a Jew and fight for survival. Will his friends on the outside, his wife and lawyer, be enough to counter the might of the Nazi machine?

Publisher: http://www.writers-exchange.com/Ascension/

Book 2: Maelstrom
Never underestimate the enemy...

Konrad Wengler survived his brush with the death camps of Nazi Germany. Now, reinstated as a police officer in his Bavarian hometown despite being a Jew, he throws himself back into his work, seeking to uncover evidence that will remove a corrupt Nazi party official.

The Gestapo have their own agenda and, despite orders from above to eliminate this troublesome Jewish policeman, they hide Konrad in the Totenkopf (Death's Head) Division of the Waffen-SS. In a fight to survive in the snowy wastes of Russia while the tide of war turns against Germany, Konrad experiences tank battles, ghetto clearances, partisans, and death camps (this time as a guard), as well as the fierce battles where his Division is badly outnumbered and on the defence.

Through it all, Konrad strives to live by his conscience and resist taking part in the atrocities happening all around him. He still thinks of himself as a policeman, but his desire to bring the corrupt Nazi official to justice seems far removed from his present reality. If he is to find the necessary evidence against his enemy, he must first *survive...*

Publisher: http://www.writers-exchange.com/Maelstrom/

Book 3: Dämmerung

Konrad Wengler is captured and sent from one Soviet prison camp to another. Even hearing the war has come to an end makes no difference until he's arrested as a Nazi Party member. In jail, Konrad refuses to defend himself for things he's guilty and should be punished for. Will his be an eye-for-an-eye life sentence, or leniency in regard of the good he tried to do once he learned the truth?

Publisher: http://www.writers-exchange.com/dammerung/

Kadesh, A Novel of Ancient Egypt

Holding the key to strategic military advantage, Kadesh is a jewel city that distant lands covet. Ramesses II of Egypt and Muwatalli II of Hatti believe they're chosen by the gods to claim ascendancy to Kadesh. When the two meet in the largest chariot battle ever fought, not just the fate of empires will be decided but also the lives of citizens helplessly caught up in the greedy ambition of kings.

Publisher: http://www.writers-exchange.com/Kadesh/

Fall of the House of Ramesses Series,
A Novel of Ancient Egypt
{Historical: Ancient Egypt}

Egypt was at the height of its powers in the days of Ramesses the Great, a young king who confidently predicted his House would last for a Thousand Years. Sixty years later, he was still on the throne. One by one, his heirs had died and the survivors had become old men. When Ramesses at last died, he left a stagnant kingdom and his throne to an old man--Merenptah. What followed laid the groundwork for a nation ripped apart by civil war.

Book 1: Merenptah

The House of Ramesses is in the hands of an old man. King Merenptah wants to leave the kingdom to his younger son, Seti, but northern tribes in Egypt rebel and join forces with the Sea Peoples, invading from the north. In the south, the king's eldest son Messuwy is angered at being passed over in favour of the younger son...and plots to rid himself of his father and brother.
Publisher: http://www.writers-exchange.com/Merenptah/

Book 2: Seti

After only nine years on the throne, Merenptah is dead and his son Seti is king in his place. He rules from the northern city of Men-nefer, while his elder brother Messuwy, convinced the throne is his by right, plots rebellion in the south.

The kingdoms are tipped into bloody civil war, with brother fighting against brother for the throne of a united Egypt. On one side is Messuwy, now crowned as King Amenmesse and his ruthless General Sethi; on the other, young King Seti and his wife Tausret. But other men are weighing up the chances of wresting the throne from both brothers and becoming king in their place. Under the onslaught of conflict, the House of Ramesses begins to crumble...
Publisher: http://www.writers-exchange.com/Seti/

Book 3: Tausret

The House of Ramesses falters as Tausret relinquishes the throne upon the death of her husband, King Seti. Amenmesse's young son Siptah will become king until her infant son is old enough to rule. Tausret, as Regent, and the king's uncle, Chancellor Bay, hold tight to the reins of power and vie for complete control of the kingdoms. Assassination changes the balance of power, and, seeing his chance, Chancellor Bay attempts a coup...

Tausret's troubles mount as she also faces a challenge from Setnakhte, an aging son of the Great Ramesses who believes Seti was the last legitimate king. If Setnakhte gets his way, he will destroy the House of Ramesses and set up his own dynasty of kings.
Publisher: http://www.writers-exchange.com/Tausret/

Glass Trilogy
{Paranormal Thriller}

Delve deep into the mysteries of Aboriginal mythology, present day UFO activity and pure science that surround the continent of Australia, from its barren deserts to the depths of its rainforest and even deeper into its mysterious mountains. Along the way, love, greed, murder, and mystery abound while the secrets of mankind and the ultimate answer to 'what happens now?' just might be answered.

GLASS HOUSE, Book 1: The mysteries of Australia may just hold the answers mankind has been searching for millennium to find. When Doctor James Hay, a university scientist who studies the paranormal mysteries in Australia, finds an obelisk of carved volcanic rock on sacred Aboriginal land in northern Queensland, he realizes it may hold the answers he's been seeking. A respected elder of the Aboriginal people instructs James to take up the gauntlet and follow his heart. Along with his old friend and award-winning writer Spencer, Samantha Louis, her cameraman, and two of James' Aboriginal students, James embarks on a life-changing quest for the truth.
Publisher: http://www.writers-exchange.com/Glass-House/

A GLASS DARKLY, Book 2: A dead volcano called Glass Mountain in Northern California seems harmless...but is it really?

Andromeda Jones, a physicist, knows her missing sister Samantha is somehow tied up with the new job Andromeda herself has been offered to work with a team in constructing Vox Dei, a machine that's been ostensibly built to eliminate wars. But what is its true nature, and who's pulling the strings?

When the experiment spins out of control, dark powers are unleashed and the danger to mankind unfolds relentlessly. Strange, evil shadows are using the Vox Dei and Andromeda's sister Samantha to get through to our world, knowing the time is near when Earth's final destiny will be decided.

Federal forces are aware of something amiss, so, to rescue her sibling, Andromeda agrees to go on a dangerous mission and soon finds herself entangled in a web of professional jealousy, political betrayal, and flat-out greed.
Publisher: http://www.writers-exchange.com/A-Glass-Darkly/

LOOKING GLASS, Book 3: Samantha and James Hay have been advised that their missing daughter Gaia have been located in ancient Australia. Dr. Xanatuo, an alien scientist who, along with a lost tribe of Neanderthals and other beings working to help mankind, has discovered a way to send them back in time to be reunited with Gaia. Ernie, the old Aboriginal tracker and leader of the Neanderthals, along with friends Ratana and Nathan and characters from the first two books of the trilogy, will accompany them. This team of intrepid adventurers have another mission for the journey, along with aiding the Hayes' quest, which is paramount to changing a terrible wrong which exists in the present time.
Publisher: http://www.writers-exchange.com/Looking-Glass/

Haunted Trail A Tale of Wickedness & Moral Turpitude
{Western: Paranormal}

Ned Abernathy is a hot-tempered young cowboy in the small town of Hammond's Bluff in 1876. In a drunken argument with his best friend Billy over a girl, he guns him down. Ned flees and wanders the plains, forests and hills of the Dakota Territories, certain that every man's hand is against him.

Horse rustlers, marauding Indians, killers, gold prospectors and French trappers cross his path and lead to complications, as do persistent apparitions of what Ned believes is the ghost of his friend Billy, come to accuse him of murder. He finds love and loses it. Determined not to do the same when he discovers gold in the Black Hills, he ruthlessly defends his newfound wealth against greedy men. In the process, he comes to terms with who he is and what he's done. But there are other ghosts in his past that he needs to confront. Returning to Hammond's Bluff, Ned stumbles into a shocking surprise awaiting him at the end of his haunted trail.

Publisher: http://www.writers-exchange.com/Haunted-Trail/

Hyksos Series, A Novel of Ancient Egypt

The power of the kings of the Middle Kingdom have been failing for some time, having lost control of the Nile Delta to a series of Canaanite kings who ruled from the northern city of Avaris. Into this mix came the Kings of Amurri, Lebanon and Syria bent on subduing the whole of Egypt. These kings were known as the Hyksos, and they dealt a devastating blow to the peoples of the Nile Delta and Valley.

Book 1: Avaris

When Arimawat and his son Harrubaal fled from Urubek, the king of Hattush, to the court of the King of Avaris, King Sheshi welcomed the refugees. One of Arimawat's first tasks for King Shesi is to sail south to the Land of Kush and fetch Princess Tati, who will become Sheshi's queen. Arimawat and Harrubaal perform creditably, but their actions have far-reaching consequences.

On the return journey, Harrubaal falls in love with Kemi, the daughter of the Southern Egyptian king. As a reward for Harrubaal's work, Sheshi secures the hand of the princess for the young Canaanite prince. Unfortunately for the peace of the realm, Sheshi lusts after Princess Kemi too, and his actions threaten the stability of his kingdom...

Publisher: http://www.writers-exchange.com/Avaris/

Book 2: Conquest

The Hyksos invade the Delta using the new weapons of bronze and chariots, things of which the Egyptians have no knowledge. They rout the Delta forces, and in the south, the unconquered kings ready their armies to defend their lands. Meanwhile in Avaris, Merybaal, the son of Harrubaal and Kemi, strives to defend his family in a city conquered by the Hyksos.

Elements of the Delta army that refuse to surrender continue the fight for their homeland, and new kings proclaim themselves as the inheritors of the failed kings of Avaris. One of these is Amenre, grandson of Merybaal, but he is forced into hiding as the Hyksos sweep all before them, bringing their terror to the kingdom of the Nile valley. Driven south in disarray, the survivors of the Egyptian army seek leaders who can resist the enemy...

Publisher: http://www.writers-exchange.com/conquest/

Book 3: Two Cities

The Hyksos drive south into the Nile Valley, sweeping all resistance aside. Bebi and Sobekhotep, grandsons of Harrubaal, assume command of the loyal Egyptian army and strive to stem the flood of Hyksos conquest. But even the cities of the south are divided against themselves.

Abdju, an old capital city of Egypt reasserts itself, putting forward a line of kings of its own, and soon the city is at war with Waset, the southern capital of the Nile Valley, as the two cities fight for supremacy in the face of the advancing northern enemy. Caught up in the turmoil of warring nations, the ordinary people of Egypt must fight for their own survival as well as that of their kingdom.

Publisher: http://www.writers-exchange.com/Two-Cities/

And More (7 books total).

Series Page:

https://www.writers-exchange.com/hyksos-series/

Scythian Trilogy
{Historical}

Captured by the warlike, tribal Scythians who bicker amongst themselves and bitterly resent outside interference, a fiercely loyal captain in Alexander the Great's Companion Cavalry Nikometros and his men are to be sacrificed to the Mother Goddess. Lucky chance--and the timely intervention of Tomyra, priestess and daughter of the Massegetae chieftain--allows him to defeat the Champion. With their immediate survival secured, acceptance into the tribe...and escape...is complicated by the captain's growing feelings for Tomyra-- death to any who touch her--and the chief's son Areipithes who not only detests Nikometros and wants to have him killed or banished but intends to murder his own father and take over the tribe.

LION OF SCYTHIA, Book 1: Alexander the Great has conquered the Persian Empire and is marching eastward to India. In his wake he leaves small groups of soldiers to govern great tracts of land and diverse peoples. Nikometros is one young cavalry captain left behind in the lands of the fierce, nomadic Scythian horsemen. Captured after an ambush, Nikometros must fight for his life and the lives of his surviving men. Even as he seeks an opportunity to escape, he finds himself bound by a debt of loyalty to the chief...and his own developing love for the young priestess.
Publisher: http://www.writers-exchange.com/Lion-of-Scythia/

THE GOLDEN KING, Book 2: The chief of the tribe of nomadic Scythian horsemen is dead, killed by his son's treachery. The priestess, lover of the young cavalry officer, Nikometros, is carried off into the mountains. Nikometros and his friends set off in hard pursuit.

Death rides with them. By the time they return, the tribes are at war. Nikometros must choose between attempting to become chief himself or leaving the people he's come to love and respect to return to his duty as an army officer in the Empire of Alexander.
Winner of the 2005 EPIC Ebook Awards.
Publisher: http://www.writers-exchange.com/The-Golden-King/

FUNERAL IN BABYLON, Book 3: Alexander the Great has returned from India and set up his court in Babylon. Nikometros and a band of loyal Scythians journey deep into the heart of Persia to join the Royal court. Nikometros finds himself embroiled in the intrigues and wars of kings, generals, and merchant adventurers as he strives to provide a safe haven for his lover and friends. With the fate of an Empire hanging in the balance, Death walks beside Nikometros as events precipitate a Funeral in Babylon...

Winner of the 2006 EPIC Ebook Awards.
Publisher: http://www.writers-exchange.com/Funeral-in-Babylon/

Sequestered
By Max Overton and Jim Darley
{Action/Thriller}

Storing carbon dioxide underground as a means of removing a greenhouse gas responsible for global warming has made James Matternicht a fabulously wealthy man. For 15 years, the Carbon Capture and Sequestration Facility at Rushing River in Oregon's hinterland has been operating without a problem...or has it?

When mysterious documents arrive on her desk that purport to show the Facility is leaking, reporter Annaliese Winton investigates. Together with a government geologist, Matt Morrison, she uncovers a morass of corruption and deceit that now threatens the safety of her community and the entire northwest coast of America.

Liquid carbon dioxide, stored at the critical point under great pressure, is a tremendously dangerous substance, and millions of tonnes of it are sequestered in the rock strata below Rushing River. All it would take is a crack in the overlying rock and the whole pressurized mass could erupt with disastrous consequences. And that crack has always existed there...

Recipient of the Life Award (Literature for the Environment): "There are only two kinds of people: conservationists and suicides. To qualify for this Award, your book needs to value the wonderful world of nature, to recognize that we are merely one species out of millions, and that we have a responsibility to cherish and maintain our small planet."

Awarded from http://bobswriting.com/life/
Publisher: http://www.writers-exchange.com/Sequestered/

TULPA
{Paranormal Thriller}

From the rainforests of tropical Australia to the cane fields and communities of the North Queensland coastal strip, a horror is unleashed by those foolishly playing with unknown forces...

A fairy story to amuse small children leads four bored teenagers and a young university student in a North Queensland town to becoming interested in an ancient Tibetan technique for creating a life form. When their seemingly harmless experiment sets free terror and death, the teenagers are soon fighting to contain a menace that reproduces exponentially.

The police are helpless to end the horror. Aided by two old game hunters, a student of the paranormal and a few small children, the teenagers must find a way of destroying what they unintentionally released. But how can they stop beings that can escape into an alternate reality when threatened?
Publisher: http://www.writers-exchange.com/TULPA/

Strong is the Ma'at of Re, A Novel of Ancient Egypt
{Historical: Ancient Egypt}

In Ancient Egypt, C1200 BCE, bitter contention and resentment, secret coups and assassination attempts may decide the fate of those who would become legends...by any means necessary.

Book 1: The King

That *he* is descended from Ramesses the Great fills Ramesses III with obscene pride. Elevated to the throne following a coup led by his father Setnakhte during the troubled days of Queen Tausret, Ramesses III sets about creating an Egypt that reflects the glory days of Ramesses the Great. He takes on his predecessor's throne name, names his sons after the sons of Ramesses and pushes them toward similar duties. Most of all, he thirsts after conquests like those of his hero grandfather.

Ramesses III assumes the throne name of Usermaatre, translated as "Strong is the Ma'at of Re" and endeavours to live up to the sentiment. He fights foreign foes, as had Ramesses the Great; he builds temples throughout the Two Lands, as had Ramesses the Great, and he looks forward to a long, illustrious life on the throne of Egypt, as had Ramesses the Great.

Alas, his reign is not meant to be. Ramesses III faces troubles at home--troubles that threaten the stability of Egypt and his own throne. The struggles for power between his wives, his sons, and even the priests of Amun, together with a treasury drained of its wealth, all force Ramesses III to question his success as the scion of a legend.

Publisher: http://www.writers-exchange.com/The-King/

Book 2: The Heirs

Tiye, the first wife of Ramesses III, has grown so used to being the mother of the Heir she can no longer bear to see that prized title pass to the son of a rival wife. Her eldest sons have died and the one left wants to step down and devote his life to the priesthood. Then the son of the king's sister/wife, also named Ramesses, will become Crown Prince and all Tiye's ambitions will lie in ruins.

Ramesses III struggles to enrich Egypt by seeking the wealth of the Land of Punt. He dispatches an expedition to the fabled southern land but years pass before the expedition returns. In the meantime, Tiye has a new hope: A last son she dotes on. Plague sweeps through Egypt, killing princes and princesses alike and lessening her options, and now Tiye must undergo the added indignity of having her daughter married off to the hated Crown Prince.

All Tiye's hopes are pinned on this last son of hers, but Ramesses III refuses to consider him as a potential successor, despite the Crown Prince's failing health. Unless Tiye can change the king's mind through charm or coercion, her sons will forever be excluded from the throne of Egypt.

Publisher: http://www.writers-exchange.com/The-Heirs/

Book 3: Taweret

The reign of Ramesses III is failing and even the gods seem to be turning their eyes away from Egypt. When the sun hides its face, crops suffer, throwing the country into famine. Tomb workers go on strike. To avert further disaster, Crown Prince Ramesses acts on his father's behalf.

The rivalry between Ramesses III's wives--commoner Tiye and sister/wife Queen Tyti-- also comes to a head. Tiye resents not being made queen and can't abide that her sons have been passed over. She plots to put her own spoiled son Pentaweret on the throne.

The eventual strength of the Ma'at of Re hangs in the balance. Will the rule of Egypt be decided by fate, gods...or treason?

Publisher: http://www.writers-exchange.com/The-One-of-Taweret/

The Amarnan Kings Series, A Novel of Ancient Egypt

Set in Egypt of the 14th century B.C.E. and piecing together a mosaic of the reigns of the five Amarnan kings, threaded through by the memories of princess Beketaten-Scarab, a tapestry unfolds of the royal figures lost in the mists of antiquity.

SCARAB - AKHENATEN, Book 1: A chance discovery in Syria reveals answers to the mystery of the ancient Egyptian sun-king, the heretic Akhenaten and his beautiful wife Nefertiti. Inscriptions in the tomb of his sister Beketaten, otherwise known as Scarab, tell a story of life and death, intrigue and warfare, in and around the golden court of the kings of the glorious 18th dynasty.

The narrative of a young girl growing up at the centre of momentous events--the abolition of the gods, foreign invasion, and the fall of a once-great family--reveals who Tutankhamen's parents really were, what happened to Nefertiti, and other events lost to history in the great destruction that followed the fall of the Aten heresy.
Publisher: http://www.writers-exchange.com/Scarab/

SCARAB- SMENKHKARE, Book 2: King Akhenaten, distraught at the rebellion and exile of his beloved wife Nefertiti, withdraws from public life, content to leave the affairs of Egypt in the hands of his younger half-brother Smenkhkare. When Smenkhkare disappears on a hunting expedition, his sister Beketaten, known as Scarab, is forced to flee for her life.

Finding refuge among her mother's people, the Khabiru, Scarab has resigned herself to a life in exile...until she hears that her brother Smenkhkare is still alive. He is raising an army in Nubia to overthrow Ay and reclaim his throne. Scarab hurries south to join him as he confronts Ay and General Horemheb outside the gates of Thebes.
Publisher: http://www.writers-exchange.com/Scarab2/

SCARAB - TUTANKHAMEN, Book 3: Scarab and her brother Smenkhkare are in exile in Nubia but are gathering an army to wrest control of Egypt from the boy king Tutankhamen and his controlling uncle, Ay. Meanwhile, the kingdoms are beset by internal troubles while the Amorites are pressing hard against the northern borders. Generals Horemheb and Paramessu must fight a war on two fronts while deciding where their loyalties lie--with the former king Smenkhkare or with the new young king in Thebes.

Smenkhkare and Scarab march on Thebes with their native army to meet the legions of Tutankhamen on the plains outside the city gates. As two brothers battle for supremacy and the throne of the Two Kingdoms, the fate of Egypt and the 18th dynasty hangs in the balance.
Finalist in 2013's Eppie Awards.
Publisher: http://www.writers-exchange.com/Scarab3/

And More (6 books total).

Series Page:
https://www.writers-exchange.com/the-amarnan-kings/

The Pyramid Builders, A Novel of Ancient Egypt

The third dynasty of the Old Kingdom of Egypt saw an extraordinary development of building techniques, from the simple structures of mud brick at the end of the second dynasty to the towering pyramids of the fourth dynasty. Just how these massive structures were built has long been a matter of conjecture, but history is made up of the lives and actions of individuals; kings and architects, scribes and priests, soldiers and artisans, even common labourers, and so the story of the Pyramid Builders unfolded over the course of more than a century. This is that story...

Book 1: Djoser

King Khasekhemwy has two sons, Djoser and Imhotep, but their destinies are very different. One will become king and the other his architect and the power behind the throne. Together, they plan to build something new, a great tomb that will be the wonder of the world. But not all is peaceful within the kingdoms of Egypt. Djoser's son Sekhemkhet will inherit the throne, but there are others that seek power and set their plans in motion, and they care nothing for the architectural ambitions of their king.

Ordinary men and women inhabit Djoser's Egypt too, living their own lives, dreaming of power or simple happiness, but sometimes these dreams do not harmonise with the plans of kings...

Publisher: http://www.writers-exchange.com/djoser/

Book 2: Sekhemkhet

Sekhemkhet faces the daunting prospect of following on from the glories of his father's achievement. He desires an even bigger pyramid than that of Djoser and orders Imhotep and Den to build it. However, the king finds it easier to build a tomb than to raise heirs to follow him on the throne, and a cousin seeks to take advantage of Sekhemkhet's precarious position and challenge the king.

Not all is well within Den's family. He is married, but love from an unexpected source threatens to destroy the success he has so laboriously built up. Will he sacrifice love for ambition, or can he find a way to have both?

Publisher: http://www.writers-exchange.com/sekhemkhet/

Book 3: Khaba

The throne of Egypt has passed to Khaba, an old man who seeks only to secure his family's position. Construction of a pyramid tomb is a secondary consideration, and the fortunes of those who desire to build them languish as he refuses further innovations. It is left to his grandson and heir, Huni, to dream of greater architectural glories.

Architect Den has achieved love, but at the cost of ambition. He and his burgeoning family struggle to survive, his relatives seeking out love of their own even as they look for opportunities to further their careers. The promise of a return to fulfilment is offered, but will they be able to grasp it?

Publisher: http://www.writers-exchange.com/khaba/

And More (10 books total).

Series Page:
https://www.writers-exchange.com/the-pyramid-builders-series/

We Came From Konigsberg
{Historical: Holocaust}

Based on a true story gleaned from the memories of family members sixty years after the events, from photographs and documents, and from published works of nonfiction describing the times and events described in the narrative, *We Came From Konigsberg* is set in January 1945.

The Soviet Army is poised for the final push through East Prussia and Poland to Berlin. Elisabet Daeker and her five young sons are in Königsberg, East Prussia and have heard the shocking stories of Russian atrocities. They're desperate to escape to the perceived safety of Germany. To survive, Elisabet faces hardships endured at the hands of Nazi hardliners, of Soviet troops bent on rape, pillage and murder, and of Allied cruelty in the Occupied Zones of post-war Germany.

Winner of the 2014 EPIC Ebook Awards.

Publisher: http://www.writers-exchange.com/We-Came-From-Konigsberg/

You can find ALL our books up on our website at:
http://www.writers-exchange.com

All Max's Books:
http://www.writers-exchange.com/max-overton/

www.ingramcontent.com/pod-product-compliance
Lightning Source LLC
Chambersburg PA
CBHW071355250626
47159CB00004B/1627